THE
DOMINANT
IDEA

AND OTHER STORIES

HERBERT E. STOVER

EDITED BY DEBRA REYNOLDS

CATAMOUNT
PRESS

an imprint of Sunbury Press, Inc.
Mechanicsburg, PA USA

CATAMOUNT
PRESS

an imprint of Sunbury Press, Inc.
Mechanicsburg, PA USA

For information about special discounts for bulk purchases, please contact Sunbury Press Orders Dept. at (855) 338-8359 or orders@sunburypress.com.

To request one of our authors for speaking engagements or book signings, please contact Sunbury Press Publicity Dept. at publicity@sunburypress.com.

FIRST CATAMOUNT PRESS EDITION: February 2023

Set in Adobe Garamond | Interior design by Crystal Devine | Cover by Lawrence Knorr | Edited by Debra Reynolds.

Publisher's Cataloging-in-Publication Data
Names: Stovert, Herbert E., author.
Title: The dominant idea and other stories / Herbert E. Stover.
Description: First trade paperback edition. | Mechanicsburg, PA : Catamount Press, 2023.
Summary: These "lost" stories of Herbert Elisha Stover (1888–1963) were found in a bucket in the rafters of his barn decades after his death. Debra Reynolds has meticulously transcribed them and carefully filled any gaps missing due to their deterioration.
Identifiers: ISBN : 979-8-88819-090-6 (softcover) | ISBN : 979-8-88819-091-3 (ePub).
Subjects: FICTION / Short Stories (single author) | FICTION / Mystery & Detective / Cozy / General.

Product of the United States of America
0 1 1 2 3 5 8 13 21 34 55

Continue the Enlightenment!

The mistakes of life are costly;
All lessons we must not forget.
But our words and deeds that come to naught
Are what we will most regret.

Robert Mazurek
Rebersburg, Pennsylvania
February 2023

CONTENTS

CONTENTS

FOREWORD

By Lawrence Knorr

Herbert Stover was best known for his full-length historical novels full of action and historic figures, always with a twist of romance. However, before he sold his first novel to a New York publishing house after World War II, Stover struggled as an upstart writer of pulp fiction short stories, the vast majority of which were written in the 1920s and early 1930s. Rejection after rejection came back in the mail, and Stover, now in the Depression, turned his focus to his education career. The letters and stories were put away, largely forgotten.

After Stover's death, his property exchanged hands. One day, in the early 2000s, the current owner was exploring the old barn on the property and found an old wooden bucket in the rafters. It contained pictures, letters, and typed stories that had been returned to Stover. But, the gentleman did nothing with these stories until the Fall of 2022, when author Guy Graybill and I visited to take pictures of the former Stover homestead. The bucket was graciously given to Sunbury Press, and the adventure began!

Debra Reynolds was handed the project of transcribing, editing, and patching the stories, where there were gaps due to the erosion of the paper. Silverfish had done their worst, but fortunately, preferred the pulp rather than the ink. Most of the stories were nearly complete. A couple required Debra's creativity to "become Herbert Stover" and fill the missing page or two.

What follows is a volume of stories, lost for nearly 100 years! They are mostly contemporary detective / police action-adventure tales, almost always with a twist of romance. Stover also liked the technology of the day, and included automobiles, airplanes, trains, and telephones to a large degree. The stories are remarkably fresh and are entertaining to this day, providing a window into the mind of a young man who would decades letter become one of the region's most famous authors.

LAWRENCE KNORR
Boiling Springs, Pennsylvania
February, 2023

INTRODUCTION

By Debra Reynolds

When I first heard that Sunbury Press was planning to bring back Herbert Stover's works, I had never heard of him. I bought and read *Song of the Susquehanna* and was delighted by Stover's tale with its rich historical detail and evocative language.

When I was asked if I was interested in joining the project, I was excited. Some unpublished stories had been discovered, which needed editing and some reconstruction. Time, water, and bugs had damaged them. As I delved into them, it became a bit like a treasure hunt, striving to understand where letters and words were missing. Interestingly enough, insects seem to dislike ink. I often found that they ate completely around letters.

I started with easier pieces, those most complete, and moved on gradually, finishing with pieces where great chunks were missing. By that time, I almost felt I knew Stover. His voice and character came through strongly in the stories he wrote and the choices he made for his characters. Also, I became aware of many little idiosyncrasies he had as a writer, the words he used frequently, those he often misspelled, and even the problems he had typing them. It's not possible to know if the machine was at fault or Stover's own hands, but the little touches of humanity in the pages I worked on endeared him to me and made me feel even more part of that great body of writers who have come before me, like Stover, and those who will continue when I, like Stover, am long gone.

We joked about Stover whispering in my ear, telling me what he had intended, and I think he did in a very real way—not as a ghost, but in how clearly his voice comes through in his writing. I learned a great deal from this project, and I'm grateful for the opportunity to peek behind the curtain to 'know' a little bit of a writer who died the year I was born.

With thanks to Lawrence Knorr of Sunbury Press for taking a chance on me; and to P.J. Piccirillo, who brought us together.

Debra Reynolds
February 20223

WHETSTONE GAP

JOHN GALE was fully awake now, his short heavy-barreled rifle at the ready. He had pushed the candle across the table so its light fell on the doorway and left him in the shadow. His lean face grim, his wire-hard body tense, he waited for the sound that had cut through the steady drumming of the rain and the undertones of the sighing pines.

Minutes slipped by. Gale opened the breech of his weapon and saw the gleam of a cartridge. He closed the action with a snap of his wrist. Then it came, sharply insistent—a rapping at the door.

"Please," a voice called. "Hurry."

Full of distress and panic, it was a woman's voice, and Gale paused just a moment in surprise before he leaped to the door and flung it open. Driven rain whirled in with a woman who turned and tried to push shut the door behind her against the blackness and the storm.

"Don't let them—"

Gale slammed the door, turned, and saw his visitor was a girl. Water dripped from her hair and ran in rivulets from her torn skirt. Her hands, raised to thrust back her hair, were scratched by briars. She leaned against the wall and tried to smile. Gale stepped to his bunk and snatched off a blanket, but when he approached her, he saw her eyes widen with something like fright as she studied his rough clothing and his lean height. He smiled.

"Don't be scared, Miss. Just wrap yourself in this and come to the fire."

She followed him and stretched her red hands to the blaze. "Yes," she said. "I was—I am frightened. I—"

1

Gale poured some coffee he had kept warm at the side of the fireplace into a cup and handed it to her. "You drink this; then we'll talk."

He noted the low tones of her voice, her struggle to keep hold of herself. He took a second blanket from the bunk and hung it over a line to make a screen; then, he placed a flannel shirt and a pair of overalls on the table.

"Now," he said gently. "You best get them wet things off. You can wear my things till yours are dry."

She picked up the garments, the blanket still about her shoulders. Half behind the screen, she came back.

"I'm Dorothy Merrill," she explained. "They kidnap—"

Once more, the door swung open, this time with a wrench. A man stood in the opening, blinking in the light, a huge uncouth figure with an odd flat-looking face. As his vision cleared, he saw the girl clutching the blanket to her throat.

"So there you are," he snarled. "Come on, get goin'."

Gale had been partially concealed by the blanket. The intruder's hand flashed to his hip when Gale stepped into view. The girls' warning scream was cut short by the blast of Gale's rifle. The slug tore away the fellow's hat, and he followed it into the night, his steps drumming on the rocky way. Gale fired another shot after him, the yellow flash cutting into the darkness.

"Lady," Gale's voice carried a deep chuckle. "If you wanted that bird to travel, you sure got your wish. This gun of mine talks terrible when you're at the wrong end."

Her face was white with fear. He urged her again. "You get dressed. I'll bar the door, so our visitors'll have to be more polite."

When she rejoined him, Dorothy looked like a slim boy in his clothes. She drank more of the coffee and then told her story. She had ridden to a friend's home on the outskirts of town. Returning to her home, some men had stopped her in a grove of cottonwoods in a draw with a query about the road. The next instant, a blanket had been thrown about her head. Despite her struggles, they had tied her to a horse, and then she had been forced to ride until she was nearly exhausted. Then, tired as she was when she was permitted to dismount, she had to walk long hours along winding trails until they came to a cabin. Two days later, she had managed to crawl through a window and traveled blindly until she saw the light in Gale's cabin.

He heard her through. "You say your name's Dorothy Merrill. You any kin of Frank Merrill, the banker in Rapid City?"

Her face lighted. "Yes, he's my uncle. I live with him. My parents are dead. I've been away at school, just came back. Do you know him?"

Gale stared into the fire a little. His lean features were set hard; his answer came slowly. "Not very well."

Aware that she was watching him closely, he picked up a splinter, and began to draw in the dust of the hearth.

"You're in the Hook country, ma'am, maybe forty miles from Rapid City. It's a rough mess of hills with a mountain round them like a big fishhook. Them kidnappers likely rode clean round, came in here the back way. The Hook's bad for horse flesh."

"You'll take me home?"

She leaned forward eagerly. He nodded slowly. "But, I guess you'll have to walk. We'll go north over the ridges. South'd be smoother going, but we'd run into Flat George and a fight. I figure that was George a while ago making his little fuss. Horses wouldn't help much, even if we had 'em, which I don't."

He stood up. "You'd better get to bed. You'll need rest to travel."

Long after her breathing told him she slept, Gale sat by the fire, staring straight ahead. Merrill's niece—here. Rising finally, he stepped to the door, opened it softly, and went outside.

The rain had stopped, but the forest was full of the sound of dripping water, the rattle of the stream, and the stirring of pine boughs. He went indoors, rolled up in a blanket before the fire, and slept.

Dorothy was awake when he took up a pail. "Need some water," he told her. "Then some breakfast."

The morning was amazingly clear, with the sun lifting over the ridges in the east. From the doorway, he could look down the long draw to where it joined the flatland beyond the huge hill bastions. He crossed the clearing, dipped his pail full in the stream, and was halfway to the cabin when the vessel was nearly torn from his hand. Then came the crack of a rifle. A second bullet thudded into a tree as he leaped for shelter. A derisive laugh floated from the timber.

Rage swept through Gale as he snatched his rifle. He would have gone out, but Dorothy had swung the door shut, put her slim form against it. "Don't go out there," she begged. "They'll kill you."

Gale breathed deeply and nodded. Ten minutes slipped by as shots sounded outside, and bullets thudded into the logs of the cabin's side. They crouched low.

"Logs are thick. They're shooting uphill, and the bullets are going high." He piled his blankets to one side of the stone chimney and made her crouch there. The night before, she had been distraught; now she showed more anger than fear. A bullet ripped through the single window, sent down a tinkling pile of glass. Gale upset the table, piled all the scanty furniture along the walls near the floor.

"Long as they keep their fire up, we'll be reasonably safe. They're trying to drive us into the open. Flat George'll show his hand sooner or later. You game to hold on?"

She nodded, her eyes snapping. Half an hour later, a voice hailed them. Gale, keeping low, opened the door a crack. It was the man who had been there before. In the sunlight, his flat features looked even worse than in the candlelight.

"Gale, you bring that girl out. She's Merrill's girl, and you ain't got no call to take care of anything of his'n."

Dorothy's eyes widened. Her eyes showed her question. "They know you?"

Gale made no reply, but his face was hard set. "Come and get her, George, I'm sitting in."

He closed the door, and turned to the girl. "It's Flat George, alright. He's just a cheap crook, but he's got some hard men with him. There's a big, tall bird they call Rash Collins. I'll have to put him out of business. Rash is a tracker and can follow us once we break away."

Gale listened as the shooting died away. He picked out some loopholes in the log wall. He peered out carefully. "You sit tight there," he told the girl. I'll get some food on while we can.

He looked at her ruefully. "Nearly out of water. Do you want some, or shall I make coffee?"

"Coffee," she said. A little later, he had bacon and some cold biscuits on the table he had set up again. They ate hungrily.

Finished, Gale smiled at his visitor. "One thing, no water, no dishwashing."

A little later, the shooting began again. The firing was slow, steady. An occasional bullet came through the window. Gale knew until the outlaws shifted to the front of the cabin, little damage would be done. There, firing through the door would make the place untenable in a matter of minutes. He stationed himself where he could watch down the path. Suddenly Dorothy called him.

"There's a big man back of that tree."

Gale looked. A tall thin man wearing a black hat, stepped out from behind the pine, threw up his rifle, and fired. The bullet entered the window, and spatted against the stones of the fireplace.

"That's Collins," Gale muttered. "He's a killer, the worst of the outfit."

Gale's rifle came to his shoulder. His face was hard as it settled against the brown of the rifle stock. Collins had stepped in back of the tree again.

Suddenly Gale fired. A long piece of bark ripped from the side of the tree. The lever of the weapon swept down, and back closed. The second shot ripped bark on the other side, then a man leaped into the open, and started to run.

Dorothy uttered a slight scream as she saw the rifle steady again. The weapon roared and was answered by a scream of agony. Gale turned to her.

"Dorothy, don't be squeamish. They'll rush us after it gets dark. We'll make a plan, but mostly rest—it's a long way out and will be hard on the legs."

"I'm game," she smiled bravely. "Only it looks so—"

Just before evening, Gale made up two packs of their clothing and food. He produced a single-shot pistol and a half box of cartridges. "You take this. Trouble is I'm nearly out of rifle cartridges. I had ten, but them two I used on Collins paid off."

Near the fireplace, he showed her a log in the wall that could be moved. "We put firewood through here. The brush is close. When it's good and dark, we'll slip through. There's a big pine on the ridge you'll be able to see; make for it. I'll join you there. You keep going no matter what happens."

She nodded, finding it difficult to talk. There was something grim about Gale with the lines in his face and the coldness in his eyes.

"Wish I could figure a way to get them out front," he muttered. Almost immediately, he slapped his thigh, and pointed. There was a stone that made a part of the hearth. "Let's get that out," he told her. "The ground pitches away out front; when we're ready, I'll turn this stone loose, they'll think we're slipping away."

She brought a table knife, they worked busily, and finally, it was out, a great round stone. Gale moved it to the door. Minutes dragged, but it was getting dark slowly. Still, Gale waited. He was anxious to get away before the rush he felt sure would come, yet he wanted the full cover of darkness. Finally, satisfied, he opened the entrance, and put the packs through.

"Remember," he whispered. "Go straight to the pine. I'll roll the stone."

She crawled through, then her hand came back, and sought his. "You will be careful," she breathed. In answer he pressed the small hand.

There was a warm glow in him as he stood there in the darkness of the cabin. She was worth it. He found the door, and opened it softly. Cautiously he eased the rock over the doorstep. It made no sound on the pine needles out there. He set it on its edge, gave it a turn, and it bounded forward down the slope.

A revolver shot tore the darkness with sound and a stab of fire, then another and another. Men were running, yelling. Swiftly Gale darted back, caught up his rifle, and doubled around the cabin. It was pitch black here under the pines. The bedlam increased. Darting on, he caromed into a heavy figure that clutched at him, and bore him to the ground.

Gale fought silently like a wild thing. A fist clipped his jaw, and Gale felt his senses reeling, but he held on. The man's knees jerked up. Gale writhed just in time to keep them clear of his groin. Now he twisted his wire-hard body, jerked his opponent clear. He had time for one last desperate blow and heard the smack of his knuckles on bone, the crash as the man dropped, then he darted away.

But they were coming. Running in a direction opposite the one Dorothy would take, Gale heard them yelling in back of him. He tried to make a noise. Yellow flashes licked in his direction. Two hundred yards and the pursuit slackened, and Gale stopped. He heard men back at the cabin. After a little, he slipped up the ridge, and came finally to the pine. A queer all-gone feeling gripped him. The girl wasn't there.

He waited a full minute before he heard a rustle, then a soft whisper. "Gale."

"Shh," he cautioned, a leap of joy in his heart. He caught her shoulders. "You all right?" he demanded.

"Yes, but you?"

He laughed softly. "I ran into a sort of bear fight. Lost the rifle and the pack. Now we'll have to travel."

Dorothy had clung to her pack, and he took it now, together with the little pistol. Forty miles of rough country ahead, almost no food, a pop-gun for a weapon. Their only hope lay in really traveling.

At the foot of the far side of the ridge, they crossed a little stream where they drank deeply. "It's going to be pretty rough from now on," Gale told her. "I want to keep them from tracking."

For an hour, he led the way upward over rocky ledges. Part of the time, he pulled her, but she shut her teeth determinedly and kept going. More ridges, thickets of brush that snatched at them, open stony screes. Gale felt sorry for the girl, but he was relentless. After midnight sometime, he did stop.

"All in, Dorothy?"

She didn't answer at first. "I guess I'd better rest—just a little."

He caught her shoulders, and steadied her. "Guess we'd better hole up. Just a few steps farther."

He half-led, half-carried her into a clump of young evergreens, then ripped down branches until he had a deep bed of browse. Over this he spread the blanket. She sank down wearily.

"You'll stay close?"

"Yes," he answered softly. "Don't worry."

She woke to the brightness of another morning and the smell of woodsmoke. Gale was broiling some trout. He grinned at her. "Friday's fish day," he told her. "You have an appetite for trout?"

She was stiff and sore, but it didn't affect her appetite. They ate until there was nothing left but the bones. Gale studied their camp and frowned.

"Guess we'll have to travel again."

She smiled bravely and nodded.

The sun was hot over them in another hour, but the stiffness worked out of her limbs a little. Perspiration streamed over them as they fought through the brush up another mountainside. Flies stung them. At the top, Gale made her sit down.

"You sit quiet a while. I'm going to scout our backtrack."

He found a pine after a little and climbed it. For a long time, he studied the country, the folds of the hills, the ravines. Something was moving way down there, on the way they had come. He slipped down.

"Dorothy, I'm sorry to tell you. There's no use hiding things. One of them is following. Are you game to stay right here while I slip back?"

Her eyes widened, and her chin quivered just a little. Then, "But you've no gun. He'll be armed."

Gale touched the rope he had wound around his body. "I brought my rope with me." He put the pistol in her hands.

"I won't need this. You keep it."

She demurred, but he slipped away into the brush. Now Gale traveled rapidly. From a low brushy hill, he saw, at last. There was the man obviously trailing, and he was doing a careful job. Gale saw him come to the place where they had camped and look about.

For a hundred yards up the hollow, their passage had been through brush, and the trail was clear. Gale remembered a rocky ledge under the overhang they had walked before taking to the slope. Before the tracker left the little camp, he was on top of this, coiling his rope.

The tracker was a little man dressed in a checkered shirt, overalls, and moccasins. His peaked hat shaded his dark features. A gun swung at his hip, but he carried no rifle.

Down from the camp, at the edge of the stream, the man stopped, squatted on his heels, and rolled a cigarette. While he smoked, he studied the brush, and seemed to calculate. Gale waited, a little breathless. Finally, the fellow rose, dropped his butt into the water, and followed the trail. Closer and closer, he came, his eyes on the ground. Then Gale's noose whirled, and dropped. He snatched the man off his feet, hands pinioned to his sides.

Keeping the noose taut, Gale came down to his prisoner, took his gun, pushed it into the waistband of his own trousers, and loosened the noose. Instantly the man leaped, snatching for the gun. Gale struck straight, savagely.

This time, when the tracker opened his eyes under the sluicing of water, Gale had his arms tied. The man's small black eyes gleamed with hate. Gale was sitting, testing the edge of the big knife he had taken from the man's belt.

The outlaw's eyes took in the knife. He watched Gale test the edge with his thumb. Gale's face was grim as he drew close some twigs and leaves and kindled a tiny efficient fire. Not until then did he address his prisoner.

"Where's Flat George?"

The man did not reply. Gale lurched forward, wrenched off the fellow's moccasins, and drew his body around.

"Where's George?"

This time the man understood. He began to beg. "Don't burn me!"

"Where's George?"

"With the horses."

"Who else is tracking?"

"Sanders, but he's way back."

"Get up," Gale's voice was savage, ruthless. "I know you, punk. You're Indian Dave."

The fellow's eyes rolled in fear. With the point of the knife, Gale edged him back against the rock. "Guess I'll just slit you—won't waste a shot."

Dave gibbered his entreaties, nothing of Indian stoicism here. Gale searched him carefully, and found a piece of raw bacon, some biscuits, and a little tobacco. Carefully he cut the man's belt to pieces, slit his clothing so it would just cling if he held on to it. The outlaw's eyes followed the glittering knife. Suddenly Gale snatched away his shirt, and raised the knife.

"Dave, which one shot Sumners?"

The man writhed, and shook his head. "I was away. Mebbe George, mebbe Collins."

Again, Gale snarled but snatched loose the riata. He was raising the knife again when the fellow bounded away screaming into the brush. Gale took the moccasins, laughed.

"Guess that scare'll hold him for a spell."

Twenty minutes later, he showed Dorothy the food and the gun. He made her put on the moccasins over her battered shoes. Gale was relieved, and they traveled more slowly.

"No place to worry us anymore but Whetstone Gap. I figure Flat George'll be watching that. He won't let your ransom slip out of his fingers if he can help it."

Ten minutes later, it came. The moccasins made Dorothy's steps clumsy; now she caught a foot between two rocks. She twisted to recover her balance, then dropped with a little scream of pain. "My ankle!"

Gale eased her gently to a seat on some rocks and took off her shoe. She rolled down her tattered stocking. The ankle wasn't swelling badly, but he bandaged it tightly with strips cut from the blanket. By and by, she was smiling ruefully.

"Poor place for a camp," he told her. "I'll have to carry you a little."

He made her fasten the small pack to her back, then slip her arms about his neck. He held her under the knees and was ready to go, but she was not the slight load he had expected. Several times he was forced to ease her down for a rest. He finally did reach a place that pleased him, a slope under the pines by a stream. Here he made her a bough couch, took the little pistol, and returned after a short time carrying two grouse he had killed.

"I'd like to hunt here sometime," he told her as they ate. "These birds are almost tame. I saw a bear sign, jumped a deer, too."

Finished, he cut bark from one of the trees. Dorothy watched him with interest as he bent around the ends of this bark and fastened them with slivers of wood. When he was done, he had a small vessel that might have held two quarts of water. He filled it at the stream. Then, from the fire, he fished hot pebbles he had placed there and dropped them one by one into the water until it was hot.

"Indian stuff," he told her. "Now, let's treat that ankle."

It felt ever so much better when he had bathed it for a time with hot water.

"You're so clever," she told him. "Where did you learn to boil water that way?"

He smiled. "I grew up in wild country, hunted since I was a kid."

"Are you a rancher?"

It was her first direct question, and his face was suddenly grim. He did not answer but rose and began tidying up about the camp.

They spent the next day in camp, treating the ankle with hot water, eating some trout he caught, and some wild raspberries. Gale talked to her of ranch life, but Dorothy did not repeat her mistake of a direct question about anything that really mattered. The next morning, she was ready to travel carefully, and this time he made her don the moccasins and threw away her battered shoes.

"Today'll bring us near the Gap. There are high rocky ridges, and the only way out is through the Gap. There's where we must watch."

Near noon, he shot a small wild turkey with the pistol, and that evening, they dined in state. Gale served some berries with it. That evening, he told stories. They laughed, joked, and he kept her entertained. But he did not tell her that he knew that they were being followed again. From the ridge, he had seen tiny figures. He hadn't scared Indian Dave enough.

"Don't worry," he told her as they sought their bough beds, "we'll come through. Tomorrow night, the Gap."

When he was sure she was asleep, Gale slipped out of bed, and went up the ridge side and forward. From his vantage point, he could see, far down in the Gap, a tiny point of light. A campfire burned there. If that was Flat George, they were trapped. He looked up at the rock masses above him. He could not take her out over that. Up there, they would be targets on the bare rocks, and it was real mountain climbing stuff up there anyway.

About three o'clock, Gale and Dorothy came out on the last ridge. Gale pointed.

"There's Whetstone Gap."

Here the circling ridge, which made the Hook country through which they had come, was a vast rocky bastion, slashed through by a narrow defile through which roared a mountain torrent. The Gap was just wide enough for the stream and the narrowest of dizzy trails.

"There's a path, Dorothy, and an old footlog crosses the stream. It's kinda dizzy along the cliff but just beyond is open country and—Rapid City."

They spent what they had left of daylight in a sheltered place in the rocks. Gale was sure that Flat George was down there in the rocks, that Indian Dave and Sanders were back of them. His brain was busy, however, with a plan that would get them through.

With the dark, they stole forward. It was open here, just rocks and stunted bushes. Down in the Gap, just at the point, was a fire.

"That'll be George," Gale muttered. "Now listen, Dorothy, we'll go down this trail. I'll leave you then and cross above. Just above George's fire are loose stones. I'll climb the ridge, and start a slide. When I call, come along the trail. You've got the little gun."

They stole down the hillside, and found the trail. "Well," Gale whispered. "Here goes. Keep your chin up." He tried to make his tones bantering. She was very close in the narrow way. Suddenly her arms were about his neck, bending down his head. For a fleeting instant, her warm lips were pressed against his.

"Oh, John, be careful. I—"

She released him. Gale's arms half circled her in the darkness, but he fought back the hungriness in him. She was Merrill's niece. He tried to think of that, but he could only think of her courage, her nearness, and her sweetness. He touched her hair gently and slipped away.

The brawling torrent was almost too much for him, but he floundered across. Then he climbed out of the creek bed and started up the slope. He was halfway to where he wished to go when he dislodged a stone. The noise of its going echoed in the defile. There came a yell.

Gale scrambled now. He saw figures beneath him and heard a bellowing voice he recognized. That would be Flat George. Then dry brush was flung on the fire.

The flames licked up, lighting the side of the ridge. A gun roared, stabbing its yellow light toward where Gale fought forward. He was like a fly on the wall. Guns roared, and a sliver of stone struck his cheek, bringing blood. He jerked at one answering shot, but stones were rolling about him. His fingers bled as he fought the ascent. Now a rifle joined the six guns below. Something wrenched at his heel, nearly upsetting him. The bullet had torn away his boot heel.

The dim loom of a big rock was there at last. One more desperate scramble, and he was back of it, fighting for breath. He strained against it, but it was firm as the mountain. He forced himself to wait. A bullet struck the rock, and whined away. More brush was flung on the fire to aid the rifleman. Now he set his body, arched his back, and strained until a salt taste was in his throat. The rock shuddered, moved, and pitched from its place. Gale sprawled in the place where it had been.

A hollow roar that filled the defile lifted as the big boulder dislodged the whole slope of loose stone. The point of the mountain was pouring down with a rush of wind and a hungry roar. Screams from the path, then the fire vanished as the avalanche swept it and the watching outlaws into the depths where the stream growled among the rocks.

A minute later, Gale was on the trail. The avalanche had come down below the footlog. It was intact, but stones were still falling. He called softly and saw Dorothy's dim figure appear. He snatched her up. They were across the bridge and the rock mass when a gun roared behind them. Gale fired back twice, but there were no more shots.

"That will be Sanders and Indian Dave," he told her. They sped on down the trail. It widened. In a grove stood half a dozen saddled horses. Gale breathed his relief. A moment later, they had reached the open high country, and way below was the road leading to Rapid City.

"Dorothy," he said softly. She brought her horse alongside his, and they rode knee to knee for minutes until they caught their breath and stopped. Directly below lay the wagon road. Gale shrugged.

"Now," he said presently. Guess you can make the rest of it alone. You won't be needing me. Your uncle . . ."

She laid her hand across his lips; that little hand scratched with briars. "Wait, I know the story; knew it before I was kidnapped. My uncle blamed you for shooting a man sent on a bank errand to your ranch. His name was Sumners. You were arrested, you broke jail."

Her fingers tightened on the lapels of his tattered jacket. She shook him. "You didn't know—Sumners didn't die, and when he became conscious again, he told who had shot him. It was an outlaw. But—you were gone. Uncle was trying to reach you when I was kidnapped. I knew who you were, when Flat George called that night from the rain."

Gale was breathing like a man who had been swimming for too long. He looked back at the dark mass of Hook Mountain. Whetstone Gap did not show in the shadows. He could not trust himself to speak. Free!

"So, you knew, all along?"

He could see that she nodded.

"But," he blundered. "Why didn't you tell me?"

Her horse pawed the turf; she did not answer for a long time. Then, she turned it closer, and dropped her hand on his.

"John, John. You are so stupid. How much must I tell you? I had to know how true you were. I wanted to know for myself, just—for me—"

His arms were suddenly about her. He bent over the warm form—shape—of her as she swayed toward him.

"Dorothy, Dorothy, how can you care?"

Her soft lips answered him. Slowly the round moon was climbing, painting them in a soft tender glow. Prairie, moonlight, all passed by as they rode forward toward the lights of the waiting town.

A SMUDGE OF RED

CLAY SHADWELL draped his long legs more comfortably over the Mains House banister and puffed rapidly on his pipe in the faint hope that the smoke screen thus set up might turn Dad Mains from his advertised determination to talk murder. Shadwell had come to Cassville to fish, and it was only the fact that Mains knew more about trout than Shadwell ever hoped to learn that made him tolerate the garrulous old constable's insistence.

"They're bringing in a patent detective," Dad began, settling himself comfortably and firing the half of cigar he held in his mouth to the accompaniment of a half dozen loud puffs.

Shadwell's lips twitched at Main's characterization of the detective expected to come and solve the mystery of the death of John Coates, retired saloon man and erstwhile country gentleman. A week before, on the very day of Shadwell's arrival, Coates had been found dead in his garden with a tiny bullet wound in his temple. Coates was by way of being the village's only celebrity; when he retired from the saloon business in a neighboring city, he had purchased the old Bradley farm on the outskirts of Cassville and had turned it, by means of an ample expenditure, into a country estate.

The manner of his untimely taking off was, of course, the principal subject of talk in the entire village. No one had heard the shot even though Coates' man of all work, Frank Forbes, had been at work on the other side of the house, and Wesley Bryce, a local carpenter, had been putting in some window frames in the second story of the house next door. It had been Bryce who had reached the body first, and he had called first Forbes, then Mains in his capacity of peace officer. To date, local and county officers had added nothing by way of real knowledge to the Coroner's finding: that the dead man had come to his end "as the result of a rifle shot fired by a person unknown."

"I've figgered that the feller that did it used one of these silencers on his gun," Dad went on. "And he did it to settle a grudge. A goodish lot of people had it in for Coates when he first came here with his carousing crew. His booze and fast women didn't go down well with the people hereabouts."

Shadwell nodded gravely. He had seen Coates on several occasions and had not been pleased with the man's loud bluff manner, but in three years, the people had come to regard the man as a fixture that must be tolerated. They turned out soberly for his fast car, put up with his arrogance, and made up for it by charging him double the price for what they sold him in produce and labor. Shadwell had seen the dead man lying in his home and even glanced at the wound itself, a tiny puncture just above the right temple, made by a twenty-two caliber rifle. If he entertained any theory, it was that one of the fast women who sometimes frequented the place had shot him.

"Forbes was telling something about a kind of Black Hand letter Coates got a while before he was killed," Mains offered next.

This was new, and Shadwell turned to the old Constable. "Did they find the letter?" he asked.

Mains shook his head. "It wasn't in his desk when the Sheriff searched it. I was there, and they didn't find anything."

Shadwell returned to his pipe, and Mains relapsed into silence until the clock inside the lobby struck nine with more noise than chime. Shadwell rose and stretched his long length. "I'm going to try Freeman's Run in the morning," he remarked, then as he turned to go inside, he noticed the dejected look about Dad's shoulders. He laid his hand on the old man's shoulder. "If I catch the murderer, Dad, I'll turn over that reward the commissioners are offering."

Freeman's Run was a disappointment the next morning. The trout were in no mood for striking at any of the flies Shadwell offered them, and at nine o'clock, he struck off to the south from the stream, meaning to cross the low ridge to South Fork on the other side.

A faint path wound up the side of the ridge through thickets of varied growth, laurel, then a stand of young sugar maples, then thick masses of hemlocks. He followed the windings methodically, seeing things that caught his attention here and there: late arbutus and early columbines. Then, when he had taken several steps into the brush to examine some tea leaves, he found a cane. Someone had cut a young white oak sapling and trimmed it carefully. The tip, still three-quarters of an inch thick, had been shaved of its bark and a portion of the wood, and about it was a ring as though the maker had thrust a circle of metal on it. Shadwell turned it over in his examination. He had seen Mains use that sort of cane, with the end tipped with the brass case of a twelve-gauge shell so commonly used for reloading in this section.

A hundred yards up the slope, he came to a place where a stump and some limbs told him the cane had been cut. Whoever cut the cane had been coming down the mountain, he reflected aimlessly. He turned and looked back. He could see Freeman's Run flashing in the sunlight through the thickets. When he turned again to the climb, a puff of breeze fanned his face. He drew in a breath of the air, only to expel it suddenly, for now, he caught the unmistakable reek of carrion. This was a watershed, and it provoked him to think some dead thing was near. He resolved to locate the thing, whatever it was, and report it when he reached the village again.

Following his nose, he literally pushed through the thickets for several hundred yards, paralleling the ridge top. Finally, he came into a thicket of hemlocks that seemed to cluster about a small opening in which was a heap of brush. He turned over the brush with his stick and found what he had been hunting. It was the carcass of a dog, evidently a pointer, now dead for some time.

Suddenly he remembered something Dad Mains had told him. John Coates had lost a valuable dog sometime before his own death; it was believed that someone had stolen the animal, and here was the solution. He turned the animal over, then gave vent to a low whistle of surprise. Squarely in the middle of the dead animal's forehead was a tiny hole like that made by a small caliber rifle bullet, and when he bent to examine it closer, he saw that, in the space that a quarter would cover about the puncture, the hair had been clipped close to the skull.

Shadwell did not tell anyone in Cassville his discovery. The detective from the city was there and had begun his observation late in the afternoon. Shadwell found Mains, and together they visited the Coates garden and carefully examined the scene of the crime.

"Over there was where Wes Bryce was working when he saw the body." Mains pointed in the direction of a neighboring house. "He had crawled up on a ladder and called down to Mrs. Fowler that he saw something over at the Coates place that looked queer. Then he hurried over and found the dead man.

Shadwell took his bearings carefully. From the position in which the dead man lay, he would have guessed that the shot must have come from the direction where Bryce had been working, but people had been about, watching the carpenter all during the eventful forenoon. It was possible that the dead man had spun around when he was struck; in that case, the shot could have come from the house or the clump of woods so near it.

The next morning a bombshell of news exploded in the little community. Beacon, the detective from the agency, carelessly dropped the news that he had found a threatening letter in the dead man's effects. Shadwell's opinion of the man's skill dropped promptly when he learned of the fellow's garrulity. At once, everyone was talking about Black Hand, and the detective promptly began to make good. He unearthed a number of things that the town knew and winked at, chief among them the fact that Anthony Romeo's daughter had been a constant visitor to the Coates house before the murder and that only recently she had gone to the city to "accept a situation." The Romeos lived with a small colony of other foreigners in the railroad company's houses about a half mile from Cassville, and Anthony enjoyed a reputation for shiftlessness. No one knew how he lived, and promptly with the starting of the Black Hand idea, his name became coupled with it, but when Mains and the detective called at the Romeo house, he was not there. His wife, comely despite her greying hair and rotund figure, could give no idea as to when he would be back. She seemed frightened into something near to speechlessness.

Back in Cassville, Mains promptly slipped the detective and came to Shadwell. "When that woman said she didn't know where Anthony was, she lied," he declared when he had finished his narrative. "I was watching her close, and once she looked over in the direction of Railroad Hollow, let's go over there."

This time, Shadwell responded promptly to the constable's words, but instead of following the old man's suggestion, Shadwell led him to the place where he had found the dog. Evidently, no one had been near the carcass. Mains was all for reporting the find, but Shadwell shook his head.

"There's something funny about this business. Even if the fellow wanted to kill this dog to get him out of the way, why did he clip this hair off?"

He drew a length of wire from his pocket and began to probe down the hole in the dog's forehead. Perhaps a minute slipped by, then he rose. "Whew," he exclaimed in disgust. "That's awful, and I didn't strike a bullet either. A doctor in France showed me how to probe."

By common consent, they drew away from the place and sat down to thrash the thing over. "Dad, you've been at everything connected with this. Did you see the bullet that killed Coates?"

Mains shook his head. "They didn't find it at all. I saw Doc Garvey go after it, but he couldn't find it."

Shadwell allowed his pipe to go out. All traces of his usual indifferent self had disappeared; instead, his features looked keen, hawklike, and there was something in his manner that made Mains get up with alacrity when he spoke.

"Let's go round up that Italian, Dad; I'm afraid that detective is going to make a mess of this."

A long detour brought them finally within sight of the railroad shanties down by the track. Shadwell signaled to Mains to keep back and stole near the buildings. He had just settled himself when he saw a boy, perhaps about fourteen years of age, come out of the Romeo house and go in the direction of the woods. A moment later, both Mains and Shadwell were following cautiously through the woods. At first, the boy appeared to loiter; then, when he was sure no one was about, he struck off rapidly in the direction of the Railroad Hollow. Years before, an old logging railroad had run up this narrow, deep ravine; now, it was thickly filled with young hemlocks. The boy rounded a shoulder of rocks and disappeared.

The cover at the opening of the ravine was so scant that both pursuers stopped, waiting for the boy to get into the hemlocks. Perhaps five minutes slipped by, then suddenly, the boy reappeared coming back.

Shadwell flashed a glance at Mains; they shrank back of a hemlock and watched. When the boy came abreast, Mains wanted to leap out, but Shadwell restrained him. He passed so close that both men saw he was carrying a rabbit. Shadwell grinned.

"Tony's hunting; the kid did his job pretty quick."

Twenty minutes later, they saw a figure slip across the hollow in the gloom of the dense shade, and cautiously they stalked it up through the hemlocks. Shadwell drew Mains close.

"I'll slip round him; give me five minutes, then you make a noise. I'll head him off above."

Shadwell made no noise as he slipped along the ridge to the right. There was no movement in front, but when his watch told him the time was up, Mains crashed his foot into a pile of dry brush. Instantly he heard the sound of running feet ahead, then a yell of startled surprise and terror. When Mains came up, he found Tony down, Shadwell kneeling on his chest.

"He ran up this old path like I thought he would, and I nabbed him."

Mains promptly snapped on the handcuffs he had carried for three years in the hope of using them, and Shadwell allowed the man to rise. He was surprised to find that Romeo was older than he had fixed in his mind. To one side of them lay the rifle he had knocked from the Italian's hand. He picked it up and handed it to Mains without a word. The weapon was a twenty-two repeater, and it carried a silencer.

"We've got him," Mains exclaimed delightedly.

"Don't be too sure," Shadwell countered.

They marched the protesting Tony back to town, and that evening, Beacon put the man through the third degree, as he called it, while Shadwell and Mains looked on. After two hours, the man owned that he had sent the letters demanding money but flatly protested that he had not killed Coates.

"These people know old Tony for ten, maybe twelve year," he sobbed. "I no kill. I use the gun, kill a rabbit, maybe. It's against the law for me to own gun. I hide it—no kill."

A little later, he owned that his daughter, Mara, had come to the Coates house, owned that he thought she had been too intimate with the dead man but oddly seemed to bear no resentment. He declared she was now in the city working.

That night, Shadwell did not go to bed until late; he sat in his room, pulling away at his old pipe for hours. When he finally sought his bed, he had a line of action mapped out for the next day.

Mains accompanied him to the Coates garden and explained things again. Shadwell's eyes caught something that lay several yards away, a common garden rake with a red handle. He picked it up.

"Was this here when they found Coates?"

Mains scratched his head a moment. "I can't be sure, but I think it was over there where you picked it up."

Shadwell examined the tool. There was nothing unusual about it; only near the tip of the handle, the paint had been scraped away as if someone had tried to force a ring of metal around it. Suddenly an idea flashed in his mind as he saw an indentation in the soft soil of the path where Coates had fallen.

"Dad, I want to try something. You go back out of sight while I fix something, then when I tell you, come out and walk down this path, just as Coates did."

Mains obeyed a trifle doubtfully. Shadwell picked up the rake and leaned it back against the grape arbor so the teeth stuck up in the path. When he stepped back, he saw that the implement was almost entirely concealed.

"Now, Dad," he called and stepped aside.

Mains advanced a trifle doubtfully along the path, looking over at his friend. Suddenly, he stepped on the upturned teeth of the rake; the handle described a swift vicious five-foot arc and would have struck the constable on the head if Shadwell had not leaped to catch it.

"I forgot and left the rake there, Dad," he explained a little sheepishly, and Mains stared after him doubtfully when he left a few minutes later without further explanation save to pat him on the back and declare, "You get the commissioners' reward, Dad. Don't forget that."

Shadwell's errand took him to the office of the local doctor who had assisted the County Coroner. "Doc" Garvey was in but not in a very amiable frame of mind.

"Yes," he jerked in answer to Shadwell's question. "I examined the wound, and no, I didn't find a bullet." Anybody with sense would know the wound was caused by a twenty-two bullet. If you or any other would-be detective want to split a hair on the fact that I didn't open the man's skull to find the lead, why split and be—"

"D—nd to you," finished Shadwell with a grin that won a shadow of an answering smile from the grim-faced Garvey.

As Shadwell went down the walk, he felt he could really learn to like Garvey. He liked the man's blunt directness. Now, he had another errand. In an hour, he left the jail after a conference with Romeo, which had been expedited by the fact that Romeo was delighted to find Shadwell spoke Italian after a fashion.

The evening's fishing resulted disastrously, for Shadwell broke his pet rod by what Dad Mains called fool carelessness. Stating that he was going back to the city to get another rod may have seemed a flimsy excuse to Dad, but nevertheless, Shadwell caught the evening train out of Cassville and did not return until the evening of the second day following.

Shadwell had a different errand in the city. Instead of visiting sporting goods stores, his errand took him into a part of the city at night where lights showed behind drawn blinds, and the sound of revelry came but faintly to the streets where policemen walked in couples as a matter of course. A pair of these policemen looked at him doubtfully when he accosted them, a doubt that disappeared when they caught a better look into his clean, purposeful face under a streetlight. Ten minutes later, he entered a dimly lighted, soft carpeted hallway, and a little later, he sat opposite a thin-faced girl who lolled on a huge monstrosity of a carved golden oak bed and smoked one cigarette after another, only stopping at times to allow the sharp hacking cough that occasionally racked her to have its way.

"You are Mara Romeo," he told her, "just come from Cassville."

It was all of an hour later that he walked down the carpeted steps again. The hall was warm, but it was not that which caused him to wipe his brow occasionally. In the gaudy room above, the girl had wept and stormed and finally confirmed all that he had guessed. He had left with his ears full of her curses when she realized what his grim insistence on the truth had forced from her.

Dad Mains was surprised the following morning to find that Shadwell had returned without a new rod but was prompt with the suggestion that Wes Bryce could fix the broken one. Together, they invaded the old carpenter's shop and found him busily at work. Shadwell had been in the place before on other occasions.

Bryce was more than a carpenter; today, he had been at work at a forge in the far end of the narrow shop, the entire side of which was occupied by a long workbench. He came forward affably enough in answer to their greeting, and Shadwell had a moment in which to study his face as he advanced. The pale eyes were set surprisingly far apart and seemed to strain to assist the grizzled beard that nearly covered his features in hiding whatever emotion might have been revealed otherwise. Bryce enjoyed a reputation for the closeness of mouth and purse and expert workmanship.

"Mr. Shadwell broke his fishing rod, Wes, and I told him you could fix it."

Bryce took the broken joint of split bamboo and examined it.

"Have to be glued up and spliced," he commented. Going to the workbench, he took up a short piece of pine board and laid the rod on it. Then he caught up an odd-shaped tool and swiftly drew a mark on either side of the rod joint in the soft pine.

Shadwell sat down on the edge of the bench where he could watch better. When Bryce had taken up a rabbet plane and started cutting a groove in the board, he reached forward and picked up the tool Bryce had just laid down. It was an odd-looking affair, with a thick handle set like the top of a T to a five-inch piece of round steel that tapered gracefully to a needlepoint.

"This is that patent scriber of yours, Bryce?" Shadwell asked casually. The tool was well known about town, for Bryce was the inventor.

The old man grunted laconically, and Mains explained the tool to Shadwell. "Bryce makes them for a tool company. You see, the T handle gives a good grip, and the thing's long and slim, so it can be sharpened easily. He's got a special temper for the steel too."

Mains showed a pardonable pride in his fellow townsman's invention and led Shadwell to the other end of the bench where a pile of unfinished scribers lay. Shadwell studied them carefully from the needle tip to the handle, which instead of being screwed on, was forced through a metal ring a half-inch wide that formed the other end of the thing.

"What's it used for," he began, then answered his own question.

"To mark lumber, of course." He laid down the one he held. Mains walked back to Bryce, whose back was now turned. Instantly Shadwell picked up one of the tools that lay to one side. As yet, the handle had not been put in. The steel of this one seemed less bright, as though it had been used. One glance inside the ring, then he thrust the tool quickly into a pocket of his coat and walked over to where he, too, could observe Bryce.

The carpenter had finished a groove in the board into which the rod joint fit accurately. "I'll have to glue this up, then I'll wind it, and you'll find it first-rate," he commented. "You can get it tomorrow at about noon."

"That will be fine." Shadwell's voice was friendly. There was no excuse for remaining longer; he turned toward the door.

"Cost you one dollar," Bryce hastened to say as they were leaving.

Late that evening, a group gathered in the office of John Chase, Justice of the Peace. Beacon, the agency detective, lounged in a chair and chewed a cigar methodically. Doc Garvey sat near the edge of another chair as though expecting instant summons to the bedside of a patient. Shadwell sat near the end of the justice's desk and drummed a tattoo with his fingers that evidently annoyed the others who had been asked to come by the constable. Presently footsteps announced the arrival of others. Chase went to the door and admitted Mains, who was accompanied by Wes Bryce. The two latecomers took seats, and as if by accident, Mains had the one nearest the door. Shadwell rose.

"All of us here have had something to do with the case of the Coates murder." He looked around, and no one spoke, but out of the corner of his eye, he thought he saw Bryce wet his lips.

"Bryce, here, was the first to get to the dead man. Mr. Beacon is the detective in charge. I may say that I've been helping Mains follow out a couple of clues, and gentlemen, I've something to show you."

He stepped to a wall cabinet and produced a common garden rake from its shadow.

"This was found near the dead man; now I want you to watch."

He leaned the rake up against the wall with the teeth out and leaning up; then he stepped on the teeth. Instantly the rake handle whipped up with terrific force only to be caught in Shadwell's hand.

"This is the thing that killed Coates."

Beacon smiled ironically. "Garden rakes don't make bullet holes," he said derisively.

Shadwell did not answer this thrust. "I believe the man that killed Coates had provocation that the law will recognize when they try the murderer. Coates had debauched a girl of this village. I saw her in a neighboring city; she'll be here for the trial. I don't know that I blame the man who killed Coates much."

Bryce had leaned forward in his chair, but all eyes were on Shadwell. Suddenly he produced something from his pocket and slipped it on the rake handle. He held it up for the others to see.

"Now do you see?" he asked.

One of the Bryce scribers with its long needle-like point had its end hook forced on the rake handle, so the tool projected at right angles. Shadwell stood the rake up on the floor.

"This rake leaned into a clump of bushes. Coates had to walk past it or tramp on a flower bed. He didn't see the rake; he stepped on the teeth, see!"

Shadwell stepped on the teeth and dodged; the sharp point buried a full two inches of its length in the pine siding of the room.

A murmur swept around the little group, then Bryce leaped for the door. Mains was too quick for him.

"I did it," the old carpenter screamed. "And I'd do it again; he ruined Mara, I—"

Bryce's eyes rolled like those of a person in a fit, and tiny flecks of foam appeared at the corners of his mouth.

"Mara Romeo is really his daughter," Shadwell went on evenly, "illegitimate, of course, with Romeo's wife before her marriage. Romeo has bled Bryce secretly for twenty years on account of the girl. I learned that in the city. Then when Coates ruined the girl, Bryce killed him."

Bryce's low moanings had stopped; he sat now by Mains, his narrow shoulders slouched forward hopelessly. With a certain air of pity, at last, Mains roused him and led him out.

Two days later, Shadwell and Mains were fishing on Freeman's Run. They finally sat down to untangle some flies. "There's a lot of things you did that I didn't understand, Shadwell, about the way you caught Wes Bryce, but there's just one more I'll bother you with."

Shadwell smiled at the old Constable; he knew after that, there would be others and others. "Well," he said.

"How were you so sure—after you hit on the idea that the fellow who killed the dog was practicing for the murder, trying to find if the hole would look like a bullet did it—that Wes Bryce was the fellow that did it? There's dozens of them things in town."

Shadwell laughed again. "In the first place, Bryce was the first man there. Even then, I wasn't sure until we went to his shop."

Mains' eyes were full of admiration. "What made you sure then?" he asked.

"That rake handle was painted red, wasn't it?"

Mains nodded.

"Well, the scriber I picked up last in Bryce's shop had a little smudge of red paint inside the loop where the handle goes."

For a moment, there was the silence of astonishment on the part of Mains; Shadwell was studying the smooth surface of the water in front of him, and his face was that of a dreamer of great catches.

"Now, if I can drop this fly on that big trout just above that eddy, I'll bet—"

Mains snorted impatiently.

"That old boy will strike like blazes when he sees it," continued Shadwell. And, rising, he cast with the enthusiasm of one who is concerned only with the business of fishing.

THE SHADOWED HOUSE

CARROLL GAGE suddenly leaned forward across the real estate agent's desk, a smile on his usually rather brooding face. "Fuhrman, I don't believe you want to sell me the Blair place! Do you know you've talked about cottages on Pine Creek, old farms, and everything except the property I want? What's the matter with it?"

"Nothing, absolutely nothing," Fuhrman declared. "There was a little more profit in the other places, that's all." From a drawer in his desk, he produced some papers. "I have everything ready here." He tapped the papers with his finger, but Carroll was talking again.

"Sam, ever since I began to want that place, I've been discouraged in the matter of buying. My friends act as though the thing was hoodooed; it's funny, too, with all the cottages in the Narrows, that it hasn't been snapped up long ago. Tell me, what's the matter?"

Fuhrman shrugged his shoulders. "Not a thing, you can take my word for that; but the place is run down, needs a lot of repairs and all that. There's a fine spring, a wonderful view, but of course, I'd prefer selling you a developed property."

Half an hour later, Carroll left the office with the deeds buttoned in his pocket. When he heard the sound of a motor horn just as the plant whistles blew, he took out the papers, snatched his hat, and ran down to meet his wife, who had come for him in the car.

"I've got the Blair place, Nell," he announced triumphantly. Under the pretext of examining something in the bottom of the car, they managed a surreptitious kiss. He elaborated on the possibilities of the old house all the way home.

"You'll be wild about it when you see it! A lonely old house, weather-beaten and shrinking from the sun into the blue-green shadows of the pines. Back through the trees, you can see the silver flash of the creek, and back of that is the mountain. It'll make the sort of background we want for the house when we get it fixed up."

He could not tell her the fascination the old place had for him, like a shabby old friend waiting patiently for his arrival. Neither did he tell her that he felt Fuhrman was reluctant to sell, for despite what he had said, Carroll still doubted a little.

When the weekend came, they drove out, following the road that wound through mountain gaps and along a foaming stream for miles. They came to where the Narrows widened, making a place for the sites of summer cottages. There, the stream slowed, resting in long, deep reaches where he planned to fish.

He watched Nell's face when they swung from the main road and came into the clearing. She was delighted and at once began to exclaim over its possibilities. "It looks lonely," she declared. "Like someone that's waited a long time for friends."

They busied themselves through the remainder of the afternoon, clearing out little, cutting a little brush, and doing what they could to make the place presentable. "It looks as though it belonged already," she told him as they stood by the car, ready to return home.

"I'll have Powers out one of these days to look the house over. He can use the lumber of the old barn."

It was getting dusk, and a glance at his watch surprised him. The twilight was unusually early due to the grim ridge to the west. A shade of disappointment entered his mind. He liked the sunset and evening hours on the porch. Already, shadows were stealing in among the pines. Nell drew close to him. "It's getting a little chilly, and I do not have my coat," she explained.

Once out of the Narrows, into the main valley, they were surprised at how light it still was. Across the hills, they could see the last of the setting sun. Carroll became aware that Nell was now more animated than she had been in the Narrows. She was chatting about dozens of things for the remainder of the trip but did not refer to the cottage before they reached their home.

Abel Powers was the best woodworker in the little furniture factory Carroll had established in Fairhaven. Shortly after the factory began operations, Powers had appeared with his chest of tools; from odd jobs about town, he gravitated naturally to the factory. He was a valuable man in every way, but Carroll had never made him foreman for one reason. He displayed a violent temper when anyone crossed him or asked questions about his past.

Carroll liked and trusted him; and had never seen him in temper until just before Carroll's marriage to Nell Gardner a few months before. The old man had made up for that by building the young couple a beautiful gate-legged table. Despite the peculiar paleness of his eyes, his grey hair and beard gave him a benevolent look. When he told Powers of his purchase of the property, and his plan to fix it up, Powers said he would pack his tools and be ready when his employer was.

Carroll and Nell announced the purchase of the Blair place to their more intimate friends with the promise of a housewarming when the house was habitable. Carroll and his wife were popular in the little city where she had grown up and to which Carroll had come six years before. Their marriage was peculiarly acceptable because both were orphans without knowledge of their parents. In true melodramatic fashion, Nell had been left on the doorstep of the Gardners when she was a tiny infant; and they had reared her as their own. Carroll had come from the west and was perfectly frank about himself. He, too, had been reared by foster parents, who had left him the small capital with which he went into business. They had never told him of his real parents. Nell and Carroll's social set was immensely pleased by their marriage; they made a good match for each other with no embarrassing question of ancestry between them.

Powers had made a good beginning by the time Carroll could take his wife out to the house again. He had mowed the yard, trimmed the tangle of rose bushes and walled the spring with mossy stones. He had managed a gravel walk from the spring to the house and built two rustic seats. One of them, in the shadow of the pines, was so placed that she could sit and catch glimpses of the flashing stream and where the breezes could sweep the soft pine incense about her.

Carroll's satisfaction was largely because the roof had been made weather tight, and most of the porch's framework was ready. Peeling off his coat, he went to work with Powers while Nell busied herself exploring and working about the interior.

By mid-afternoon, most of the porch rafters were in place. Powers was up on the framework, and Carroll handed the pieces of lumber to him. Somewhere about the place, the old carpenter had found an old broadaxe, filed off the rust, and fitted a handle. He was using this to cut his pieces into shape before fitting them. Nell had moved out into the yard, and neither man noticed her where she worked about the rose bushes. Carroll bent over to pick up a piece of lumber when suddenly she screamed.

In the instant he swung around, something thudded to the floor, so close in passing that he felt the wind of its displacement. Powers' yell of fright almost echoed Nell's cry, and he was down from the framing when Carroll had gained Nell's side and patted her shoulders reassuringly. The point of the heavy ax was driven deep into the floor by the force of the fall.

"I saw it, saw the board he was holding push it off the beam!" she declared.

Powers snatched up the offending tool and flung it into the yard. "I hadn't any business using that thing up there! Might have knowed it'd fall on somebody. It'd have split your skull like a punkin," he lamented with a tremor of excitement in his voice. "I don't believe I can do another lick today after this."

Carroll laughed at the pair of them but willingly called off work for the day; he was satisfied with the progress made. After supper, which they had an hour earlier than planned, Powers asked to go back to town with them. Before they started, the two men were together alone for a few minutes.

"I'm worried about that ax falling," the old man declared. "I like to have scared her into a fit." His concern was so evident that Carroll went out of his way to laugh at it. A little later, Nell joined them, and they drove home. When Carroll returned to the house after putting away the car, to his surprise, a grim-faced wife met him.

"He pushed that ax," she declared. "I saw him do it! He stirred round with the end of that board, and I screamed just in time."

He stared at her in astonishment. "Why," he protested. "It was a pure accident, a thing that might happen to any man at any time; it might happen over at the plant any day—"

"That's just why I want you to discharge him at once; you can't tell when he might do something dreadful!" She seized his coat lapels and shook him excitedly. "Tell me you will," she pleaded, but she saw his face was set. "His white eyes give me the creeps, and Carroll—there was murder in them today!"

Carroll found it hard to go against her wishes. He argued and cajoled and told her he couldn't and wouldn't punish an old man who had done faithful work for an accident in which Carroll was sure he was guiltless. "I just can't, even to please you," was his final word, and when she went to bed, there were tears in her eyes, and he felt like a brute.

With their first quarrel in mind, Carroll did not go out again until Powers reported it done, with the request that he be given several weeks off. He wanted to go fishing on a stream up in the Narrows, several miles from the Blair place. Carroll was glad to assent.

Nell forgot a good part of her resentment when she saw what the old craftsman had done to the place. Things were even better than they had planned; Powers had done marvels with poor lumber and little help. About the two sides was now a wide porch, and every line of the place blended into the surroundings without clashing. A truck brought out some furnishings, and they busied themselves arranging things when it arrived. That done, Carroll went over to the stream. Nell went out into the yard to work at the rose bushes again.

The sun was pleasantly warm, and she enjoyed a pleasant feeling of privacy. Several cars went by, but she was screened by the pines between. She became so engrossed that her first impression from outside brought surprise. She was a little chilly. The sun was on its way down, and she was now in shadow. Getting up a little stiffly, she moved out into the sunshine.

Suddenly, she brought her hands up to her mouth as though she wanted help to repress an outcry as she took in the uncouth shape made by the shadow of the house. Incredibly flat, it stretched over the yard. The shape of the porch gables and the perspective of the lines of the roof made the fantastic shape, she knew. The whole thing was ridiculous, yet, when Carroll appeared, she had an odd impulse to cry out to him not to step on the shadow.

He greeted her with a cheery hail. "What are you staring at, old girl? Seen a ghost?"

She shook her head, and noticing his wet and bedraggled appearance, she cautioned him. "Don't track all that wet and mud into the kitchen." She watched him step into the ghastly shadow. When she went in, she passed around the house on the pretext that she wanted to see her bench in the pines. When she went outside again sometime later, she saw the shadow had shifted. It was now perfectly normal and uninteresting. She wished she had noted the exact time she had seen the thing.

Twilight was punctually early but with a tardiness of denser shadows that seemed unnatural. After supper was over, they sat on the porch. The breeze moved the pines to soft whisperings; the chatter of the stream came to them as a cheerful overtone in a symphony of sighing lower notes. Nell drew her chair a little closer to Carroll's.

"What's that?" she suddenly demanded, her hand on his arm.

A thin swish as of parchment wings, and a vague shape swung by, then another, and another, like a flock of uncouth birds. Her hand tightened on his arm before he replied.

"Only bats. Common or garden-variety bats, young lady. Supposed to be carriers of Satanic messages, bad tidings, and bedbugs," he answered lightly, covering the fact that he did not like these nocturnal creatures a bit better than she did.

They retired early, but Carroll noticed that Nell did not fall asleep at once. Into the stillness, vague noises began to break, with an eeriness bred of the house and place. Down in the cellar, something moved about with thin rustlings as though mice were dragging things across sheets of paper; once, a swinging bat brushed against the screen. He heard Nell's sharply indrawn breath at the sound. Sleepily, he resolved to have the crowd out before they spent another night in the house. That would serve to break her nervousness. His second resolution was to set some mousetraps in that infernal cellar. The mice were still moving when he fell asleep. Sometime in the night, a voice roused him; Nell, talking in her sleep.

"Don't," she muttered hoarsely. "Don't get in the shadow. It's shaped like a coffin—don't!" Her voice had mounted to something like a scream with her last word, and he shook her awake.

"Nell, you're getting my goat; you're acting like a child," he remonstrated. He lectured her for some minutes before he realized she was crying. When she fell asleep again, one of his hands was tightly gripped in hers.

The next morning, without telling Nell, he descended to the cellar with a flashlight. He peered here and there into the corners and cracks in the masonry. In a dark corner, something that glistened moved slowly; and before he could grasp a stone or a club, a huge blacksnake disappeared through a crack in the wall. Ugh! he shuddered—of course, it was harmless, but he disliked the slithery thing, and if Nell saw it, she would be scared into a fit.

She brightened considerably when they were home again. He began to sense a rising irritation in his attitude toward her. The Blair place was not discussed in their conversations, and finally, she discovered that there was a visit to friends out of town, which should be paid at once. Since Carroll agreed with her, she made plans to go.

Doctor George Lent was Carroll's closest friend in the city despite the disparity in their ages. Lent was old enough to be Carroll's father. The two men had many things in common, one of them being a perfect passion for trout fishing. The day Nell left, the pair of them left for a fishing trip, planning to stay at the Blair place.

Lent was immensely pleased with the changes in the old house and showed a mild concern when Carroll told him he believed Nell was coming to dislike it. "Go slow," he advised. "A woman's intuition is a wonderful thing, beyond a man's comprehension entirely." Several times during a long evening on the porch, Lent seemed on the point of confiding something; but in the end, he did not.

Their luck was good, and they were on their way back to town with well-filled creels when Carroll remembered that he had not looked up Powers. He turned to the doctor to mention it when the steering wheel seemed to loosen in his grasp. The car shot to the side of the road, crashed through the guard rail, and plunged to the streambed a good ten feet down. It struck right side up, and both men were hurled clear with little injury. Lent bandaged a cut on Carroll's shoulder. He had pulled up the young man's shirt sleeve when he gave a barely suppressed start.

"What's that on your shoulder?" he asked, touching a tiny red crescent on the sunburned skin.

Carroll laughed. "You're a bum doctor if you can't see that's a birthmark!" he replied.

When the car was brought to town, Carroll and Doctor Lent went to the garage to learn why the thing had gone over the bank. "Someone tampered with your machine, Mr. Gage," the foreman replied to the query. "The nut on the end of the steering column was removed, and the steering gears became unmeshed. No, it wasn't an accident," he declared at their looks of astonishment. "I went over this machine myself a few weeks ago, and I put on a locknut. Someone tampered with it."

The two men left the garage and walked up town toward Carroll's home. The machine had stood for nearly twenty-four hours—there had been plenty of opportunity for the mischief.

Lent went in with Carroll on his insistence. "I can't understand it, Doc," Carroll burst out. "There seems a hoodoo on my owning the Blair place! First, I have trouble getting it; then Nell dislikes it; then someone fools with my car."

He smiled ruefully at his friend. "I won't dare tell her I found a six-foot blacksnake in the cellar."

Lent nodded. "Hardly. You forgot to mention that your carpenter nearly killed you with an ax out there, too," he added dryly. "I guess it's my business to tell you something unpleasant, Carroll. I've practiced medicine in this section for thirty-five years, and I have at least a fair memory. I know why Fuhrman held off, he's sold that place three times in the past four or five years, and it's come back each time. There was a murder here a long time ago. The Blairs were a decent, hard-working young couple that lived there. It was rumored that they had some money, and one day three devils went out there and killed them in cold blood."

"Murdered," Carroll interrupted.

Lent nodded. "Yes, heads split open with an axe. They got two of the men and finally hanged them. A degenerate named Sanders did the killing. He had a murder lust. Afterward, he maimed the two cattle and the horse. They took the money, but somehow a little year-and-a-half-old boy escaped. He was found the next day and later was adopted by some kind people and taken out of the country. They caught Sanders and Moyer, but the other man, who used to work in the lumber camps, got away. I remember seeing him several times before the murder. Beyond the fact that he had queer, pale eyes, there had been nothing against him. The others were a bad lot and got what was coming to them out the back of the old jail."

"Haven't they heard anything about the boy since?" Carroll asked curiously."

Lent smoked a long time before he answered. "The people who adopted the boy gave their names only to the court officials. They didn't want the story to follow him. No one has heard of him since."

After Doctor Lent had gone, Carroll sat musing over the situation for a long time. It might be possible that the sinister nature of the Blair place had come to Nell by intuition; perhaps she knew more than she told him. At any rate, he'd sell at the first good offer. Yet with this decision came a vague regret—he hated to give it up. Even now, he could hear the murmur of the water, catch the scent of the pines, and see the lonely house in the mellow light of the sun.

A letter from Nell advised him that she would be home in two days, and obeying an impulse the following morning, he secured his repaired car and drove out. The sun was warm, and his spirits lightened as he caught sight of the place, caught some of the peace of the quiet scene. There was certainly nothing menacing in the rose bushes, the rustic seats, and the wide porch with the deacon seats Powers had made. Things were all right and would be better after a little house party.

Parking his car, he went to work. His first task was to go into the cellar, where he had the luck to get the blacksnake within ten minutes. Then he went to what was left of the barn and hunted bats until dinner. As he was eating, he thought of Powers, and when he finished, he struck off on foot to visit the old man.

Despite the heat and the rough going, he made quick time once he left the highway. Ahead of him, he caught sight of the little shack where Powers stayed. A figure was moving about in front of it. An impulse to mischief possessed him. He would leave the trail and surprise the old man. Nothing was difficult about the task, and he came out back of the little building. He crept around it; Powers was busy over a long narrow wooden box. Carroll smacked his hands together with a report like a pistol shot.

Something like an animal snarl came from the lips of the old man as he wheeled, and Carroll was aghast at the expression on the man's face. The pale eyes blazed with devilish fury, the lips drew back from the yellow teeth, and his right hand went back to his hip.

"Powers!" remonstrated the young man." Only a little joke; I wanted to scare you. Don't look so infernal mad." He tried to laugh, but it fell flat at the sight of the man's fury.

"That was a hell of a trick," snarled the old carpenter. "You've been watching and spying on me for months. What do you want?"

Carroll stared at him with the uneasy knowledge that probably nothing he could say would mollify this blind rage. "I came up to ask you back to work, that's all."

"I've quit; quit right now. You git to hell out of here! Git."

Carroll's temper flared up dangerously, but he mastered it and faced the old man's brandished hammer without a quiver.

"All right, Powers, I'll go. When you cool down, come and see me, and I'll apologize for scaring you."

He plodded down the trail with his mind full of blended emotion. The old cuss had a right to be a little cranky but not as devilish as all this. Nell's phrase popped into his head, "white eyes." They had been; white with a hard, cruel hate. He recalled how Powers had pushed back the box with his feet, how his hand had gone back to his hip for a weapon. He was scared out of his senses, yet that was odd; Powers did not seem to be easily scared.

Angry, Carroll walked faster than he thought and returned to the cottage sooner than he expected. The sun was throwing heavy shadows, and now Carroll's eyes caught a queer resemblance that brought him up, staring. The shadow of the house, with its gabled porch roof and the twisted perspective of its lines, formed a shape on the yard, the outline of a coffin.

So that was what Nell had seen. As he looked, a queer, uneasy feeling possessed him. Lent's story of the murders came to his mind. He knew it was ridiculous, but it required an effort of will for him to cross the shadow and enter the house.

So far, Carroll had not become used to the twilight's early coming, and this evening, it surprised him at his supper. He did not light a lamp but pulled on a coat and went out on the porch. As he smoked, he thought of Nell and their first evening in the place where they had planned to be so happy. He was vaguely uneasy about her; somehow, they were not as close as they had been, and he blamed this house business. Tonight, he wanted her, longed to reach out in the dusk and touch her smooth hand. Carefully, he reviewed all that had happened, everything purely accidental, even to the shape of that infernal shadow. He'd sell the place then, as soon as he could.

The first evening stillness passed; on the edge of the woods, rustlings began; across the stream, a screech owl uttered his ghoulish cry. After a little, a fox on the opposite ridge barked cynically. Carroll found himself fighting a tense feeling as he watched and listened. The shadows seemed like heavy piled velvet. Here and there, they seemed to move; once, he fancied he heard a step. Disgusted with himself, he knocked the ashes from his pipe and went indoors.

Once in bed, he dropped into a light sleep, but almost immediately, it seemed he was awake again. He resisted the temptation to turn on his flashlight. Outside, everything was as still as the death that had once come to the place so terribly. Suddenly, and again without reason, he knew something was out there, creeping in, soundlessly, in the shadows.

With this knowledge, his nervousness left him. He was cool with purpose as he drew on his clothes, thrusting his flashlight in his hip pocket and taking his revolver, a light calibered weapon he had brought to kill rats. The stairs did not creak as he descended.

On the porch, a board creaked softly, then utter stillness, then a cautious step. Carroll gained the doorway and flattened himself against the wall where the door would swing back. He remembered that it was not locked.

A board creaked again, followed by a silence that was trying; then footsteps like those of a padded-footed animal stole along the porch and paused outside the door. The knob turned so softly that he could hear the lock tumblers falling; a light puff of air struck his face as the panels swung back toward him. Again, the padded footfalls. In the darkness, he could make out a crouching figure that crossed the room as though carrying some bulky object in its two hands. It halted at the stair door, then a sound of fumbling and a light thump as if something had been placed on the floor.

The roots of Carroll's hair prickled, but his hand was perfectly steady as he brought his revolver to bear on the bulk of the intruder. The man's breathing was apparent, and another sound, as of something crawling. Involuntarily, almost, Carroll's finger tightened on the trigger; he fired into the ceiling.

The yellow stab of fire from the discharge cut the blackness and blended with the roar came an animal-like scream. Next instant, he was fighting a thing that mouthed curses in a shrill whine and that bit and scratched like a thing possessed. Shoving him clear, Carroll swung his revolver down on the man's head. He sank to the floor and lay still.

In the stillness that followed, something on the floor by the stairway moved with the sound of dragging rope. Carroll's fumbling fingers found his flashlight. On the floor at his feet lay Powers, and a shudder swept through Carroll at the sight of the death planned for him, for crawling across the floor were two huge rattlesnakes, their scaly, blotched bodies glistening evilly in the light. At Carroll's movement, they coiled near the box in which they had been brought.

Shuddering with repugnance, Carroll fired into the mottled coils, then finished the job with a club snatched from a corner. When he had lit the kerosene lamp, he saw that the rattles had been cut from the snakes.

Powers was beginning to stir when an automobile roared up outside. Quick footsteps crossed the porch, and Doctor Lent burst into the room. He took in what had happened at one glance.

"I was uneasy when I heard you came out here alone," he explained. I hurried out as soon as I could."

He bent over Powers, made a swift examination, then beckoned to Carroll. "Help me over to the couch with him. One of his own snakes bit him," He pointed to the already swelling hand and wrist.

Once on the couch, he made a closer examination. "Bad heart," he muttered, "can't use strychnine."

"I surprised him," Carroll explained. "Guess he fumbled when he let the snakes out."

With a sudden movement from the couch, Powers was trying to sit up, but they pushed him back. The man's eyes flamed as they rested on Carroll.

"He's been trying to get me, Doc—he's Dan Blair's boy, the baby we didn't kill."

Carroll started forward, but Lent pushed him back. He bent over the stricken man. "You're Fraser, aren't you?"

Powers nodded. "I wanted to get him before he got me, Doc. I've lived through Hell since Sanders put the axe to his people." His eyes widened with fear, then narrowed with cunning, his lips set. Doctor Lent bent closer.

"You're going to die, Fraser. Come clean. The snake got you, and your heart's bad. Tell it all."

Fraser moved his swelling hand and screamed with pain. "I didn't kill them; Sanders did that. I got away, thought I was safe, and got married. My wife was sick after the baby came. I guess I talked in my sleep or something; she knew, and the shock killed her. I brought the baby away here and left her at the Gardner's. After that, they were always after me. I was all over—it was Hell, Doc. Years and years. I came back to Fairhaven to see what became of my girl. I didn't know who he was," he snarled toward Carroll, "till I saw that mark on his shoulder a week before he married my girl. I thought he'd been watching me! I didn't want a Blair to have my girl! I'm going to Hell on account of them, Doc!" The poison was working fast; his arm had lost all semblance of a human member. The doctor slit his shirt sleeve to the shoulder.

"I tried three times to get him, missed every time. He was after me, up in the hills today—I—" He sank back, groaning. His staring eyes closed. Doctor Lent turned to Carroll.

"I didn't know for sure who you were, Carroll, until I saw your arm after the car went over the bank; then I knew."

He motioned toward the man on the couch. "Insane—paranoia, moodiness, delusions kept him moving. He's Nell's father. He's lived a lie and claimed the name Powers, but what he says is true. You've got to bear up for her and keep her from knowing. You love her enough, I know."

The couch creaked. Fraser had started up with a wild stare in his eyes, but the lucid moment had passed. The blotched arm rose slowly. His voice rang with a clear, deadly menace.

"Throw the ax down, Sanders, and leave the kid alone or—I'll blow you to hell, quick."

With the snap of the last word, the man's whole body gave a spasmodic lurch. He fell back, and by the time Lent had reached his side, he was dead.

THE DOMINANT IDEA

KINCAIDE MOVED down the aisle in advance of the trainmen, his long weather browned face set in a scowl. Amused faces grinned at him through the smoke clouds, but the grimness on his face, and the long swinging arms of the drifting laborer, stopped any further audible comment.

Outside on the cinders along the track, Kincaide waited for the train from which he had just been ejected. He claimed he had lost the check, given him in exchange for his ticket, a few miles out of Emporium. The windows began to march by in slow procession a few feet from his face. Suddenly he saw, sticking alongside the glass in the window frame, the outline of a check with one corner torn away. Behind it was the heavy face of the man he had heard addressed as Butch by his rat-like partner, who occupied the seat with him.

Involuntarily he began to walk with the moving train—it was all clear now. Butch had lifted the check from his hatband while he slept. The heavy red face was gone. Kincaide moved a little faster. The windows were flashing by in blurs of light; all the vestibules were shut; then came the last coach, and decision and opportunity came to Kincaide together. Leaping, he caught the brass railing on the observation platform. The pull of the train swept him off his feet, but he managed to scramble aboard.

Through the glass in the door, he saw the conductor and brakeman approaching in the second coach from the rear. The railing of the old observation car helped him again. By the time the trainmen reached the rear platform, he was crouched along the ventilator, holding on tightly against the pull of the wind. Above the roar of the speeding train, he heard the sharp slam of the door a few minutes later and knew the men had gone inside again.

In his wanderings, Kincaide had often ridden freights and, from master hoboes, heard a great deal about riding passenger trains; but this was his first venture taken on the impulse to follow Butch and get even.

The coaches were rocking drunkenly now. Attempting to stand up, he nearly pitched from the roof and thereafter crawled on his hands and knees. His sole desire was to gain the platform ahead of the baggage car, where he would be out of the tearing wind that tugged at his garments and buffeted him like something malignant. The train rounded a point of rocks and shot out on a spidery bridge. Kincaide looked once at the swirling hungry water thirty feet below, lit into long patches by the lights of the train. Dizziness made him lie flat, clinging with tense fingers to the running board above the ventilators, nor did he look down again until they were running through a long dark aisle of timber.

A full three-quarters of an hour passed before he reached the platform. Once, he had to stop while the local discharged some passengers at a flag station. Passing from coach to coach was the worst, but it was done at last. Below him was the small blind platform ahead of the combination baggage car and smoker. Cautiously, he lowered his body until he clung to the edge of the roof by his work-hardened fingers, then dropped with a grunt of relief.

It was easier here. Ahead the tender lurched, and occasionally a glare of light flashed heavenward as the fireman opened the firebox to shovel in coal. The train was making few stops. They were following the river and on the right grim wooded bluffs swept up toward the sky. Kincaide knew something of the country here; he had come the other direction on a freight months before en route to the mid-western grain fields. The rocking motion made him feel sleepy. He dozed until each time the whistle sounded for a station, he came back to consciousness and cautiously watched the discharge of passengers.

Two hours passed. The train stopped ten minutes in a rather large town with a long-deserted platform. Thirty minutes later, they crossed the river. The country was comparatively flat now, with clumps of trees looming against the skyline. The whistle sounded a long wailing call.

Kincaide could not see the river, but the light shone on long parallel lines of steel, the upper tracks of some long distribution yard. A tiny box-like station loomed up, and when the train stopped, Kincaide's heart leaped. Butch and his smaller partner dropped from the steps; the iron grating banged shut. Kincaide dropped off on the other side of the track and crouched down and watched, for the second time, the lights first march by, then quicken until they became a broad band of yellow light.

Kincaide probably did not know the meaning of impulse, and he certainly had not been fully awake when the conductor demanded his ticket and told him to get off. Even when he moved down the aisle, he had been in a fog, half asleep. The sight of the outline of the check he instantly recognized had brought him fully to his senses. For the rest, he was dominated by a savage desire to get even. Before he had fallen asleep, he had noted Butch and his companion by their loud, wrangling conversation. Now he crouched low along the track until the taillights of the train winked out far down the track.

In the shadow of the tiny open station, the two men talked for a long time. They rolled cigarettes and smoked them through. The big man's voice was a low boom as he talked; the other's was whining, petulant. Suddenly Butch's tones rose, and he swore viciously.

"It's a scant mile across the river and easy pickin'. We've got easy pickin' and a good two hours before the rattler goes back north again. Come on, quit your belly-achin'."

Kincaide caught the whole sentence, caught the little man's sharp "Shh."

"To hell with keepin' still," Butch announced. "There ain't another guy in two miles of here."

Footsteps crunched on the cinders, and the pair moved off across the tracks, passed a line of box cars on a siding, and entered a road. Kincaide followed cautiously. Driven by impulse, he took no chances. His ups and downs among the drifters of half a continent had taught him some measure of caution, but whenever he caught Butch's heavy arrogant tones, he tightened his fists involuntarily.

The road led to the dark shadows of a bridgehead. A hundred yards below was another bridge, and Kincaide recognized the place at once.

Lockville was the town across the river; he knew it by the two bridges, one for the inter-urban trolley, the other for regular traffic. His quarry had stopped at the entrance of the railway bridge, and Butch was talking again.

"You're gettin' as meek as that big bird I snitched the check from tonight, Slim. Hain't you got a sign of guts anymore?"

Kincaide swore softly to himself and stole closer. From his new position, he could hear Butch's lowered tones and follow the plan he was outlining. The post office—that was it, and the precious pair were yeggs. That meant they were heeled and dangerous to tackle without help. If he only had a gun!

With Kincaide following closely but keeping in the shadows of the steelwork, the trio crossed the bridge. Kincaide remembered something of the town; years before, he had worked on a road gang near it. Now he paused where the bridge debouched on Main Street while the yeggs, keeping ever in the dense shadows, went on. For the first time, the foolishness of the chase came over him—to chase a pair of armed and desperate men for the sake of the price of a railway fare. Coming upon them in the act of robbery would be simple suicide. Suddenly, with a new idea, he stepped out of the shadow of the steelwork and began to run. This was a county-seat town, and he remembered the jail's location.

He was prepared to rap for a possible ten minutes, but scarcely two had passed when the outer door was flung open with a suddenness that found Kincaide unprepared with his story. Five minutes later, in the waiting room, he told it to a young fellow who explained that he was the deputy sheriff while he dressed with speed and dispatch.

"Got a gun?" he queried, and when Kincaide shook his head, he gave him a heavy revolver. The two ran out into the quiet street. As they hurried, the deputy explained that Kincaide was to take the street and he would come by way of the alley. Before they could separate at the alley nearest the post office, there was a sudden tapping on the pavement like the rattle of a policeman's nightstick, then the drum of running feet. The deputy swore under his breath.

"Making for the bridges. Hurry. I'll follow them," he ordered. "Be ready to head them off if you get there first."

As Kincaide gained the bridge, two figures emerged from an alley and halted for an instant. Before Kincaide could get into action, they dashed away parallel with the river in the willows that fringed the bank. A moment later, the deputy came up.

"Get across the river," he directed. "I'll chase them out of the brush, and they'll try to get over by the railroad bridge."

Before he reached the first pier, the sound of a fusillade in the willows fringing the river made him swing around. Two more spurts of fire, then dark figures ran out on the slender railroad bridge. Kincaide broke into a run, but the others gained on him. By the time he was across, they had disappeared into the gloom of the tree-fringed road. Locating the quarry here was virtually impossible. Then loud in the comparative stillness, brush cracked. Almost instantly, Kincaide fired a shot into the air, and an answering shot told him by the stab of fire that the two yeggs were just ahead.

Crouching by the side of the road, he waited for them to make a move. Here in the gloom of the trees, it was deathly quiet with a menacing, charged stillness. Beyond and a little to one side, he could make out the yard tracks and the loom of a line of box cars. Five minutes passed, then two shadowy figures emerged from the trees near the box cars and disappeared. Kincaide scrambled up and began to run forward.

Haste proved his undoing. Trying to keep his eyes on where the yeggs had disappeared, his foot caught on something, and he fell sprawling, the revolver hurtling away into the darkness from his out-thrust hand. When he tried to rise, his foot was fast, he found, in the frog of a switch. He wasted precious minutes unlacing his shoe and extricating his foot. Fumbling about in the darkness in search of the lost revolver was futile. He released his shoe, slipped it on again, and then cautiously approached the line of cars.

For what seemed a long time, he listened, then he caught a sound, the careful sliding of a car door. Cautiously, lest his crunching the cinders under foot might be heard, he stole along the cars keeping close to them where the shadow was the densest. The car from which he thought the noise came was just ahead. His heart gave a throb when he noted the half-open door. From the interior came the sound of stertorous breathing.

Kincaide reconnoitered carefully; then a boyhood tic came to his memory, a hoax used when they played ball over a shed roof. The danger would be chiefly in getting into the car through the door. His chin set stubbornly. Back in the willows, the deputy might be lying dead—he must take the chance. Picking up a lump of coal, he weighed it carefully in his palm and then tossed it over the car.

The sound of its falling was followed almost instantly by a cautious movement from the interior. He tossed another piece, then, taking his desperate chance, leaped for the opening and threw himself inside by a powerful twist of his body.

So far, Kincaide had scored. Save for the sound of cautious breathing, the interior was deathly quiet. Under his fingers, he felt a chip, and he picked it up. The scraping of his nails must have been heard, for a revolver bellowed in the narrow space, filling the car with acrid powder smoke. Kincaide tossed the chip to the far end of the place, and another shot followed. Almost instantly, he leaped like a football tackler for the position of the spurt of fire. He collided with one of the yeggs, and something metallic struck the side of the car. Devoutly he trusted it was the yegg's gun. His clutching fingers felt cloth, there was a sound of ripping, and his quarry eluded him. Both yeggs began to swear viciously. Kincaide realized he was between them and that scored in his favor; they would not dare any more shooting. What he dreaded now was a knife.

A little light filtered into the interior through the door opposite the one through which Kincaide had entered. The cursing stopped, followed by a charged quiet, then a whisper, followed by a movement near the door. This time, as he launched himself forward with all his force, he got his man, and from the weight and strength of his adversary, he knew it was Butch.

Kincaide was a big man, but the yegg was powerful. Locked in a straining embrace, they rained short-arm blows into each other. It was straight rough-and-tumble fighting with nothing barred. Back and forth, they strained and came to the floor with a thump that shook the car but failed to separate them. Kincaide's coat went at the shoulder where Butch tore at him; a moment later, one rip of Kincaide's iron fingers tore away the yegg's shirt in one sweep. He found the outlaw's hairy throat just as

Butch's thumb came against his cheekbone. Sheer animal rage convulsed Kincaide. Butch was trying to gouge eyes out. He jerked back his head and snapped his teeth almost shut on the big yegg's thumb. Butch gave one yell of pain, then Kincaide's fingers closed on his windpipe, while with the other fist, he beat the fellow's jaw with savage short jolts.

So far, Slim had made no move. Kincaide jerked up his knee sharply and thrust it home in Butch's gross stomach. The big man yelled again, but Kincaide bore down relentlessly as he felt his fingers loosen on his throat grip.

"Slim—light—knife him—quick!"

Kincaide's fingers found the throat again as the yellow beam of a flashlight bored through the interior. In the light, he saw the glint of steel. Desperately he bore down with his knees until he dared to release his fingers for an instant. It was enough. Kincaide wrenched off the heavy shoe he had not relaced and threw it, with all his strength, at the man with the knife. Came the thud of the hobnailed shoe on flesh, the sound of a fall, and one rasping gasp of agony. With a sudden rush of strength, he grabbed Butch's head, brought it down with a thump on the planking of the car floor, and the big yegg's body went limp in his grasp.

Kincaide was still leaning against the side of the car, trying to get back his breath, when the door was pushed wide open, and the deputy flashed an electric torch into the interior. He let the light fall first on the two yeggs, then on Kincaide with his torn garments and battered face.

"Well—I'll be—damned!" he exclaimed fervently after a moment. "You beat me to it, got them single-handed."

He flashed his light over the interior again. "Where's your gun?" he demanded suddenly.

Kincaide grinned ruefully. "I lost the darn thing back on the tracks when I fell."

Something in the yellow path of the flashlight caught his attention. Stepping forward, he picked up Butch's old hat. In the band, a blue conductor's check was still stuck, and one corner was torn away. Kincaide drew it out with satisfaction.

"Well, you son of a gun," he addressed the reviving Butch. "I got you." Bending, he stuck the check under the yegg's nose.

"He slipped it from me on the rattler last night," he explained to the puzzled deputy.

An hour later, the two would-be post office robbers were behind bars in the town, which slept on peacefully despite the stirring little drama that had just been played in its streets. Kincaide had just finished putting on a new shirt the deputy had given him when the man reappeared from the office holding two handbills which he passed to Kincaide.

"Look familiar?" he inquired as Kincaide's face lighted.

Kincaide nodded. "Butch and Slim, all right." Then his eyes glanced to the top of the bills and caught REWARD FOR THE ARREST AND APPREHENSION OF.

"Come in the office and sit down," the deputy said. "I've got a proposition."

Despite his declaration, the peace officer sat for a full five minutes before he had a word to say, then he cleared his throat loudly.

"I'm running for sheriff this fall, Kincaide. If I'd a caught those two birds in there single-handed, I'd have gone into office like a breeze, see?"

Kincaide nodded even though he did not comprehend what the man was driving at.

"Well, there's a total of about five hundred dollars reward on them which we split when it comes in a couple of months." He leaned over and tapped Kincaide on the knee.

"I wonder if you might be willing to take all the reward and let me have the glory all to myself." I've got the cash in the safe, and I'll take the chance of collecting, too."

For a reason, Kincaide could not comprehend, the officer's face was red. Five hundred dollars! It made his head swim, a three-summer stake because he wanted back his check.

"Sure, Mr. Sheriff," Kincaide tried to keep his voice nonchalant, afraid the officer might change his mind. "Money talks; I'll be obliged to you."

Five minutes later, the two men shook hands, looking into each other's eyes. "You've got the real stuff, Kincaide," the deputy announced. "You're either a mighty brave man or—." He did not finish, and Kincaide clumped off feeling a sneaking sort of pity for a man who would pay good cash money for such thin stuff as glory.

In the waiting room of the drowsing depot, he found a bench and composed himself to sleep for the remainder of the night. The bundle of bills bulked pleasantly against his side. His plan had come to him suddenly, to ride north and catch that night local south, then to offer the conductor the lost check and rub it in real good. He patted the packet of bills again. Far up the tracks, he heard the long-drawn, lonely whistle of a train. Five hundred dollars, his summer's stake. He sat up wide-eyed, sleep gone in the new emotion that gripped him.

For five years, Kincaide had been a drifter utterly without the responsibilities that hold other men. The night's events, and the danger, all had come from his drifter's attitude that time and place were two things given to be passed. He had followed his impulse and was satisfied but five hundred dollars . . .

In the dimly lighted room, the vision of the mortgaged mountain farm was mighty plain, the ramshackle springhouse with its icy spring, the thin, stony fields, and the green fringe of the jealous pines. The old folks—nostalgia gripped Kincaide with tremendous force. He drew in a breath through his nostrils sharply, as though in the smoky room with its reek of stale odors, he caught the fresh perfume of the pines and the scent of wood smoke.

Over at the ticket window, he pounded excitedly on the window ledge to rouse the sleeping agent.

"Gimme a ticket," he demanded, fumbling with his huge roll of bills.

Up the track, the mournful whistle of the train sounded again.

"Gimme a ticket," he repeated, "Home."

"Come up for air, fellow. That station ain't on this line," the ticket agent snapped crossly. Kincaide explained patiently where he wanted to go, with most of his attention riveted on the steady roar of the approaching train.

MERCY JHOT

BEHIND HIS ridiculously inadequate breastwork of a hatful or so of stones and earth, Clint Howard tried desperately to concentrate on shooting the man who lay hidden in the thicket of hemlocks and birches across the pasture field. The heavy sun bored a hole in the back of his neck, and his head ached abominably. But the headache was not new. The thing had been with him for the last two weeks since Bess and he had quarreled.

Knitting his brows, he crawled closer to the little mound. What was it Bess had said that morning? It was so hard to remember things, and this getting into town and then being involved in chasing this murderer had confused him. His whole body twitched when he finally did remember. He half raised his head from the protecting mound.

"It's too late, Clint, too late." It was easy to recall how she looked, the set of her little chin. Bess usually meant things when she looked that way.

"Too late," the words drummed soundlessly in his ears, a litany of pain. It was too late for Saunders, who had quarreled with Black Dan Rand that morning, for Saunders was lying in the spare bed at his home with blood on his white hair. Too late for the three others shot down by the murderer in his day-long fight with his pursuers.

The sun pressed heavier. Clint's garments felt like level-warmed weights resting against his hot skin. Moving slowly in his discomfort, he remembered another thing and managed to get out his watch and examine it anxiously. It was time for the men who had gone for the machine gun to return. He hoped they would hurry and get here before some reckless posse member exposed himself to the devilish accuracy of the murderer's shooting. He twisted round, scraping his cheek on the ground to keep under the scanty cover. To his left and a little to his rear, he could see the ragged line of the posse, each man behind such cover as he could find. Near the end of the line, he could see Sheriff Greener. Fascinated, Clint watched the officer shove his rifle forward slowly, then empty the magazine as fast as he could pull the trigger. Near the middle of the line, a man became too interested in the sheriff's shooting and exposed himself from behind the tree that had sheltered him. Instantly, from the thicket, a single shot crashed out, and with a scream of surprise and pain, the posse member dropped to the ground and crawled to safety as fast as he could move. The shooting quickened all along the line; Clint fired once. There was a slight tug at his shoulder, followed by a report from the thicket. A bullet had ripped his coat.

Perhaps it was too late, but Bess could not have meant this way. A sudden presentiment came to him that this murderer in that fringe of hemlocks and black birches would send a steel jacketed bullet through his aching head before night or the machine gun came. He wondered idly what a bullet would feel like; there would be little pain, he felt sure, only shock.

Bit by bit, Clint built up the happenings of the day for the hundredth time. He had come to town that morning—it seemed weeks ago—to get something for this confounded headache. The crowd about the Saunders place had attracted him. He could see, vividly, when he closed his eyes, the splotch of dull red on Saunders' white hair and hear Greener swearing in the posse in terse solemn phrases.

"You men will get three dollars a day and expenses," the sheriff had added.

Clint cackled softly to himself as he thought of the promise. What would Bess do with the three dollars? Doubtless, it would be paid to her. Flowers, that would be it; carnations, likely, at three dollars a dozen—or was it two dollars a dozen? He could not remember because of his head. He remembered that he had not told her how his head ached—he must do that without fail. Again, he straightened up a little, and a bullet whined by almost instantly. He returned hurriedly to his prone position and his review.

Rand had been fought all through the day; he had fallen back steadily from cover to cover until now they were entering the Narrows. Once in that place, the whole countryside could not root out the quarry. Three dead, four others hurt so far—that devil in the brush could shoot. An automobile horn sounded raucous in the roadway, and Clint's head cleared. That would mean the machine gun had been fetched from Boalsburg, and the end. Sheriff Greener planned to spray the cover with it.

From the far end of the line, the sheriff sprang up and ran. There was no shot from the thicket, and, with a leap of his heart, Clint understood—Rand was escaping.

To the right was the nearly bare slope of the ridge fringed with laurel along the course of an old road. Clint saw his opportunity, seized it, and gained the bushes by a quick scramble. Just a little ahead was the point of rocks covering the rear of Rand's hiding place. There he could cut off the outlaw's retreat. Clint knew the deadly thicket well from having hunted through it. In its very center was a depression, fully a yard deep, with a sort of natural ditch leading out into the open space in the rear. The hollow had saved Rand from the bullets of the posse, and Clint knew the man's movements would follow the ditch.

He made the last dozen yards on all fours, expecting each moment to feel the jar of a bullet, but he gained the rocks without drawing a shot. Here he tumbled into a sort of stone fort built by boys. Stones had been laid up loosely in the openings. He shoved his rifle barrel through a chink and waited.

The momentary clearness of his head was passing now. He felt queer and sick from the intense throbbing in his head, but he fought the thing. Here on the rocks, he held the key to the situation concerning Rand, and he strained every nerve to concentrate. If the murderer slipped out when the machine gun went into action, Clint could get him. He edged his rifle barrel a trifle farther front.

The sun was beginning its long slide now. Still, the minutes dragged for the watcher on the rock. All along the line, shooting had practically stopped. There was no sound or movement from the thicket where Rand lay. Suddenly the machine gun went into action with a rattling burst of sound that surprised Clint even though he had expected it. Hemlock limbs rained down like grass before a mowing bar; then Rand began to shoot. A yell from the sheriff's line told Clint another man was hurt. He wanted to shoot, to rake the thicket to put an end to the sinister crouching thing hidden there.

Another burst from the machine gun. Clint's eyes were clear now, alight with his desperate purpose. His fingers gripped the rifle as though they would sink into the wood and metal. Something was moving in the thicket. For a moment, he thought it was twigs falling from the machine gun fire a moment before. Five minutes passed, and he caught a glimpse of khaki—Rand had worn a shooting coat. Clint fired instantly. From the ditch, Rand leaped erect. His clothing was in tatters. There was a dark blotch across the side of his face. Even at this distance, Clint could see the man's face was distorted like a beast.

Seconds, minutes-long, passed while Clint tried desperately to hold his rifle on his quarry, but the sight had become a haze. He saw the outlaw's rifle leap to his shoulder; he tried desperately to press the trigger; then, the whole world seemed to explode in a splintering, jarring crash. To Clint came a vision of Bess's face that morning. Then he crumpled down, his body asprawl on the dead leaves that carpeted the tiny amphitheater.

* * *

Bess Howard moved mechanically about the bungalow through the long droning heat of the day. Small, of a fragile prettiness that could warm to the soft flush of a wild rose, she was not unlike the bungalow. It had seemed so jaunty ten years before when the Howards returned from their honeymoon. Now the brutally revealing sunshine showed the once gay cretonne faded and frayed, the rugs worn and colorless, the upholstery growing ragged.

"I'm getting as shabby as the house," she told herself resentfully, staring at her reflection in the hall mirror. Her frown deepened the tiny lines between her brown eyes. She noted the shadows under them and the droop at the corners of her pretty, petulant mouth. "I'm getting to look old," she wailed half-aloud. Her fists were clenched by her sides, and her lips carried the droop of bitterness and discontent.

The day seemed unreal, interminable. She had not meant half of what she had said to Clint that morning, but their quarrel had been a little more savage than usual. She had said it was too late. When her emotions were high, she was prone to threaten, but as the morning wore on, it seemed she had spoken more truly than she had thought. She was through with Clint beyond hope of reconciliation.

He had given her no idea when he would be home that morning. At noon, in a tone of icy virtue, she called his office to be told he did not answer. Her eyes snapped as she turned away from the instrument. This had happened before.

"Golf or pool," she muttered angrily.

Still in a cold rage, she ate a little toast and drank a cup of hastily brewed tea; then arrayed herself in the one frock she considered presentable, a cheap but vastly becoming voile. A little brush of rouge, an almost imperceptible stain of lipstick and she was a pretty, vivid woman again. Her mouth curled up into a winsome smile at her reflection.

It wasn't as if she had to endure this sort of thing. She didn't have to deliberately nurse what, at first, had seemed an incredible dream. Ten years of this and—the memories of her rosy bridal expectations turned her smile sardonic. Ten years ago, Clint had everything to recommend him; a small but growing lumber business; he was liked, handsome, debonair; and she was the prettiest girl in town. Nothing ever had gone *very* wrong—not until lately, but nothing had gone entirely right. Business was always dull when she wanted things. Clint always promised them for the next year, unheeding her recitals of clothes, furniture, and motor cars owned by her friends. Lately, he had taken to drinking. He had always liked to go about, but now he was drinking more and more, unheeding her reproaches. Unpaid bills were gathering like autumn leaves. Her disgust was too deep to permit her to get to the root of the matter.

Well, she was done. She would tell Ross Wyndham so; he understood. Wyndham had made her lot bearable by his understanding, patience, and efforts to keep her amused and entertained. Beneath that was his growing feeling for her, poorly concealed. Within the last two weeks, it was terrifyingly open and above board.

It was intoxicating to know that your bare word was enough to have a man give you all the things that were desirable. The knowledge of what she could do, gave her an odd air of triumph as she moved about. It gave her the courage to acknowledge the bow of the austere Miss Rote, who lived next door, with a hard impertinence. She knew the whole neighborhood commented on Wyndham's frequent calls. Well, no man had ever looked twice at the Rote sisters, that was certain.

The only person who had not seemed to care about Wyndham was Clint, she told herself angrily. So far, she had kept within the letter of the law. She had listened sympathetically to Wyndham's explanation of why his wife had divorced him; she had failed to understand him.

This evening Wyndham would come again. With a feeling of delicious terror, she asked herself whether he would ask her to go away with him and what her answer would be if he did. The afternoon paper, with its account of the battle out in the hills, went unheeded.

All day her resentment had simmered, the sullen heat rising in her as she prepared an unappetizing dinner. She felt sure Clint would be late. The stove's heat flushed her face and made her hair cling to her temples in tendrils. She waited an hour past the time and then pitched the meal into the garbage can, drinking only a little black coffee. Food choked her. Her anger had reached a point where she must vent it somehow. "Maybe he's left me," she told herself. "I hope so; I'm well rid of him." She did not know rage could hurt so; only by hurting Clint could she dull the steely agony of her discontent.

The sound of a car, and a step on the porch, made her heart leap; but it was Wyndham. She stiffened as he entered the dusky living room. Slim in her light dress, she stood rigid as he entered, one hand pressed against her breast.

"What's the matter?" he asked, startled.

"Clint hasn't come home." Her dark head went up defiantly.

"I'm done with him." Then, slowly, "You haven't seen him today?"

"No." A point of light kindled in his gray eyes and grew to a blaze as he looked at her. "I just got into town. I came straight to you, Bess. I, I need you."

"Thank you," she tried to make her voice mocking, without success. His intensity frightened her.

"You'll go with me now, Bess." His voice was uneven; his restraint moved her tremendously. She could not meet his eyes.

"What's the use, Bess? You can't stand this anymore. You've the right to be happy, and I can give you everything, Bess!"

She laughed uneasily. "Oh, well, as you say, I can't stand things anymore."

She tried not to shrink at his stifling embrace, his hot kisses, though something she could not define fought within her. Woman-like, she was suddenly ready for the great plunge but not for some of the lesser things. They talked for a half hour. In the end, he went away to return for her and a bag when it was darker.

After he was gone, she went about her packing. It seemed to her that another woman was doing the little tasks, another in whom she had little interest, but at last, it was done.

* * *

The car swung smoothly into the long grade and began to climb. Bess was tremendously glad the town was behind them. For hours, they swept through wooded hills and skirted steep banks. The sound of the motor boomed in the hollows. Once, far distant, she heard a sharp report, then another, as if an engine backfired. Neither paid any attention to it. They talked little; occasionally, he drew her close and kissed her. She felt unresponsive, detached, as though some other woman was speeding along in the dark.

After the first hour out of town, the road Wyndham had chosen was unfamiliar, but she had paid little attention and could care less. They had been out in the valley for a time; now, the machine had re-entered the hills. They passed through a frowning gap, and a stream flashed dimly to the right of the road. Occasionally she saw the bulk of a cottage.

"Where are we?" she asked.

"Culvey Narrows," he answered. She leaned forward suddenly.

"Why, why," she stuttered. "We're only a few miles from town, what—?"

He laughed easily. "Right, Bess. We doubled and came back. I've a little cottage up here, and I didn't want to come straight out to it."

He swung the car from the highway, entered a narrow lane and came to a stop within a few hundred yards of the road. Bess felt herself suddenly numb; what did it mean? Was he tricking her?

"But, we're going away, we're—"

"Sure," he evaded. "We'll go tomorrow. I didn't want a night drive."

He got out. "Just stay put, Bess. I must straighten up the place a little and find a light." He tucked a rug about her, rummaged in the back of the machine, then left in the direction of a dense bulk of shadow.

Minutes passed; a light flamed up in a cabin, and through a window, she caught glimpses of Wyndham as he moved about. What he had said turned over and over in her mind. He had brought her back near to town, and the rising misgiving within her would not be pushed down. Above everything else that had moved her to leave her home was the desire for freedom, not a great affection for Wyndham. She liked him and was fascinated by his understanding and deference, but she had not gone away with him because she cared. He simply constituted the possibility, financially and otherwise, of getting her freedom back. Now she sat in the car, her evening resolution weak, her mind full of doubts. He would be coming now, soon. She shivered a little.

A rectangle of yellow light showed, then Wyndham's figure. He approached the car with quick steps.

"All ready, Bess. Guess I was pretty long about things."

A sudden numbness seemed to possess her limbs as she stepped out of the car. He seized her in his arms. She suffered his kisses in the same detached fashion she had before; then, her dismay deepened; she smelled liquor.

At the door, he released her. In the center of the living room was a table piled with things: plates of sandwiches, glasses of jellies, fruit, and a frosted pail from which stuck the necks of bottles.

"Filled up the car with this stuff before I came for you, Bess. Thought we'd have a little celebration all our own."

Her spirits lifted a little as she looked over the table. She was reminded that she was hungry; she had eaten very little all day. She began to eat, but she could not help seeing that he ate little and drank a great deal. The room was warm. Wyndham smoked cigarettes, and she saw him through a blue haze. Her appetite suddenly left her. He came round the table and put his arm about her.

"Little girl looks worried," he declared. "Come, cheer up; we're celebrating."

She tried to smile, to respond, but his words were thick, and the odor of the liquor on his breath nauseated her. In desperation, she drank some wine herself. Delighted, he urged more on her and drank himself.

"Got to have a good time tonight. Tomorrow must be all business," he urged. "Conference tomorrow afternoon." He was drunk, she knew, but she did not miss his reference to tomorrow afternoon. Through the haze of cigarette smoke, she saw him as down a long perspective, an evil spider, waiting, waiting. Nausea swept over her. What a fool she had been—was. And now she must pay.

He bent over her again; his fumbling hands sent a chill along her spine. He drew her to her feet and led her across the room. Suddenly she could stand it no longer. Wrenching free, she backed toward the table, but he followed.

"Mustn't spoil the party," he ordered. His thick voice was low, but the light in his eyes frightened her.

"No, no. Have a good time tonight. Tomorrow—"

He caught her again; she struggled furiously. His fingers bit into the flesh of her shoulders until she wanted to cry out. Another wrench, then he struck her. The light in his eyes was sheer drink madness now. She had had no idea that liquor could craze a man so soon.

"Treat 'em rough," he declaimed. "Caveman stuff, you'll like it, my dear."

Again he struck her, brutally hurling her to the couch. For a little while, he stood over her, leering. "Now you'll be good—I like 'em meek."

He crossed to the door and locked that. "Got some gin in the cellar. Going to mix you a real cocktail, then you'll be a good sport."

A trap door in the area way to the kitchen led to the cellar. Using a flashlight, he went down the steps. From the couch, Bess could see his every movement until he disappeared, then she moved with all the speed she could compass. The trap door went shut with a hollow clump, and she dragged forward a wooden chest until it rested on the trap. From below, Wyndham was cursing and thrusting up on the boards with all his strength almost before the chest was in place. She leaped for the door; he had locked it but had not removed the key. In a moment, she was outside in the velvet blackness of the night, running, stumbling, falling, but always trying to get away from the cottage.

How long she traveled, she could not tell. Once, she blundered into the creek. Briars snatched at her dress; stones bruised her feet. Somewhere up the stream would be town and her home, but she had only a hazy idea of how far it was. Whenever she stopped, wave after wave of pain and loathing racked her. She was fast becoming hysterical.

At last, she stumbled and fell under some pine trees. The clean odor of the bed of needles seemed to clear her brain. She would go back to Clint and confess. He must believe her; she had had her lesson. Utterly exhausted, she wept from sheer weariness until she slept.

A soft breeze stirred the trees. Bess came out of her troubled sleep with a shiver. In the east, a faint grayish light showed across the gaunt ranges. Her vitality was at its lowest; huddled there under the whispering pines, she wept in self-pity. How could she go back? Clint couldn't believe her. She saw everything clearly now. She and Clint might have made something of life if either of them had been strong and been above the petty bickering that had ripened into the present trouble. Clint, poor Clint, with all his high hopes, he had failed; and she had helped him fail. Poor Clint—the tears slid down her cheeks.

The shadowy hills began to outline themselves more clearly against the sky. With pain like a knife in her heart, she thought of Clint as she had first seen him, gay, laughing, handsome. Her first tenderness for him came back to her poignantly. She wanted him terribly, the old gay Clint, even the sodden sullen Clint of these last two weeks. Blindly she gained her feet and started forward, every step an agony to stiff muscles. She must move on, get back to town, her home, and Clint.

She had not gone a full hundred rods when she stopped in dismay. Somehow in the night, she must have become confused and moved in a circle; just a little ahead was a cottage she knew and, before it, Wyndham's car. Numbed with disappointment and fear, she stood still and just then, from the door, came Wyndham. He saw her almost in the same instant and dashed forward, yelling threats of what he would do if she did not stop, for she started to run. Over her shoulder, she saw him stumble and fall. He must still be crazy drunk. Then he turned back to the cabin to appear in a few seconds. In his hands was a gun.

Fear drove the stiffness from her muscles and gave wings to her feet. The ground was fairly open along the creek, but there were clumps of thorn trees and piles of rocks. She swung away from the open space and entered the belt of pines. The dark shade seemed friendly to her; perhaps she could get away. Just then, she saw something else and shrank behind a friendly trunk. Down near the stream, behind a pile of rocks, lay a man. Even at a distance separating them, she could see his clothing was in tatters. Dark blotches were on his face and clothes. It was what machine and rifle fire had left of Rand.

Even as she looked, he slowly raised himself and the rifle beside him. He gained his feet and sank back. He was like a dying snake that would strike to the last. Fascinated, Bess watched. The man was watching something, struggling to get his rifle in position. She glanced in the direction the man was looking. Wyndham was coming at a stumbling trot, his gun ready. Her voice would not obey when she tried to cry out; she turned her head. In the still morning air, the rifle report was like the crack of a giant's whip! A second passed, then another shot. When Bess summoned the courage to look, two figures lay prone and still like bundles of clothing that had become loosened in falling.

Sometime in the dark, Clint, in his tiny amphitheater of rocks, had fought his way back to semi-consciousness. With the first vitality of the morning, he fell and crawled to the road below and started downstream, driven by a blind instinct to get help for himself and to capture Rand. In his head, a demon beat a tremendous drum that filled the entire world with pain. Unmindful that he was taking the wrong direction, he kept on. Staggering to the side of the road, briars clutched at him; he wandered off into the pines. Across his face was a smear of dried blood. He still clutched his rifle.

He must get to the others; they'd let Rand get away, which would be unthinkable. He fell and lay still for a minute, fighting to regain consciousness of what he wanted to do. What was it? Oh yes, he must get Rand, or the murderer would escape; poor old Saunders with the blood on his white hair. Bess would be wondering where he was for so long and be angry. He gained his feet. In his pain and bewilderment, he had strength for but one idea at a time; momentarily, he forgot Rand.

Bess would be wondering, be bitter if he had kept her waiting. He wished she could put her cold fingers on his aching head. Perhaps then he could think clearly, be rid of this fog. She used to do that before they had quarreled so much. He shambled on; then, somehow, he heard a cry. He collapsed momentarily; when his eyes opened, he began to mumble. Cool fingers moved on his forehead, he sensed the fragrance of the pine needles on which he lay, and at last, he knew it was Bess who pillowed his head on her lap and crooned over him.

Sheriff Greener had found them; Bess's flight had led her into the pines and, minutes later, to Clint, unconscious. Greener had known Clint and Bess all their lives, and in a moment, he had her story. His decision was characteristic of him.

"Listen, Bess, the posse will be up in a minute, and Clint'll come round. I guess you're cured. Tell Clint you came out to find him. He'll believe anything you tell him. Wyndham got what was coming to him. Can you go through with it?"

Clint's eyelids fluttered as she nodded her head for fear of tears. Men were appearing back in the pines.

Back in the little bungalow, the desire to confess everything had died easily in Bess when she saw the happiness on Clint's face when Greener explained how she had come out to hunt her husband, frantic with uneasiness. Perhaps, she promised herself, sometime when their newfound happiness was more secure, she could tell him, but now—she would not tempt fortune further.

That evening she helped him out to the porch into a chair. He pointed to the west, where the sun was going down red.

"That's a good sign, Bess."

Together they looked a long time at the gorgeous riot of reds and golds. Her fingers tightened on his. She fought back a little shiver as she thought of the evening before. After a little, he drew her brown head down close to him. Gradually the colors faded into the impartiality of the dark.

THIN SIBILANCE

JOAN FERRIS swung her roadster in between the sandstone posts and stopped. The place was beautiful, with its great sprawling house and the green of broad lawns and trees. It was like Mark Breining himself, in its air of being tremendously alive, too much so to be restful. But she had not come to Windacres to rest.

A man was coming now, walking swiftly through the spruces. "Joan," he called.

His voice suited him; she thought as she stepped out of the machine, eager, big, dominating. He towered over her slim height. His snowy shirt was open at his brown throat; he looked as though the winds of high places had swept him clean.

"You must have been looking for me," she said with a smile. Her hand lifted to put a tendril of brown hair back under her small hat. His big arms swept around her.

"Looking for you! Don't be foolish. Just existing until you came."

He kissed her half a dozen times, then held her off admiringly. She wriggled free.

"That'll be enough, Mark. I believe I feel sufficiently welcomed. Tell me, did you welcome them all this way?"

He laughed. "Surely! I always do, especially when they have brown eyes and—"

"Well," she interrupted. "They must have all seen and know I'm here."

He answered her rueful smile with a laugh. "No, you're safe; those spruces shut off the view. Come on."

Leaving the car standing, he took her arm and together, they went in. "Here she is," he called as they entered the hallway, and the guests came trooping in. Joan knew them all, the Ventres, Breining's sister, two or three others, and Polly Catherwood, blond, slim, satirically smiling. She kissed Joan.

"Warm entrance, Joan," she whispered under cover of the perfunctory caress. "Keep him coming; he's good to his women."

"Judas kiss," Joan whispered back.

For a while, the group chattered. Wilton appeared, his face wrinkled but his uniform immaculate, and took her bags. She moved toward her room. Suddenly a French door to a porch opened. Joan stopped, facing the man who had entered.

"Dan," she spoke half-aloud. A queer, faint feeling swept over her. No one had told her Dan Gaines would be here. He was bowing now. Nearly as tall as Breining, Dan was blond, slim and straight. In his eyes was a look of weariness that his smile did not hide.

"This is nice, Joan. I didn't know you were coming."

She tried to carry the thing off lightly but stumbled in what she said. "I didn't know—"

Then Wilton broke in. "Beg pardon, Miss, you're to have the new room."

Glad for the interruption, Joan followed the man to her room and, there, changed rapidly. Breining had told her he wanted to show her the orchards.

For the next two hours, she almost forgot what had brought her to Windacres in Breining's enthusiastic display of his property.

Everywhere there were apple and peach trees, rows and rows of them laden at this season with tiny green fruit. They stretched away interminably.

"Millions of stomach aches," she said, and he laughed.

"Yes, now, but in harvest, they'll be red on the trees, red in the baskets. Red, I like it for a man's color."

He took her for a circuit of the place; showed her packing houses, a cooper's shop, and storage cellars. Not once did he refer to her or hint at an interest beyond delighting her with the place. With his strength and enthusiasm, Mark Breining fitted here just as his white shirt, whipcord breeches, and puttees did.

No wonder Breining loved his place, she thought as she dressed for dinner that evening. In town, he had told her of it, and others had amplified his descriptions. The original farm had been in his family, and he had acquired others rapidly, planting them at once. He played the market for money to further his schemes. Now, when others were broke, he was coming into his own. He had vision. She stared at herself in the broad mirror of the dressing table. Yes, Breining had what she wanted, what she needed—property, money, energy. He was the man who got what he wanted. That he had told her masterfully.

She looked at her image for a long time. A month ago, he had said he wanted her, and she had laughed at him. Now, she was in his house; she had answered his invitation with its implications. It wouldn't be long.

Her eyes suddenly were troubled. Dan Gaines was here, and she wondered why. Had Breining brought him there to taunt him with his victory?

Dan was waiting at the foot of the stairway when she came into the hall and crossed to meet her.

"I didn't think you'd come, Joan." He smiled that infectious boyish smile of his, which his tired eyes belied. She knew he was covering his hurt.

"Why?"

She tried to make her counter casual, but her voice broke a little. Dan's being here made things suddenly hard, almost impossible. She wanted to say something to help him, to smooth his rumpled hair, to straighten his tie. Dan was always that way, just careless, ever kind. She had known him always. His gray-blue eyes met hers.

"Because you can't go through with it," he answered slowly as though choosing his words from a long list.

Impulsively she rested the tips of her fingers on his arm.

"I must. Dan, don't hate me too hard. It's money—"

Wilton appeared. Joan remembered that he had been with Dan's family in better days.

"Dinner is being served," he announced. "Mr. Breining cannot be with us, a slight accident to a workman. He wanted Mr. Dan to take you in for him, Miss Ferris."

Joan was glad that the excellent dinner dragged along interminably so that the bridge games were cut short. Out here in the hills, they were all sleepy early, and she wanted to be alone.

The next morning, they assembled at breakfast. Breining liked to have his guests together at the morning meal, and he was full of apologies for his absence the night before. He explained that a man had been injured and it was necessary to take him to a hospital. He outlined plans for his guests. There were horses, a trout stream, and places to walk.

Polly Catherwood was suddenly interested in the fruit business. "You must show me the place, Mark. I really must see it."

If their host resented being captured, he did not show it. "All right, folks. I'll make a horticulturist out of her in a few hours. Just be at home here."

Joan resented Polly's throwing herself forward, but she also felt relieved; until she found that all were paired off but she and Dan.

"I'm afraid you'll have to ride with me, Joan. I know you don't fish. We'll get a pair of horses and see the view from Hall's Ridge."

They rode slowly through the orchards and turned down a winding road, a leafy green tunnel, at the foot of which they splashed through a small crystal stream. Grouse scuttled away; once a rabbit crossed the trail leisurely. "They're not afraid," Dan told her, "because we're on horses." Presently they were climbing. He chose one road at a fork.

"You were here before, Dan."

"Yes, I owned one of these farms once. Breining bought it at sheriff's sale."

She was sorry she had asked the question. They rode for a moment, then he commented dryly. "Breining usually gets what he wants."

Joan resented the fact that her cheeks were suddenly warm. She brought her riding crop down on her horse and forged past Dan up the rough road. He followed. Once he called to her that the road was too rough for speed, but she did not heed.

Near the top of the ridge, it was much worse, and she was ready to pull her horse in when it suddenly veered to one side and reared. She heard a sharp hissing sound; then, she was thrown through the air. The world went out in a blinding shock.

When she came up out of that well of blackness, she was cradled in Dan's arms. She felt no pain, but she was badly shaken.

"Am I hurt?"

He smiled down at her. "No, you landed in some brush. Can you stand?" He helped her, and she steadied herself. "I must get the snake that scared your horse."

She saw it when he stepped forward with a stick, a thick mottled thing, triangular head raised, rattles erect. Again, the thin sibilant challenge of death, like the rattling of myriads of tiny, very dry seed pods in unison. Dan dispatched it with a blow of the stick and held it up.

"Don't blame the horse, Joan. A snake's bad medicine."

They tied the horses to some trees and went on afoot, up the few rods to the summit. For a long time, they sat drinking in the view.

"I'm mighty sorry about the fall," he told her. "I fancied you might have wanted to come out with me for a talk."

She did not answer, but inside her, there was a tightening, a girding of her strength. Her resolution had cost too much; she had counted the cost too much to turn back now. She resented Dan's presence, which made it so much harder. It had been cruel of Breining, unnecessary.

Joan and Dan had been children together. She wondered now just how much she cared for him after months of putting him out of her mind and heart. He was so kind, so sure. But he was not a success. Bit by bit, he had lost his property. Now he had but his modest position. She had known with Dan, her father's debts would be unpaid, she would be bound, and she needed freedom from the grind of managing.

"It's hard," he said slowly, "to see a girl let go, but much more so when it's one that—when it's you. You're hunting freedom, Joan, but freedom doesn't lie that way."

She rose swiftly and faced him. "Don't, Dan. I'm going through. My mind's made up. I can't face debts any longer or the grind of being hard up."

She stopped and looked at him with wide brown eyes, now almost violet. His lips were set in a straight line. Spoken aloud, her motives looked sordid, and she knew Dan realized Breining's reputation with women. She remembered his kisses, the clutch of his powerful arms.

Now Dan's arms closed about her gently. "Joan, I've always been mad about you, ever since we were kids. I'm fool enough to believe I mean more to you than you know."

She tried to keep her eyes from him, but he turned up her face. She felt tears on her cheeks, but she could not make her eyes lie. He kissed her slowly, reverently. His free hand rumpled her hair.

"You'll go back to town now," he said, "and be safe."

In the circle of his arms, she shook her head. "No, Dan. I just wanted this moment, then we'll forget. I'm going through with it."

As suddenly as he had seized her, he released his hold. "No, I don't want stolen things. Come, the horses are waiting."

Riding behind him on the way back, she could see how white his face was and the set of his jaw. He talked casually of the things they saw, and presently they were back in the rows of apple trees, then at the stable.

After dinner that evening, they danced. Breining led Joan out on the wide porch. He kissed her. "Joan, I'm hungry for you. I'm trying to play host, but it's hard when I want just you."

She was slow in undressing that evening. The room was luxurious, the rugs deep and soft on the polished floor. Once as she crossed to the dressing table, she heard a faint rustling sound below the floor but ignored it. Finally, ready for bed in a sheer gown, she drew a wrap about her and stepped to the door that led out to a small porch. It was moonlit. Suddenly from the shadow, a figure strode toward her.

"Joan." It was Breining. He vaulted the low railing and swept her into his arms.

"Don't," she remonstrated. "They'll see."

He laughed softly, pushed open the door and drew her inside. "Girl, you're maddening." He kissed her savagely, her lips, her hair, her smooth white shoulder from which her wrap had pulled away.

"Don't, Mark, don't be so rough."

He released her, crossed the room, shot the bolt in the door, and returned.

"You know, Joan, I challenged you to come out here. Tonight is ours. Tomorrow we'll drive into town, be married, but—" From beneath their feet came suddenly a thin sibilant rattling. Joan's heart came into her throat. She remembered the snake on the ridge.

"A snake," she said, eyes wide.

He laughed. "Never mind that, it's underneath the floor. We just finished this room a couple of weeks ago. The snake crawled in before the window was closed. It's shut in there."

"But, Mark, why don't you get it out? It's awful!"

Once more, he smiled. "Well, I sort of like to have danger close. It gives a zest to things. I'd hate to be the rat that gets in down there."

Joan shuddered and drew her thin wrap closer. She was afraid at the look in Breining's eyes. Dan had warned her, and now—

Footsteps sounded in the hallway. There was a gentle rap at the door. "Wilton, Miss. Telephone—long distance."

Joan heard Breining's muttered curse, but she closed his lips with her fingers. "I must go." She followed Wilton to the instrument and took down the receiver. "This is Joan Ferris," she said. "Who is it?"

No one answered. A sleepy operator said there was no one on the line.

Breining was still in the room when she returned. "Mark, I can't sleep in this room. I'm going up to Polly."

He looked at her sharply for a moment, then his white teeth flashed. "I can be patient when I'm sure of the end," he said. "Pleasant dreams. Tomorrow night, sure—in this room."

Once more, he kissed her and suddenly snatched away her dressing gown. She snatched at it, furious, but he still smiled as he flung it around her again.

"Good night, Joan. Tomorrow night's a date."

Polly Catherwood admitted Joan with a wide smile on her face. "Some people just can't sleep in the beds they make for themselves. Couldn't *you* sleep, dear?"

Joan explained about the snake. "Well," Polly drawled, "there were snakes in the garden of Eden. I believe I could sleep in that room down there if it were specially built for me if there was even a wild crocodile under the floor. It's what's actually in the room with me that bothers."

She showed Joan to a bed on a deep couch, then returned to her bed. Joan watched, for a long time, the glow of the cigarette she smoked before she slept. Polly Catherwood had depths, and she did some thinking.

The next morning the group was on time for breakfast when the bronze gong in the big dining room boomed; all but Polly and she came in presently, breathless. "Folks, I've just been in Joan's room listening to Mark's family skeleton rattling. Hurry up; I want you all to hear it."

A little reluctantly, Breining explained about the snake, and they repaired to the new room after breakfast. "He's been in there close to a month; maybe one of the men would like to get him out."

No one offered, but as Mrs. Ventres crossed the floor, the rattling came, stridently insistent in its warning. Of the guests, Dan Gaines alone did not remark. Joan heard Ventres remark to his wife, "Queer that a man like Mark'd tolerate such a thing."

That evening when they all trooped into the hallway after bridge and dancing, Polly slouched over to Joan. Dan was near them.

"Dearie, do you want the comfort of my room tonight, or?" She arched her eyebrows provokingly, and her mocking tones caused Joan to bridle and make up her mind. She had accepted Breining's challenge. This was what she had come out to Windacres for.

"Thank you, Polly. It's sweet of you, but I'll chance the skeleton this once."

Alone, at first, Joan was afraid. Not of the snake below, but since she had heard it, the thing took on itself the personification of warning. She remembered the look on Dan's face. He despised her now. Perhaps love might come; Breining had everything that attracted a woman, strength, good looks, magnetism. Something perverse in her brought the memory of Dan's kiss again. It had been like a sacrament.

Undressed at last, she looked into the mirror; then she thought of Breining last night when he had snatched away her wrap. She heard again the thin, sibilant rustle. Panic caught her. Dan had said, "There's no freedom that way."

Her fingers fumbled as she dressed again and trembled as she packed her bag. Breining would be outside in the moonlight. That telephone trick last night had saved her. Had Dan managed it, or was it Wilton helping Dan, whom he had known and loved as a small boy? She could not count on that. To Joan, Breining was suddenly sinister, waiting for her, prolonging his enjoyment by waiting. He was so sure of her. This was his house, and it shut her in. She must hurry.

Outside on the little porch, she suddenly felt weak and shrank against the building. Again, a figure had come out of the shadow and was coming to her. Then a sigh of relief broke from her lips. Next instant Dan Gaines had her in his arms.

"Thank God you were going," he whispered. Now she noticed that his shirt was torn and his hair rumpled.

"What happened?"

He shook his head fiercely. "I've just had the pleasure of thrashing our host thoroughly. He was outside here again."

Joan's fingers found his rumpled hair; then her arms went around his neck. "Take me away, Dan. I'm ashamed."

He grinned. "Joan, I got a license yesterday. There's a preacher not far away. Don't do any thinking. I can't take any more chances with you."

A swift night ride under the stars, then a lamp-lighted room, the quiet tones of the old preacher, the almost indistinct figures of the witnesses by the wall. They used Dan's seal ring for the ceremony.

Hours later, outside the city, Dan stopped the car. Joan leaned against him, reveling in the comfort his nearness brought her.

"Happy, Joan?" She nodded. "We'll be poor," he told her, "but—"

"We love each other," she answered bravely. "Dan, I wonder how I ever thought of what I would do. I was tired, then that snake made me think. I was scared. It made me see what hidden dangers were there in his house. Hold me close, Dan."

"Joan," he said after a little. "I must tell you something. This afternoon, I crawled under that room. Dearest, there wasn't a snake in the place. We heard a seventeen-year locust, sort of a cricket, you know, but it makes a noise like the real thing."

It was Joan's turn to be silent for a moment or two; then, suddenly, she laughed. She drew her new husband's head down to the level of her lips. "Just think, Dan. Here I'd planned how all our lives together I must be good to snakes. Now—now all I need is to be good to crickets!"

"And me," he interrupted as he started the car.

THE RAMBLING PAYROLL

DAN CRAIG slammed the door of the one-room office building behind him and stepped into the spring sunshine, thoroughly mad. Scowling, he remembered that McVey always asked his callers to slam the door because it nearly always stuck. His gesture hadn't been an insult after all. He regarded the lettering on the door with disfavor:

McVey Construction Company

"Stubborn old Scotch fool," he muttered. "Lose your old payroll, not my funeral anyway."

The last was almost exactly what McVey had just finished roaring at him. Down by the impounding dam, Number Two mixer sounded a little off. Dan's long freckled face cleared of its anger, and he swung away vigorously. He'd have to see what was the matter with the thing.

Craig had virtually grown up on Ross McVey's jobs. As a boy, he had carried a rod on surveying crews. Since he came out of college five years ago, he served as an engineer and general foreman. In his heart, he cherished a tremendous affection for the gruff old contractor and for Doris, McVey's only child. This loyalty to the old man had made him bring up the payroll business.

Dan realized it wasn't entirely a mistake on the part of the bank. Payday would fall on Sunday, and the bank sent out the payroll money believing the pay would be made Saturday night. McVey elected to make Monday the day, and that made the trouble.

Six thousand dollars in small bills. Entirely too much to keep in the flimsy office safe or in Ross McVey's big wallet, particularly with this gang of men about. Dan knew what the older man did not, that this was the roughest crew they had ever picked up, city toughs in the main.

"I can take care of myself and my money!" McVey had roared. "You take care of the work! Do you think I'm getting old?"

That was exactly what Dan knew. The blue eyes under the heavy gray eyebrows glared, but Ross McVey *was* getting old, and he didn't realize the latent viciousness of these new men.

Number Two mixer had stopped by the time Dan got there. He and Larned, one of the foremen, set it right presently and stood back to watch it for a while.

"Fired that fellow they called Butch, Dan!"

Dan nodded, his eyes still on the mixer. Larned went on.

"Took him up to the office just before noon. The Old Man paid him off from a roll that would choke a cow. You should have seen Butch's face."

Dan turned to Larned. "We'll have to keep our eyes open. Did Butch leave the camp?"

"Went down the road with his war bag all right. Think he went to Centerville."

For a moment, Dan thought of taking Larned into his confidence but rejected the idea. If McVey knew Dan was sharing his concern, McVey would be all the angrier.

Supper was served early in the mess hall since it was Saturday night. By dark, practically every man was gone. McVey left early in his car. Ordinarily, he would have asked Dan to go along, but the old man was still huffed. Dan grinned when he saw him drive away but shook his head.

A construction camp never seems to be occupied. The shacks stand empty during the day. Only at night, when the lights are on, one looks habitable. Dan made the rounds; they employed only one night watchman, and he was stationed on the work.

Coming finally to his room, he felt restless. On the table that served as a chiffonier stood a picture in a silver frame. Dan picked it up and looked long at the girl's face.

"You'll be here for a little vacation soon, Doris."

He grinned sheepishly and put down the picture. The silence of the whole place brought him to speak aloud. Not a very good place up here for a girl, he reflected, even though Doris had always been at home on her father's jobs. This crew was different. He thought of Butch. That fellow's face surely looked out from some rogue's gallery. McVey had allowed Butch to see the money, and the old man was by now down country somewhere.

Dan put on his hat in sudden decision. He'd walk the four miles to town and look about a bit. You could never tell what might happen down there, even though the men had not been paid off. There'd be drinking at the Blue Goose, and McVey often went there to buy cigars.

It was after nine o'clock when Dan came into the little scattered village. Lights gleamed from the Blue Goose, a sort of roadhouse on the edge of the town, which catered to the men on the construction job. There were other lights but no sign of a crowd, except at the roadhouse.

Dan did one errand, called at the home of a foreman, and was out of the town again a little before ten. He approached the Blue Goose slowly. In front were several cars, one a fast-looking touring car, another which he recognized as belonging to McVey. He moved closer, so he could look through windows into the big room that made up most of the place, and stopped, electrified.

The building stood on a small hill, its floor level perhaps four feet higher than the level of the roadway. Dan had followed a path at right angles to the highway and looked in from the side. From the front, the place would have seemed innocent enough.

Inside, the bulk of the patrons were backed against the wall, facing three men who held revolvers. On the other side was Ross McVey, facing that wall, his hands high. Another of the robbers had a pistol jammed in the old man's ribs. Butch, the discharged laborer, had just pulled the big wallet into which McVey had packed the payroll money from their victim's hip pocket.

Dan Craig had faced dangers in his life as an engineer. He had no weapon. Rage at the treatment of his boss was foremost in his mind. Two leaps carried him to the corner of the building. The man on guard there was not quick enough. Dan saw the light glint on the pistol, struck once, and saw the man sink like a sack to the ground. The next instant, he reached the back door.

Dan had been in and out of the Blue Goose a lot. As he entered, he knew the light switch was just inside the door on his right. Softly he turned the latch and felt the door loose.

None of the hold-up men saw the door open, but only a fraction of a second before Dan's hand shot up and yanked down the light switch. Even as he did that, he saw that Butch had merely turned from McVey.

Dan had played a lot of football. His one hundred and eighty pounds went forward like a catapult. Butch was thrown up off his feet and swept in the direction of the opposite door. Dan's powerful fingers snatched away the bill fold before the man dropped, limp.

A pistol roared, but Dan was through the front door. He knew he had but a few seconds. There was only one thing to do, and he did it. The nearest car was McVey's. Dan leaped in, started the motor, and backed away when the lights snapped on, and a man with a pistol ran out of the door and opened fire.

Dan's foot came down sharply on the accelerator. He would drive to the camp, call the State Police from there and get some kind of weapon. Behind him was the sharp whine of a starting motor and half a dozen shots, the last nearly drowned by the roar of the car and the yells of the men who had been held up in the Blue Goose. The bandits were after him.

The pursuing car was faster than McVey's. Dan saw that when he topped the first big hill and saw the car's lights coming on like an express train. They might overtake him before he reached the camp where he could get a weapon or help. He muttered a curse at McVey's foolishness and stepped down hard.

On the next hill, he knew he would be overtaken. He reached forward and snapped off his lights. It might be possible to swing sharply to the side of the road and let the pursuers pass, but he would need a patch of dense shadow.

Half a mile from the camp, his chance came, and he swung the machine into a road that led through the pines to the dam itself. His wheels skidded sharply, but he was a few hundred yards from the main highway when the bandits' car whizzed by.

Dan slipped out the clutch and allowed the machine to roll forward under its own momentum. Back at the Blue Goose, they would have thought of the telephone by this time. McVey would be directing the pursuit of the bandits with vigor. The roar of the car that had passed died. It had probably stopped at the camp. One man would stand little chance against them.

The car had rolled off the road and nosed itself into the brush. He guided it back. This byway ran back into the hills and then to the main highway again. It might be a good idea to drive on and stay out of the way with the money until morning, at least.

Dan drove slowly at first, then as a grade developed, a little faster. He was running through a belt of pines for the most part, his headlights a yellow fan against the dark wall. The grade ended, the machine shot ahead, then it happened. A slight stir behind him and a cold circle settled against his neck just below the ear.

A cold chill went down the engineer's spine. He had been so sure of himself. By his side on the seat lay the stuffed billfold. The pursuit had fooled him. Whoever held the pistol to his ear had been in the car the whole time.

"Stop!"

It was a woman's voice. Dan had expected a man, but he knew these gangs often had women in them, women quite as deadly as the men. A few hours before, Dan had called McVey a stubborn Scotch fool, but the engineer was Scotch himself and sometimes stubborn and foolish. His foot came down sharply on the accelerator.

The pistol lifted a little. "Shoot, and this car will break both our necks," he gritted.

He caught the beginning of an exclamation, then he did another thing; applied the brakes sharply. The car skidded, slued clear across the way, and a form catapulted across the top of the seat and dropped beside Dan.

She was struggling to get up when he snapped on the dash light. "Doris," he yelled in amazement. Then, he was out of the car, ran round, snatched open the door and gathered the girl into his arms.

"Doris, Doris," he begged. "Why didn't you tell me—" She wasn't quite unconscious. He had run with her slight weight in his arms to the headlights. Her eyes had closed; they opened slowly, looked up at him and grinned.

"Might have known it was you, Dan. Lord, what a bump."

She sat up and began to order the close-fitting hat she wore, took it off finally and shook loose her short, curly brown hair.

"My hair and hat saved me," she explained. "I couldn't see; I thought you had stolen the car while Dad was in the Blue Goose. I'd been in the back seat. Dad came down for me this evening, and I was half asleep when you jumped in."

Briefly, he told her what had happened. "He wasn't safe with the money, Doris," he finished. "Anybody might have taken it away from him. Here it is."

He showed her the wallet. "Put it in your pocket," she told him.

Now both heard it at the same time, the sound of a motor behind them. They scrambled into the machine. "That car's fast, Doris. We'll have to beat it. What's your gun like?"

She laughed and held her weapon under the dash light. It was a small caliber target pistol. "Not much good against that crowd," he muttered. "We'll have to run for it." Their only chance was getting out again to the main road.

Dan was uneasy. Any other time he would have been overjoyed to see Doris, but now he wished her anywhere else. For a mile or so, they drove straight ahead. The road swung to the left, down a small hill, and across a narrow pole bridge that rattled under their wheels. A hundred yards and there was a fork, but the left-hand road appeared to double back. Dan swung to the right. In a half mile, they were going through a gap; the mountain lifted sharply to their left, with a sheer drop on the other side.

Not far on, Dan realized they were lost. At the foot of the grade, they crossed a good-sized creek; and he knew no creek lay where he needed to go.

"Doris, we're wrong."

"Don't you know the road?" she asked, and he shook his head.

"No, we'll have to turn; go back." His head out the window, he heard plainly the sound of the pursuing car. "Listen!" Butch would know this area; he would have guessed Dan's ruse when they got to the camp. The road was getting rougher, and it would end soon, for he knew none went all the way through. This one, probably, led to some hunting camp.

Doris sat quietly by him, her handbag now on her lap, the little pistol across it. To add to his perplexity, the motor began to splutter.

"Out of gas!" he told her when it stopped entirely, and he had investigated. McVey always filled up at the camp. "We'll have to run for it."

Doris pushed the little pistol into his hand and leaped down beside him. "All right, Dan. Let's go."

Her spirit heartened him. After five minutes of scrambling along the rough road, a darker shadow loomed to the left: a cabin. There might be a gun in the place; with a shotgun, he would have almost enjoyed meeting his pursuers.

A side door was closed with a padlock, which Dan broke with a stone. A hurried search inside revealed no weapon more effective than an axe. The building was of mountain stone, fit enough for a siege if they had some way of defending themselves.

Doris caught his arm. "Listen!"

The planks of the bridge just below rumbled, then brakes screeched when another car stopped where theirs had been left abandoned. Doris stood close to Dan. Her fingers stole into his big palm, and he pressed them reassuringly.

"Keep your nerve," he counseled, and she gave him an answering pressure.

The machine's headlights came around the bed, falling on the front of the cabin. The car stopped again, and five men piled out. Before they stepped into the shadows on the sides of the road, Dan recognized Butch.

"Come out of there, you—!" A string of oaths followed, but Dan made no reply. A second of silence, then a volley of pistol shots. Dan drew Doris down along the wall out of the range of the door.

Another volley, then a long silence broken by the rumble of voices. A man stepped up near the car, then another. "Don't believe he's there." They heard the voice distinctly. "Come on, let's rush the place. He ain't got a gun."

The five toughs moved around into the glare of the headlights, pistols in their hands, and came forward.

"Wait," Dan whispered. "Stay here, Doris, I'll try—" He stole to the window that had been broken by a shot, with the little pistol ready, and singled out Butch. A scream of pain followed the snap of the little weapon. Butch went down, a bullet in his leg, and crawled for the shadow. Dan got in one more shot before the bandits gained the shelter of the darkness.

Now, from the two sides of the road, they opened a hot fire. Glass from the windows tinkled on the floor, a frying pan struck by a bullet emitted a loud *spang*, and splinters from the door were hurled across the room. Dan and Doris huddled close to the floor.

"Doris," Dan said quietly after a moment. "I'll hold them off. You get outside in the brush. Travel south. You'll get out."

"Dan, I'd get lost in five minutes out there in the dark! I'll stick. I'm safer with you."

The headlights of the car lit the scene. Dan knew there was just one thing they could do. He and Doris must slip out, get away under cover of darkness, but those headlights illumined the side door, the only other entrance. He waited until the firing had stopped, then slipped to the window. Two quick shots into the car's headlights. He wondered why he had not thought of that before.

Again, the firing. He chuckled when he thought of how angry they must be. Keeping low, he drew near the side door and pushed it slowly open. The woods came close here. Somewhere a little stream babbled. He caught Doris' arm and whispered his plan.

Five minutes later, they were outside. Keeping close to the cabin, they gained its rear without drawing a shot, then down a path to a little spring run over which he lifted her.

"Now," he said. "Wait here for me. I want to give them something to keep them busy."

He sneaked back into the cabin, then to the front window. The dim moon was up; there was enough light for him to do what he wanted. Rapidly he emptied the little pistol at the car. Glass splintered, and he hoped he had hit the tires. When the pistols opened up again, he crawled out and rejoined Doris.

The bandits were still firing at minute intervals when the fugitives were a quarter-mile away, moving swiftly through the woods. The going became atrocious. Brush clutched at them, tore their clothing, and old logs tripped them into briar patches, but presently they came to a stream, and Dan carried his charge across in his arms. They crossed a ravine, reached what seemed to be a summit, then he stopped.

"Tired?" he questioned.

He saw her nod in the moonlight. "Afraid I am, Dan. Let me rest a bit."

There could be no danger here, he knew. Those city toughs wouldn't come this far. Still, he felt sorry for the merciless way he had set the pace. He made her sit down, gathered a great heap of hemlock boughs, and spread them near the tree.

"Now, Doris, Lie down. I'll cover you with my coat."

She obeyed him, but a moment later, she spoke softly. "Dan, guess you'd better hold my head in your lap. I'm—a little—nervous."

He sat down with his back to the tree, pillowed her head on his lap and stroked her curly brown hair until she slept. Her body twitched, and she moaned a bit but didn't wake. She had been so game that Dan had not realized the strain she endured.

The moon climbed higher. The ravine dipped away into the dense shadows of the country below. He wondered where the bandits were. Little breezes played with loose leaves near him. He bent over the sleeping girl and touched her forehead gently with his lips. She moved, her arms came up about his neck, and her lips met his. "Are we safe?" she whispered.

Dan nodded.

"I'll sleep again," she told him and nestled her head closer.

After a while, he slept, too.

With the grey of the morning, he eased her head from his lap and got up on his cramped legs. There were early wild raspberries on some bushes nearby. When he returned with some berries in a leaf cup, Doris was sitting up, brushing her hair back from her face.

"Will you breakfast in bed?" he mocked with a bow. "I know you'll have fruit first."

She laughed and made him join her. They picked more berries from the bushes and finally found a small spring of icy water that refreshed them.

A little before noon, they came down the last mountainside, across a flat, and found themselves at last out on the hard surface of the highway.

"Thank the Lord," Dan exclaimed. "Now we'll wait for a lift."

The first car came from the wrong direction. A minute before it reached them, Dan recognized Larned, the foreman, in the old flivver he drove to work. He brought the battered machine to a screeching stop and leaped out.

"Well, I'll be hanged," he yelled. "I thought you'd come out somewhere up here."

He pumped Dan's arm vigorously and almost lifted Doris onto some blankets on the back seat. Then both men climbed in; Larned spun the machine around and started back.

"Go easy, Dan, when you get in. The Old Man's on the warpath." He glanced back nervously at Doris, but she smiled.

"He ain't likely to forgive you for grabbing that money. He don't like to own up it was bad business keeping it out of the bank. They got Butch and one of the others, and the State Police are after the rest, but McVey's got the sheriff down at the camp. He wants a warrant for you, Dan."

Dan smiled. "What's his charge?"

"Well," Larned drawled. "It runs all the way from kidnapping Doris to stealing his car."

They wheeled into the road that ran past the office. Most of the men were back in the hills, but there was one big car there. They could hear McVey shouting. When they entered the office, he was there with Masters, the sheriff. His face was bright red; he was obviously in quite a state. Doris ran to her father and kissed him. He hugged her vigorously, pushed her aside and glared at Dan.

"Now!" he roared. "What have you to say for yourself?"

His white eyebrows drew down in a savage scowl. Dan slammed the wallet down on the desk. "There's your money. I saw the hold-up and did the only thing I had time for. I didn't know Doris was in your car. I was trying to save the money."

McVey snatched up the wallet, stripped off the rubber band, and opened the flap. For one awful moment, both men stared at each other as they saw inside. Instead of yellow and green bank notes, the wallet was filled with a folded sheet or two of newspaper!

McVey found his voice first. "You!" he yelled. "You try to put this over on me. I'll, I'll—"

His face became apoplectic, and he choked. Then he turned to Masters. "Sheriff, do your duty. Arrest this man."

Masters was stepping forward when Doris held up her hand to stop him. She crossed the room and stood beside the young engineer facing her father. "Sit down, Dad. I've something to tell you."

McVey, for a wonder, obeyed her. "You told me about the money right after you met me, Dad. Do you remember?" McVey grunted. "Well, I was worried. The wallet worked out of your pocket in the car. I was in the back seat and saw it fall. I figured I'd take care of the money for you. I took it out and stuffed in the paper. You were busy with the car. Then I handed the wallet back to you. Remember?"

McVey nodded. "But," he glanced savagely toward Dan, "did he know this?"

Doris smiled at Dan and shook her head. McVey took in Dan's surprised, mystified look with satisfaction. "Where's the money now?" he demanded suddenly.

Doris opened the handbag she had carried in the car and had clung to since; and dumped the contents, piles of bills, before her father. She turned to Masters.

"Mr. Masters, are you going down to the county seat soon?"

The sheriff nodded. "Pretty soon; why?"

She smiled at her father, then at Dan. "Well, Dan and I want to go along. We want to get"

She stopped with a smile, and Dan finished soberly, "a marriage license."

Back at his desk, McVey fumbled the pile of banknotes and stared at them. The storm of his anger had burned out. His face calmed. After an interval, the ghost of a smile showed on his lined face. He spoke slowly.

"So, she fooled him, too," then he chuckled deep down in his throat. Rising, he came round the desk with his hand extended to Dan. "Go ahead, but she'll keep you stepping 'til—'til you're as old as I am."

A moment later, with his arm about Doris' slim waist, Dan stepped out into the sunshine. Something inside him was singing, and the birds in the trees were answering.

THE TENTH CAR

THE TENTH CAR had not gone up the mountain!

Craille raised himself on one elbow and listened. He could still hear the purr of the engine. He knew now that the machine had swung to the left across the little bridge and stood in front of the cottage there. He had neighbors, the first since he had been here.

Each night for the six weeks he had occupied the cottage, he had followed a sort of ritual, first bed, then count ten cars passing on the highway out front, then sleep. Tonight, the tenth car had been long in coming, he had nearly dropped off several times, but now he was wide awake.

There was more sound from the cottage, startlingly loud in the echoing hollows. Baggage was being transferred from the car to the building. He caught the low rumble of a man's voice, then the thinner sound of a woman's sudden laughter.

Craille told himself he liked that laugh. There was a lilting unforced quality to it that was appealing, and the woman's voice was just as pleasant when he caught it a moment later.

"Not a bit of it, Jim. Don't coax. I'm going home."

The man's rumble followed for a little. Craille found himself applauding her decision.

The car motor quickened, hummed. He caught her gayly flung "Goodbye." The bridge echoed back the thud of tires on the planks, a yellow fan of light searched the front of Craille's cottage, and the car was gone with the echoing drum of the motor against the hills.

For a long time, Craille lay there speculating. Sleep would be slow coming. Outside, the pines whispered softly in the little winds that drew down through the ravine, at the end of which his cottage stood. No more cars passed; there were no other sounds but the rattle of the brook and the pound of a locomotive miles away somewhere. Craille's new neighbor seemed to have gone indoors to remain perfectly quiet.

Craille's routine was broken the following morning again in two ways: he overslept, and he felt irritable. After he had finished his breakfast, he felt better; about nine o'clock, there was a knock at his back door.

Instinctively, Craille liked the man who stood there, a big fellow who looked a trifle disheveled despite the excellent cut of his clothing, like one who slept in his clothes.

"I'm your neighbor across the water." He gestured toward the little stream and smiled. "Sorry to bother you, but have you any milk?"

Craille held out his hand. "Glad to welcome you. My name's James, and I have plenty of milk."

The big man shook hands warmly. "Mine's Courland. I'm all the more pleased to meet you because I can't bear canned milk."

Together they went to the brook, where Craille kept his things in a box in the water. Then, supplied with milk, Courland left.

"Come over after I've had my breakfast; smoke a cigar with me."

Craille smoked a pipe thoughtfully after the man had gone, then went indoors and took some pains to change the arrangement of things there. With plenty of time on his hands, he had experimented with sections of wallboard and the open window until he had turned the room into a sort of sound amplifier. This he took apart, stacking his materials away. When he finished, he went over to the other cottage.

Courland answered his knock promptly and genially invited him inside.

"Glad I have a neighbor. My wife brought me up last night and assured me I couldn't stay, that I'd get lonesome."

Craille went inside as his host held the door open. Courland looked to be a man about fifty; the woman's voice last night had seemed young.

The cottage was a big affair, much larger than the one Craille occupied, and he was astonished at the luxury of its furnishings. There were excellent rugs, upholstered furniture, game heads, and pictures.

"Never thought you had such a pretentious place. Aren't you afraid to leave it all up here in the hills? Fire and theft, you know?"

Courland laughed. "Everything's insured. I'm in insurance, and everything's covered, down to the doormat. Ordinarily, you can't get coverage on such places, but I fixed things. If this place was to burn, I'd get my money out of it."

He laughed again, this time with a faint touch of bitterness. "Fact is, fire'd be almost luck."

Craille saved himself from commenting on this remark by asking about one of the pictures, and a little later, he departed after inviting Courland over. The man puzzled him. At times he was attractive, but something under the surface kept rising up that changed him subtly.

For the remainder of the day, he saw little of Courland, but the following morning the neighbor came over.

"Making my party call," he explained with the laugh Craille liked.

"I'm pretty well acquainted with your place. A friend of mine built it shortly after I built mine. By the way, did you buy it?"

Craille shook his head. "No, just rented it through a real estate broker. Doctor Taby sent me for my nerves. He said I had to have rest and quiet in the hills and recommended the real estate man who had this."

Courland looked Craille over, seemed to note the wiriness of his body, the lines on his thin face below the upstanding shock of hair.

"You better?"

Again, Craille nodded, but now Courland found something that interested him, a huge contour map of the section, marked off with red circles and minute lettering.

"Mind telling me what all this is?"

Craille came over. "Just a pastime. You see, I walk a lot and note the things I see. Then I come and set down everything on the map. You'll find every tree clump, every big rock listed there. I started with the cottage as a center."

Courland bent over the map. "From the lettering, you're an engineer. Is that right?"

Craille smiled. "Well, I had engineering training, but the map's a plaything. It sort of gives meaning to things. I can locate sounds. When a bird sings, I know exactly where he is, how far away he is, and all that."

Courland straightened up. "You mentioned Doctor Taby. Are you acquainted with him?"

"No, only as a physician who was recommended."

"Well, he stands ace high with the insurance companies I represent," Courland explained his curiosity. "When we have a puzzling case, we send it up to him. He's the last word. I know about this nerve stuff, too. That's why I'm up here. I figure I need the quiet. I was getting pretty shaky, working pretty hard the last year or so."

In the three or four days following, Craille could not help noticing that Courland was not getting anything out of his rest if that was what he came into the hills for. Daily he became more haggard, neglected shaving, became unkempt. He would go for long tramps in the hills, returning dog-tired. The two of them got on well together, though, spending long hours on their porches smoking and talking.

On the fourth day, Courland loafed during the forenoon but took a long tiring tramp in the afternoon. In the evening, he came over for a smoke. For an hour, he talked little; then, he turned sharply toward his host.

"James, you'll have to forgive me for being such poor company, but I'm worried I'll have to talk or go crazy!"

Craille filled his pipe slowly, lit it, and by that time, Courland was underway again.

"I'm in insurance, live in Ravensburg about forty miles from here, supposed to have a good business."

Craille nodded understandingly, and the other hurried on.

"I've been making money, but—it's taking it all. Five years ago, I married a girl twenty years younger than me. Good family, used to money, and I spoiled her. I've been spending way beyond my income, especially the last year. Of course, I never told Doris, but for a little over a year, she's been unhappy. Now I've got it figured out. We don't fit—it's the age difference."

He waved his dead cigar excitedly. "No, don't think we quarrel, not that. But I can see she's unhappy. I'm man enough to give her a divorce, but she has scruples about that. I've sounded her and know." The man's face was tense. He jumped up and paced the room.

"One day, I came home. That Blunt from the bank was there. He and Doris had been going over something. I saw her face, animated, like it used to be. When I came in, they stopped talking. Blunt looked queer. He's young—fine looking, near her age. I tell you, I'm shutting her off from what she deserves, happiness! If I knew a way of getting out of her road, I'd do anything—"

"Suicide?" Craille voiced the outlandish suggestion. Courland, in his excitement, caught at it.

"I'd thought of that. I have heavy insurance."

Craille leaped up, laid his hand on the other's shoulder.

"That was beastly of me, Courland. I didn't mean it. I only thought that had come to your mind at one time. You're tired; this rest up here will put you on your feet."

Courland's mouth twisted into a bitter smile. "Rest—I'm giving it to her! That's the best thing an old man can do for a young wife, get out of her way. I tell you, she's tired of having me about!"

It was another hour until the man quieted down and went over to his cottage. Craille thought suddenly of Doctor Taby. "Here in town, every time you stop ten minutes on a street corner, Craille, one of your problems will pass you. Get up into the hills away from such things."

That was the gist of Taby's advice. Now Craille's lips twisted slowly into a grin. He did not count cars that night to get to sleep. Across the creek was something more interesting.

The next morning, Craille was up early and off in the huge roadster he kept. Once out of the hills, he opened it up, came presently to a small city, then to a brick house set back from the street. A woman answered the door, and Craille liked her at once. She had thoughtful eyes and a wide mouth. Craille could be engaging, and people found it easy to talk frankly to him.

That evening, Courland seemed more at ease. Craille spent the evening, and Courland talked of Canada. The man had a real gift for holding attention, and he had likely read much on his subject. "A great country for a new start. If I was footloose, I'd go up there to a little town, start a store. Hunt and fish in my spare time; there'd be real people."

The next morning Craille called over to his neighbor. "I'm going to tramp round a bit, get data for my map."

Courland came down to the stream. "How far are you going?" There was a shade of anxiety in his tone, as if he disliked being alone.

"Not far," was Craille's reply. "I don't take long tramps like you. Just a mile or so."

Once out of sight of the cottages, Craille did exactly the opposite. In the woods, his small spare body seemed to slip along effortlessly. He followed the old logging road that ran from the highway a mile or more back, and where it stopped, he found something that interested him tremendously—a fresh blaze.

He was back home mid-afternoon, tired and dirty and quite prepared to work several hours over his map. But his eyes were bright, and he whistled a bit off-key as he worked. Later he produced a "Forest Use" map and studied it for a while. He nodded with some satisfaction over what he had learned.

The next day he was away again, this time in his car, and returning, he displayed a half-dozen trout.

"Tried those Narrows trout," he declared. "Come over for supper."

It evidently did not occur to Courland that a day was a good bit of time to put in, getting this amount of fish. Once, however, he looked up.

"Do you know, you're picking up. Got more color, eyes look clearer."

"You ought to go, Courland," Craille countered, but the man only shook his head.

Two days later, a passing truck brought in the mail, and there was a long manila envelope for Craille. He studied the contents with absorbed interest for a long time. Finished, he got up and paced the room for a while. He liked Courland. There were possibilities in the man.

Courland had developed a morose streak after the fish dinner and kept to himself more or less. Craille was not hard to discourage, and the two kept to their respective sides of the little stream. On the second day, Courland started for a walk, and then Craille did a mighty unneighborly thing. He neatly burglarized Courland's cottage and did not emerge for a full half-hour.

That night Courland said he was going to bed early, that he was tired. Craille noted a sort of wire-drawn look about the man's lips but did not comment.

By nine, both cottages were dark. One or two cars passed, but in the main, what sounds were heard were the little ones of the night; the eternal rattle of the stream, the soothing soughing in the pines, and once in a while, the sleepy twitter of a bird.

Craille was not asleep. He lay near his back door, which was wide open, and he was as wide awake as the door was open.

An hour slipped by, and the brook seemed to change its tune, then another hour. Lying there, Craille thought there was a stirring in the night, but that was mere imagination. Another hour, in the darkness, his sense of smell warned him. Instantly he was up and out of the door and across by the back way to the old road.

He was just in time. A light footfall on the plank bridge, then a dim figure coming into the shadows.

Craille's voice snapped like a whip in the darkness. "Halt, put up your hands!"

Courland gave a grunt of sheer surprise and fright. Craille stepped in close and shoved the muzzle of a revolver against the other's body.

"Back to the cottage, Courland. Hurry!"

Courland offered no resistance and hurried, goaded by the pistol's muzzle. The door of the building was unlocked, and Craille switched on the lights. Already the living room was filling with smoke. Gesturing in the direction of a chair with the gun, Craille leaped to the closet under the stairs and yanked it open. A dense cloud of smoke poured out.

Ten minutes later, Craille had stopped the fire set in a huge box of excelsior.

"Any fire upstairs?"

Courland shook his head negatively. He seemed unable to speak, and his face was gray. All life seemed to have gone out of him as he sat there moistening his lips with his tongue.

Craille darted up the stairs, returning in a moment, his face grim. "Well, I see you solved your problem. Thought you were clever." His eyes suddenly blazed. He stood over his captive. "Where'd you get the skeleton?"

Courland looked up stupidly, then answered. "Had it for years. A medical student gave it to me."

Craille nodded. "If you'd got away with the fire and been seen elsewhere, you'd have been up for murder. Do you see it?" Courland made no reply for a moment. Craille drew over a chair.

"Listen, Courland. You were out to beat the insurance companies. You came up here with a bunch of money in your pocket, which was paid to you on a matured endowment policy. You have a car hidden back in the hills for the getaway. I found it. Everybody knew you'd come up here. You brought a skeleton along. It's upstairs on a pile of oil-soaked waste on top of your bed. The whole upstairs is oiled. You figured the fire under the stairs would give you time to slip away clear."

Courland's eyes followed the other man, but he did not speak.

"You lost out by about ten minutes. That much to the good, and they'd have found your bones in the burned cottage. Your wife would have received your life insurance, and you'd have been well away to Canada. A new start."

Now the badgered man leaned forward. "You said your name was James; who are you?"

Craille laughed. "I gave you the wrong name on a hunch. My name's James Craille, special investigator for a number of insurance companies, yours among them."

Courland sank back in his chair. Craille's voice lashed on.

"I was on sick leave up here. You tried so hard to pull the wool over my eyes I got suspicious. Courland, you amateur crooks make me sick."

He leaned forward suddenly. "Why did you do it?"

Courland twisted round and scowled. Craille went on. "You were hard up; your story that night was true. Then you got this policy. You thought your wife was tired of you and extravagant."

Courland was not yet beaten. He jumped up and towered over the little detective. "Keep her out of this!"

Craille rose, a different light in his eyes. He put his hand on the other's shoulder in a friendly gesture. "I liked you, Courland, but you've been a fool! Didn't even understand that wonderful wife of yours. What would you do if you knew she'd been saving the money she asked you for because she knew you were squandering it and that she had it all safe? That she's been doing that for years, doing it because she loves you. That she sensed you were flying too high and didn't want to hurt your pride?"

Courland's eyes were hungry, eager. "Have you talked to her?"

"I have, and it's true. She doesn't need to know you're a crook, though. Want to go back? Have you had your lesson?"

Courland started toward the door, then remembering, returned to his chair and sank into it. "You know it's too late."

Craille shook his head. "No, I'm not on regular duty. I figure you've learned your lesson. My car's over in the shed. Go to her tonight! She's one woman in a million."

Three-quarters of an hour later, Craille was back in his cottage, ready for bed. Courland had gone with the car. The cot creaked as he lowered his weight to it. Suddenly he chuckled. He had just remembered that break of Doctor Taby's when he said Craille had to leave the city, where every corner presented its problem.

He settled deeper into his blankets. There was a welcome coolness in the nights up here. He began, through habit, to count the passing cars. Four. Outside, the little winds whispered through the pines, and the brook gossiped softly.

A string of three cars passed, five minutes, and two more. Nine cars had passed. He dozed and hovered in the borderland between sleep and wakefulness. Another car . . . .

"Ten," he mumbled with sleep-stiffened lips, and this tenth car went up the mountain.

YOU GET YOUR FIRST BUCK

WHEN THE hunter's moon begins riding the autumn skies, the disease of the itching trigger finger passes from the common to the epidemic stage among those who take to the hardwood ridges in quest of the elusive whitetail. There is no doubt about it; hunting is the greatest amateur sport; vigilant game wardens keep it from professionalism.

Among hunters now, one finds a swaggering attitude. "Where you going for your buck this year?" and the like. It's a sort of discussion of a foregone conclusion. I protest; I am not writing to these experts but the great army of the uninitiated. To those who set forth for the first time, full of hope, who wonder how to accomplish this feat. How to establish the connection between a soft-nosed bullet and one of those elusive, hard-running, buck-jumping animals that can smell a man at half a mile and beat a slow bullet hands down in a hundred yards? Even these experienced swagger birds know it's a real problem. It's not simply a case of aligning sights, squeezing the trigger, and then toting out the meat.

The beginner speculates first as to his armament. I am glad for the word of an authority recently in a magazine to the effect that: "The deer hunter is, oftener than not, over gunned." It's a grand feeling to throw a finely stocked rifle to one's shoulder, to have your eye guided down that blue barrel by fine sights, and to feel that with this weapon, you can dust a blue jay's comb at a hundred yards. Believe me; the gun can do it, but—well, there are slips.

Here in the east, it isn't once in a blue moon that you'll find your deer standing on the opposite ridge. Even if he is there, without binoculars, maybe the blamed thing does not sport a hat rack. Madame Doe may be every whit as large as her lord and master, and those batting ears are deceptive things. Don't be misled. Turn down the cannon. Buy something that will shoot straight and flat over a hundred yards, brushy yards at that, but also lightning-quick to reload.

No, brother, I don't want you to plan to lay down a barrage at a deer. But when you've fired your first shot at a deer, your bullet has gone into that vast empty space that the buck totes around with him and from which he expertly keeps his body. Slam the lever down; remember, your gun is built to work that way; they'll fit a new lever if you break it. Now, you're ready for the next jump over beyond that clump of red brush. The theory is, load fast, shoot slowly. It's a case of hurry, so you can be slow, just like a girl hurriedly powdering her nose in her room so she has time to come down the stairway slowly, gracefully.

There's another thing about that fancy shooting iron you have rejected, the one that uses those long, viciously pointed bullets. Every time I fire one, I feel myself waiting for the referee's whistle and looking for the first down signal. Brother, those things kick with freedom and abandonment that would make a mule green with jealousy. Never mind the jeers of the initiated and the council not to put your thumb over it—you're not playing football—you're going hunting. Remember, that recoil will draw your attention from the business at hand to your rifle, and you don't want that. Get something short that won't hang up in the brush; fast, neat, safe at both ends; and, if you love your fellow men, leave the shotgun and the 'punkin' at home. One of those big, soft, lead basketballs can glance around a corner and ruin a man with the right to think himself safe. Punkins remind me of the way the good wife throws a stone; it's a matter of conjecture which way the danger lies.

You have your rifle, and I hope you have enough money left for a hundred cartridges; for you're going to have not a housewarming but a gun warming. Give the gun crank around the corner your gun and one of those boxes of twenty cartridges. Have him target the weapon. When he has finished, thereafter, let the sights alone. You have eighty cartridges— your next business is practice, and I hope that somewhere, not too far away, is woodland, safe for your experiment. Shoot that new gun a lot.

We will assume you have learned the hang of it in a measure. You can't make three-inch groups at three hundred yards, but you can bunch them reasonably close, say in your hat, at seventy-five yards or so. The next lesson is harder: pick a stump that's not too big. Step off fifty or sixty three-foot strides. It's better if the stump is a bit in the brush and if there is a small hill to its back. Keep your back to it, count to three, and wheel around. Keep your eye on the stump, *not on the rifle*. Make the weapon come to your face until the sights line up, don't breathe; squeeze the trigger, and mark your shot. Let us hope it was in the stump. Keep practicing, and time your fire. You're getting on when three out of five bullets strike the stump pretty close together and low. Don't try to be too fast—I don't believe there's much chance for venison after the second shot.

You have your rifle and some practice; now to your costume. Far be it from me to advise you here, but, whatever you wear, have the good wife sew on it red cloth—bright red. I am tempted, some years, to wear red underwear. There have been times when I craved a flock of red toy balloons about my head when the next drive got warlike. Doll yourself up in red until you look like an overgrown cardinal bird gone haywire. It's simply amazing what some folks think looks like a deer.

Now, you are armed and dressed. On the opening day or the night before, let the good shot of the gang drive the car. Nothing spoils my good intentions with a rifle like the long drive to the hunting grounds. Of course, you haven't loaded your rifle, and, equally, when you got out, you didn't draw out your gun by the muzzle. Believe me, the darn thing is dangerous.

The morning is glorious, a little misty this early. The air has a heady quality, like wine. Most of the leaves are down. Facing the woods, make a resolution you will keep: not to kneel while hunting, but at all times to stand on your hind legs like a man. You don't want to show anybody how well you can imitate a deer, not here in the woods; that stunt means slow music and flowers.

Last fall, our drive worked out across an old farm grown up to thick bushy pines. Suddenly, behind a low jack pine, I saw something brown, then a touch of white. It moved, too. I kept to the cover, rifle ready, and moved forward. Closer and closer, I had only one way of knowing it wasn't a deer; it didn't run, and I didn't believe any self-respecting deer would stand in such scant cover. Yes, it was a man, an old man. He didn't wear a scrap of red; his coat was brown, and his hair was white. Beside him where he sat, on a stone, lay a copy of the game laws; his rifle was pointed through the tree. He grunted a greeting.

I answered, then said: "Brother, you've got lots of faith."

He scowled. "In what?"

"In a happy hunting ground," I answered.

He was courting suicide. His relatives should tie a cowbell about his neck and insist on sharp underwear so he'd keep scratching and ringing the bell.

If you are a still hunter, likely you'll be in the hands of a competent guide. My message isn't for you. I figure you'll be one of a party, and you'll work things this way. Most of you will string out through the woods and drive. Your best shots will be stationed on a ridge or along a road, and you will drive the game their way as you move forward.

Now is the time for a little confiding in you. Don't let them stuff you too full of woodcraft. Getting a shot at a buck deer is largely a matter of accident. All these preparations are to increase the possibility of this lucky accident. The deer are plentiful, but there isn't one behind each pine tree. There may be only a few in a square mile. But it is chance that makes hunting such a good sport.

The brethren on the watch do not deserve your envy. If it's cold, they stand and slowly congeal while you're moving and warm. If the drive is long, the minutes drag by, and it's mighty hard to keep the attention focused. When the line gets closer, your nerves insist on tying themselves into a double knot. You're afraid of two things; first, that some driver will blunder out ahead of the rest, and the other is that the deer will get by before you can shoot.

You will have to get into action—fast. The buck will come that way, and you have the split seconds while he passes. If you miss, you have thrown away the labor of the drive. The only thing good for you is to take your stand where you can see a maximum of country.

For me, at least, the fun is in the drive, but you have a fair question. What shall you look for? What does a deer look like in the cover? Well, forget Landseer's Stag. He won't look like that. Keep your eyes open for the unusual, and the thicker the cover, the more ready you must be. One moment, the woods will seem as empty of chances as the stock market; next, there'll be a scurrying rush, a flash of white tail. If the gods are good, you'll see a great rack held back along the top of the neck, and a nose stretched forward. Hold *low*, hold your breath, and squeeze the trigger. If you missed, maybe the watchers'll get him; you can scare up plenty of alibis.

For his size, a buck presents a mighty scanty target when he is intent on going places. An old hunter told me he believed a buck at speed, going directly away, was as hard to hit as a ruffed grouse. It is always a marvel to me how he manages to tuck up all that weight of meat and to present that elusive, bounding, legs flying, white-tail-bobbing spectacle of himself. Going away, he doesn't look graceful, but he's efficient.

Steady when you see him. Let me hope for you he goes away quartering. Hold low, and get the bead of your sight down into the notch. Aim where you expect his front knees to be the next second. Again—hurry to be slow. The theory is to shoot for where he isn't so that your bullet will get there when he is. Right here, brother, is one place where these fast locks on the new guns are fine; your bullet gets started fast, and there is no reason for leading.

This same old hunter friend tells me he never leads them. Well, that's all right for him. He has used the same rifle for years, thirty or more. Shooting a deer with him isn't so much hunting as mathematics. You and I must lead Mister Buck a little, even granting that it looks foolish to aim at thin air when there's so much deer in sight.

When you have gained experience, you will know that I am pleading for fine sportsmanship when I want you to hold in front. You must hit that deer in the head, neck, or front shoulders—no paunch shot for you. Shot through the abdomen, the deer will travel miles and die in horrible agony. Have a heart, don't shoot anywhere there's a big bulk. You won't get your deer if you do.

Personally, I don't hone for a standing shot. I'm not so hot with a rifle, but there's something about a standing deer. A friend of mine, a fine game shot, had a big buck step out and confront him. After his second shot, the deer departed contemptuously and unhurt. The next day this hunter dropped a smaller buck, going like nobody's business through the thick red brush.

Keep your eyes open in that line. A big buck can slip away, head down, as quietly as a wind-borne leaf. He also likes to slip back through the line of beaters, where accidents happen, when everybody starts shooting. Occasionally, you'll get a bit too keen and whip a soft-nosed bullet at a rabbit. Once on a drive, something stirred ahead in the thick brush; I fought my nerves to control and raised my rifle slowly. Hold low, I whispered to myself. Then, into the open stepped a lordly wild turkey!

Of course, it was out of season. I do have a yen for shooting turkeys, even more than deer. That gobbler strutted his stuff, and I remembered that he was not in season. A loaded rifle, a gobbler—the finest quarry in the woods—and after a time, he went away. I hope he has a large family.

Suddenly your chance comes. Your nerves are steady. You hold the white bead down in the rear-sight notch against the background of a reddish-brown shoulder. This buck is moving slowly; no need to lead. You squeeze the trigger, having remembered to hold your breath. The woods ring to the flat whiplash of your rifle's voice. Your buck bounds; he's going away. Steady, his white tail did not show; he doesn't appear in that open space ahead. You jack up another cartridge and move forward; your friends are calling. Your heart leaps as you round that clump of laurel. It can't be true! Yes, it is. There he lies, where he dropped in his stride; his antlers are a great rack; he is unbelievably sleek and brown. You have shot your buck.

Once more, allow me to confide in you. I hope you won't get him the first day, perhaps not the first season; that makes it seem too easy. Be one of those who hunt humbly and persistently before the quarry drops. Then, yours is a lengthened anticipation rich in woodland joys. Yours is the rustle of brown leaves underfoot, the distant drumming of grouse. Before your eyes is the haze on hilltops, the spicy smell of pines and a forest prospect that makes a man profoundly glad that he's alive. Yes, brother of the itching trigger finger, anticipation is a sharper joy than realization; when you set forth to get your deer.

THE SECOND CRASH

"**F**LAT?"

The first word Howard Ventnor spoke to me made me angry. I was downtown on an errand for Mr. Vincent, using his car. His last words were, "Don't take a chance with punctures. I'll be in a hurry this evening." And now, there was the left rear, a huddle of limp rubber, and a rusty nail in plain sight. No wonder I paid no attention to the car that had drawn up on the other side of the street.

"No," I snapped. "I've just put on the coffee, and I'm waiting for it to boil."

The man laughed, and I looked up. He was standing, his hands on his hips, his white teeth showing. Then he swept off the light-felt hat he was wearing.

"In that case, I'll stay for breakfast. That is if there's plenty of coffee."

I laughed, and he joined in. "I'm a car man. I'll change the tire for you. No need to call a garage."

He had the machine on the jack in a jiffy, quicker than I thought such things could be done. I explained what Mr. Vincent had said as he worked.

"In that case, we'll repair the tube."

It didn't look hard, he was so quick and expert, but in a matter of minutes, he had the tire off, the tube out and patched and the spare in place.

"Now, get in, sister. We'll run around the block for some free air. I'll drive."

The moment he took the wheel, the machine seemed changed. The engine purred, and we went fast but dodged the bumps, so I relaxed with a smile.

"I know this old bus; sold her to your old man. You tell Vincent he needs a new machine. I've tried to sell him for the last month, but he's slow."

Back, finally, to where his new car was standing, he got out; and I slid into place back of the wheel. I thanked him, and he grinned, showing those wonderful teeth.

"Don't thank me. I'm glad for the visit—Miss Hope Barnes."

I stared at him in surprise, and he drew my driver's license from his pocket and gave it to me.

"You had that lying on the seat," he explained. "I always look out for prospects." He passed me his card.

"I'll be round one of these evenings to show you the new car."

I started the engine, prepared to let in the clutch. He looked at me tantalizingly and drawled, "Thanks for the visit and say—I like small girls with red-brown hair." I let the clutch in. "With dimples," he finished as I shot away.

I thought I was angry all the remainder of the day, but occasionally I'd catch myself smiling at the way he had gone about things. I was leaving Mr. Vincent's private office about closing time, and I ventured a question.

"Mr. Vincent, who has the agency for your car here in town?"

"Spring Motor Company," he answered, then smiled. "They've got a live young bird on as a salesman. The other day, he nearly made me think my car was a total wreck. Wanted to sell me a new one."

"Are you changing cars?" I asked.

He laughed. "Haven't the faintest idea. But if that confounded young Ventnor gets me in tow, I'll have to, in self-defense. He's the smoothest thing in town."

That was my introduction to Howard Ventnor. I tried to get him out of my head, but two days after our meeting, I was in my room when the landlady called up to me. She said that a man was waiting to see me. I went down to find him on the front porch, and standing by the curb was a beautiful seven-passenger car.

"Called to give you your demonstration, Miss Barnes. The boss turns over all woman prospects to me, you know. Of course, I know girls like you prefer big machines, and here yours is."

Of course, I had to laugh, and I really enjoyed the ride we took in the huge machine. Ventnor had a gift with machinery; the car he drove always responded like a live thing. He brought me back early.

For the better part of a month, he kept up the fiction of trying to sell me a car for the pretext of taking me out for the most wonderful drives. Then we began stopping at places for lunches and dances.

So far, the men I had known were either employers or the young men with whom I worked. I had been in Lock Haven for nearly three years when I met Ventnor. I worked in the big paper mill offices; my immediate superior was Mr. Vincent. I had always liked a good time. Dad used to go out with me before I went to business college. Mother had been dead for years. The crowd about the big mill was fast enough to make any girl gasp at times, but we stuck together.

"This gang always gets home," Big Jim Parkes used to say, and that was our battle cry or, rather, a pleasure cry. All the girls smoked, and most of us drank a little, all largely to be thoroughly devilish. None of our bosses cared what we did, so long as we were efficient in the offices.

But now, I was pairing off with Howard Ventnor. He fascinated me. His laughter, his easy way, and the flash of his even teeth under the clipped mustache seemed different. He seemed to belong to the big world outside somewhere, and I liked the frank way he played with me. Sometimes he'd rumple my mop of red-brown curls like a kid; sometimes, he'd be sober for an hour at a stretch. Several things I noticed—he was older than I thought; there were odd lines at the corners of his mouth. The other thing, well—

Howard had taken me to a party at a roadhouse on the Island, and most of our gang was there. We danced, but Howard's face was red. There was a touch of surliness about him, and I wondered what was wrong with him. A little before twelve o'clock, Big Jim Parkes came up to me.

"Hope, Mae and I are going home a little early. Won't you come with us?"

I looked at him, surprised and a little resentful. "But," I began. Jim grinned and held up one of his huge hands.

"I'll speak to Ventnor. Mae and I'd like company, kid. You just sit tight."

He moved away, and I saw him find Howard at the punch bowl. I hurried over. Howard was scowling. Jim had a hand on his shoulder.

"So, we're not taking chances," Jim was finishing. "Hope goes home with us."

For just a moment, I saw something in Howard Ventnor's eyes that frightened me, a queer, wolfish light; and he seemed to be measuring Jim, who stood over him smiling. The look passed.

"Jim wants you and Mae to go home with him, Hope. It will be all right with me."

All the way home, I was resentful and said little. I was wedged in the single seat of Jim's roadster against the door, and I was wondering. When we reached town and my boarding house, Jim got out. Mae kissed me goodnight, and Jim followed suit.

"Ventnor was a little lit up tonight, Hope," Jim said. "Mae and I figured we'd better look after the kid, that's all," he explained.

Mae French was one of the older girls, and I liked her as much as I did Big Jim, but I went into the house wondering. The next day I picked up some more news. Howard Ventnor's car had side-swiped another machine on one of the Island bridges, and there had been a fight and several other things. Two days later, I lunched with Mae French and was dying to ask questions. When we reached our dessert, she looked up brightly.

"Spill it, Hope; you've got a lot of questions on your mind. Come along, ask, sister."

I colored, but I asked my question. "Mae, what's wrong with Howard Ventnor when he's been drinking?"

Mae fished out a cigarette, studied it momentarily, then lit it.

"Well, Hope, none of our gang is too good, but they play. Ventnor's bad when he's had liquor, just plain bad and reckless. No girl's very safe when he's been drinking. He'll do anything. Sober, he's a good sort, but he's been in a good many scrapes when he's drunk. Some of our girls can tell you if they would."

Why do young people resent advice and the truth Mae was telling me? I don't pretend to know, but it angered me.

"Mae," I snapped. "You just don't like him, and neither does Jim."

She smiled. "No, girlie, you're wrong. I like Howard Ventnor, fine. Jim don't, but I do. He, I mean Howard, has played round too much, though, and we don't like to see him use you as—" She leaned forward suddenly, and what she said cut like a knife thrust. "You know, of course, that he's married."

My dry lips framed the word. "Married."

Mae nodded. "Has two children, too."

To that moment, I had not analyzed my feeling for Howard Ventnor. I thought I just liked him. Now my world seemed spinning. I tried to light a cigarette, take it nonchalantly, and hide my feelings from Mae, but in the end, my head went down on the table, and I cried my heart out.

Mae was a brick. She came round and hugged me. "Poor kid, we'd ought to have said something sooner, but we all thought you knew what he was. We didn't dream. Didn't you find out about him?"

I shook my head. I had made no inquiries about him. I had just taken for granted that he was free and playing the same sort of game I was, light-heartedly. By and by, I took myself in hand and went back with Mae to work.

For nearly ten days after Mae and I had talked the thing over, I threw myself into my work. During the days and at night, I went everywhere I could, to dances and parties. I was the wildest spirit in our crowd, but I was trying to push down the misery in my heart.

Then Howard came to me with a smile and a new car, and I went out for a ride. Never once did we allude to anything between us. He seemed content to be near me but was not as light-hearted as he had been. I saw the lines were deeper about his eyes. When we came back to my boarding house, we sat for a few minutes before I left him.

"How's business out in the plant?" he queried suddenly.

I laughed. "Really, I don't know. Mr. Vincent hasn't confided in me, you know."

He fooled with the ignition and turned it off and on. "It's pretty rotten with us lately. Has me worried."

Two evenings later, he was back again. Once more, we drove, and this night he frightened me. He stopped the car and wheeled around.

"You know, Hope, I've a notion to chuck things. Dad did, you know. These smashes I've been in don't help me. I get to thinking about them until I'm wild, then the booze helps for a bit. Hope, you're the only hope I have—Hope, let's chuck everything and get out together!"

There was a savage intensity about him now. "How about your family?" I queried coolly.

He sneered. "I've plenty of money, but it's in trust with my brother, who owns the agency for which I sell. If I lit out, he'd turn it all over to my wife. He believes in her.

"Hope, I love you. Yes, I know you'll say that's an old gag, but it's true. You're all I think of. Let's take the car and just go on, not come back."

Something inside me was choking me. I wanted desperately to do just what he said. A high tide of wildness was surging through me. I met his recklessness with my spirit. But outwardly, I was cool. I laughed.

"Let's—but get me back in time for the office in the morning. I've got to earn my living, you know." Then I turned hard. I was fighting myself and him.

"Say," I said. "Just ring down the curtain. I can wait for the last act. Just now, I'm plain sleepy! Home, James," I mocked.

He took one look at me and turned. We went back to the city at the fastest clip I had ever traveled, and he nearly dumped me out at the boarding house. I climbed to my room, threw myself on the bed and cried my eyes out.

The girls in the offices began leaving on their vacations. I wasn't ready, for I'd squandered my paycheck, as usual. Two of them had rented a cottage somewhere in the hills, and one was Mae. She made me promise to come up to see them over the weekend. Saturday came, finally, and I planned I would go.

Just after I reached home, Saturday noon, Howard drove up.

"Say, Hope, let me run you up to the girls for the weekend. I understand Mae and one of the others are up in the hills."

I was glad. It would save hiring a car. "You're on, Howard. When can you go?"

"Be ready at four."

My bag was packed, and I had waited half an hour when he arrived. He was driving the roadster he had driven to the dance from which Jim and Mae had brought me home. The rumble seat was piled high with things covered with canvas. But when I ran out to get in, I saw that his face was red, and there was a reckless light in his eyes.

For the moment, I was frightened. Then I thought, I'll be out to the girls' place in a short time; what difference does it make?

We left the city a-sailing. I have a poor sense of direction, and I assumed he knew where the girls were. We went through Flemington, then Mill Hall.

Howard Ventnor had appealed to me by the way he treated me when I was out with him, none of this rough stuff. Directly after we had left Mill Hall, though, he began almost violent love-making. I scolded him at first, but he did not seem to hear. He'd turn to me, and the car would angle off the road. Then he'd dodge back onto the highway again.

We passed through the first string of mountains; then through a small town I'd never seen. I turned to him.

"Where are we?" I demanded. "The girls aren't over here!"

Howard laughed and slid to the side of the road. He fished out a bottle, took a drink, and offered the flask to me. I shook my head, and he put it back. For a moment, he inspected me with mock gravity.

"Hope, you've got a great head on you. You're right; the girls aren't over here. You and your curly hair, and both dimples, and my humble self, are going for a weekend at my cottage." He slipped the machine into gear and rolled on with one arm thrown around my shoulders. No, I wasn't frightened; I was angry clear through.

"Stop!" I demanded, but he merely laughed and went on. I threw off his arm. For the moment, I hated him, hated the liquor reek on his breath, hated myself for being caught in such a simple trap.

Again, we entered the mountains. This road clung to the side of the hills, and steep banks pitched down to a brawling stream. Howard's arm went about me again. I was desperately angry. He managed to kiss me.

"If—you do—that again—I'll—"

I didn't finish my threat. He swept me close and crushed his mouth against mine. I struggled and struck him, but he laughed and jeered. We swept around a curve, and then I acted. I didn't care; all I wanted was to get even.

For just one moment, I hated Howard Ventnor, hated him as I never knew I was capable of hating anyone. Nothing mattered, just so I stopped that jeering laughter. The bank was to the right. I thrust out my arm, seized the steering wheel, and gave it one desperate push.

Too late, Howard saw and released me, but his frantic clutch at the wheel came when the wheels had already leaped the low embankment. Just a moment, the great machine seemed to cling, then it crashed down the sharp slope, smashing the brush and snapping small trees as it went!

I must have been hurled clear of the machine. I landed in a clump of small hemlocks that broke my fall, but I was partially stunned. When I became fully conscious, there was a sharp stabbing in my ankle. I was lying by the side of another road, this one through the woods and a man dressed in high boots and khaki was kneeling over me. His thin, keen face was brown from the weather. His voice was anxious.

"You hurt?" he asked anxiously, and I shook my head.

"What happened? Steering gear broken?"

Again, I shook my head. "No, I did it."

The anger faded out of me, but anxiety had not yet come. I was completely indifferent to Howard Ventnor and what belonged to him, but I asked casually, "Is he—killed?"

The forester laughed. "No, he's walking about his car, swearing. No, I guess he isn't dead. Shall I call him?"

"No, no!" I protested vigorously. "Get me away from him!"

He stood up suddenly and moved toward Howard and the damaged car. I tried to stand, failed, and crawled around the tree out of sight. Minutes later, the forester passed me, and then I heard the sound of a machine on the woods road.

Later, I learned that Howard's machine wasn't damaged much; and it wasn't a half-hour until it was out on the road above where I was hidden. I could see the machine through the thick branches and hear the two men.

Howard must have offered the forester money. I saw him shake his head. His voice was cold. "No, I don't want any money. You can get back to town."

Then Howard said, "Well, call that girl up. I've got to get her back to town."

Again, the cold voice. "I'll attend to that, mister. You just move on."

I was close enough to see Howard's face turn red. "Oh," he sneered. "You want her?"

That was exactly as far as he got. The sound of the blow was like a pistol shot, and Howard went down flat. After a moment, he scrambled up, crawled into his car, and shot away down the mountain.

The other man was very gentle with me when he came back. He helped me into the seat of his small truck. "I'll take you to my place. My name's Dan Giles; I'm a forest ranger."

His place was an old house set among pines. It was small, clean, but obviously man-kept. My ankle hurt pretty badly.

"I'll take you into a bedroom. You get your stocking off, and I'll have hot water ready in ten minutes."

His brown fingers were amazingly strong and gentle. He fixed up the ankle expertly, for he had a first-aid kit, bandage rolls and all. I asked about them.

"Have to fix up the men sometimes," he explained. "It isn't hard to do a simple strain. Now, I'll call a doctor. There's one in Loganton."

"No," I protested vigorously. "Don't. I'll be alright if you let me stay here for a few days."

His face flushed. "Why, I'll be glad to have you stay as long as you will."

My ankle was slow to heal. Monday, it was some better, and Giles helped me outside for a while. He was proud of his place. In addition to his duties as a ranger, he had a small nursery where he raised ornamental trees. He told me with pride that his sales amounted to more than his salary.

"I like to see them grow," he said as I looked over the rows of small evergreens standing like soldiers.

I tried to help him about his kitchen. He had to be away on Tuesday, and I baked a cake. He was tremendously pleased, and I, from then on, tried to please him more. He was tired of cooking for himself. On Wednesday, we tidied up the kitchen and made a pretty good job of it. My ankle was improving, but I dreaded going back to town. They would already wonder about me in the office, but I could not go back and face the others. Then Thursday came the blow. Giles came in with the mail. There was a newspaper.

"Here's the weekly county paper," he said. "Maybe you'd like to see it."

I turned to it eagerly, covered a column or two, and then the lines leaped out at me.

Howard Ventnor a Suicide, Coroner Finds

The little living room reeled around. Giles had gone out, so fortunately, I was alone. By and by, I steadied enough to read on.

> Ventnor, a local automobile salesman, was recently in a motor crash. He had spent a day and night in the local hospital, from which he was then discharged. He returned to his home, where he was found dead from the effects of poison. It is believed that he brooded over the effects of the automobile accident and killed himself in fancied remorse. Search is being made for his companion at the time of the accident.

That was as far as I could go. Howard Ventnor had killed himself on account of me. I was his murderer! I, Hope Barnes, had killed a man. Clutching the paper, I staggered into the kitchen. A fire was going, and I threw in the paper and dragged the stove lid into place. Suddenly the whole earth reeled and rocked sickeningly. I fell into a well of darkness.

Dan Giles told me afterward that the doctor said I'd been pretty badly shaken up when we went over the bank, but it was days until I was rational again. Giles had called in a woman, and they nursed me through two long weeks between them.

As I became stronger physically, I was more and more troubled by my problem. What should I do? By this time, there would be an investigation on about Ventnor. Would there be a trial? Could they do anything about me?

Giles came in about sunset and sat down beside me. He was smiling. "You're better?"

I nodded and turned a bit on my pillow. "Mr. Giles," I began.

He put his hand over mine. "Everybody round here calls me Dan. That mister makes me feel sort of silly."

I managed a wan smile. "Well, then, Dan. Does anybody where I came from know about me?"

"That's our trouble," he said earnestly. "You see, I didn't even know what your name is. You said to call you Hope, but it could have been a nickname. I supposed you came from Lock Haven, but that's all I knew until I found the name Hope on one of your handkerchiefs. I don't know your surname."

I breathed a long sigh of relief. So thus far, I was safe.

"What did you tell the woman who helped you?"

He began to fidget about. His face was like a beet. He stammered. "Well, she's sort of funny. I figgered she'd talk, you and I being here together. So, I told her we were—"

He got up, walked to the window, returned, and sat down. "Well, I told her a cock-and-bull story. Said we were engaged, that I was bringing you here to see this place, and the car went over the bank."

I wanted desperately to laugh, even as worried as I was. In the end, I smiled. "Good, that's fine, Dan." He was so relieved he made another turn round the room. "What am I going to do to repay you?" I said. He shook his head and smiled.

After that, he whistled around his work in the kitchen and whistled when he came in to say good night. Mrs. Edwards was to go home in the morning. I insisted on his paying her out of my money, and he finally acquiesced. Then I remembered I didn't have enough for the doctor.

That night I fought with myself. What should I do? Go back to town and face the trouble or—. Suddenly I was face-to-face with the most awful temptation. A husband could not be made to testify against his wife. Dan had said we were engaged. If he married me, I'd be safe. But Dan had been wonderful! What right had I to wreck his life?

The next morning my mind was made up. I was improving. Mrs. Edwards went home. I got out of bed as soon as I could. No need to tell what I did, but I used every wile I knew on Dan. Just one week after I got out of bed, Dan Giles and I were married in the Centre County seat, and I returned to the little house his wife.

And, despite my conscience, I was happy. I saw now that I did not love Howard Ventnor. I loved Dan, my husband. I had tricked him, but

I knew I loved him with all my heart and soul. And he was happy, happy as a king. There were no questions about my former life, but I told him as much as I could. The only thing I hid was the story of Ventnor's death.

"I don't want postmortems, Hope. You're my present and future Hope, old girl," he said, rumpling my hair. "Let's go out and see the trees."

Then one day, three weeks after I was married, he asked me to go along to Lock Haven on some business. "You can run around while I do my work, Hope. In the evening, we'll go to a show." I couldn't refuse. We went, but it was like going to a funeral for me. Still, I felt safe from the consequences of my ride with Howard Ventnor.

Thirty minutes after Dan left me alone, I ran into Mae French, and she bore me to her boarding house room. "I'm dying to talk to you!" she declared.

I told her a preposterous story of my meeting Dan and my marriage.

"Gee," she said. "Take me over to those mountains. Maybe I can catch somebody, not a lounge lizard! But honestly, Hope. I'm so thankful you broke away from Ventnor in time." I said nothing, and she hurried on. "You knew about his death, didn't you?"

"A little I read in the papers," I managed casually.

Mae snorted. "Another one of his drunks. He, and another married sport, had two girls down to Williamsport. Ventnor side-swiped the lower Island bridge. His partner got the girls away, but one nearly died in the Jersey Shore Hospital. Ventnor thought she was dead. That's why he poisoned himself."

Dan and I went to the show, and Mae went along. We got back to the hills in the small hours of the morning, but I could not sleep until I had told him.

"Pretty good time, Hope, wasn't it?"

I nodded. "Dan, I want to tell you something. You'll want to turn me out, then, but—"

He assumed a mock-startled expression, but I hurried on.

"Listen, Dan. When I married you, I thought I had been party to Howard Ventnor's suicide. I married you to, to—because I—Dan, I didn't love you when—"

He caught my arms and turned up my face. "But, Hope, you love me now, don't you." He seemed satisfied by what he read in my eyes. "Hope," he said softly. "I've something to confess, too. I knew all about you. You see, you babbled a good bit when you were sick. And I knew Howard Ventnor, knew him that day on the road. But Hope—I was willing to marry you on any terms." He shook me gently. "From the first, I was wild about you." He grinned. "Two swindlers. She marries him for protection; he marries her because he's willing to take her on any terms."

Suddenly he was sober. "But, Hope, you love me now, don't you?"

I threw both arms around his neck and hugged him. "Dan, Dan, you're wonderful. How could I help it?" Then his strong arms were about me. He swept me up close. The last cloud was gone; I was happy and content without measure.

UNDRAPED

AS BRENT CALDWELL turned his car in on the drive, Ted Aldice ran down the steps of the bungalow, and was rods away before he turned, waved his hand, and called something that sounded like "safe keeping."

Aldice was in and out often; the bungalow was never locked, so there was nothing unusual in the appearance of the would-be sculptor. Besides, Brent was preoccupied. This was the day—his first open house to Doris.

He stepped from the roadster with pride in the closely clipped lawn, the beauty of the shrubbery, and the way the rambling bungalow fitted into the setting. Doris was bound to like the spaciousness of the place and the peace under the big trees. Inside, everything was immaculate, the long-beamed living room with its trophies and pictures, the worn leather furniture, everything in its place, in perfect order. Mrs. Walcott and her niece were jewels, and they'd done a good job. A clock on the mantle chimed, and he started; he did not know it was so late. Doris and her people would be here in a scant half-hour.

He hurried to the kitchen, where Mrs. Walcott explained with a smile that things would be just right. Her niece would wait at the table. Satisfied, Brent took a turn through the other rooms to be sure Doris would find things just so. This would be their home for much of the year, and he wanted her to love the place and know that one could live in an artists' colony and not be frowzy. Even the view was right; he reflected as he glanced from the living room window at the blue of the lake. Now, he must dress.

His bedroom was on the side of the building and opened from the end of the reception hall. He hurried, changing to immaculate white flannels after a hasty shower. Standing before his mirror, knotting his tie, he whistled softly through his teeth. Suddenly he started as if cold water had poured down his back. Reflected in his mirror from the bed was the figure of a woman.

Brent had lived among these artists, painters, and writers long enough to accept the unexpected, but this was too much, particularly today! He turned slowly.

The girl was asleep and had evidently been that way while he had dressed. A thin coverlet was thrown across her, but her slim, graceful back was innocent of covering, and so was a foot and the greater part of a smoothly-turned leg. The dark head was almost concealed by the soft pillow into which it was sunk.

Brent was angry—this day of all days! It was Aldice; that fool had brought her here. He tiptoed to the door. He would open it, slam it, rouse the girl on the bed, and tell her to get out. His hand was on the knob when a car stopped out front. There was the sound of voices. He caught the booming tones of Forbes, Doris' father.

Too late, he took a last glance full of exasperation at the calmly sleeping figure. Then he pushed the door shut behind him.

Four people alighted from the car, Doris, her father, her mother, and Aunt Sue. They were noisily glad to be here, they assured him. He led them up the steps to chairs on the broad porch.

Doris was radiant. "Brent, it's marvelous, that view of the lake through the trees, the lawn. And the house! Brent, you'll have to show me every stick of it, all the rooms so that I can plan. Oh, I'll even have to be shown the closets, every girl's wild about closets!"

He patted her arm reassuringly. "Yes, dear, after lunch."

Forbes heard the word lunch and rose. "Brent, we've had a long ride. I'd welcome a chance to wash up a bit."

Brent led them to the reception hall. Forbes laid his hand on the knob of Brent's bedroom door. "Is this a bathroom?"

A cold chill of panic swept through Brent. It would be a predicament to have his future father-in-law open that door and catch one glimpse of those pink and white shoulders on the bed.

"No, no, Mr. Forbes, down the hallway."

Forbes did not seem to notice his excitement but moved off. Brent strode after him and opened the door of the bathroom. "Here you are; help yourself."

He had left the ladies standing by the bedroom door, and as he turned, he saw Doris had twisted the knob. He strode forward, the door already half-ajar, and closed it firmly.

"Doris, that's my bedroom. I don't want you to see my housekeeping. Even Mrs. Walcott leaves that place alone." He tried to chuckle.

Mrs. Forbes laughed. "Doris, you'll have to learn that no man likes the intimacy of his housekeeping to show. Time enough for that, later."

Doris laughed, caught Brent's arm, and moved away from the door with him. He repressed a sigh of relief, patted her hand and echoed her laugh, relieved.

Forbes rejoined them. "Mrs. Walcott will have lunch on the dot," Brent told them. "I can't have you miss seeing my garden; let's go out."

"Well, a successful landscape gardener should have his own place just right," Forbes commented in heavy facetiousness. "Let's go."

Brent had looked forward for a long time to the pleasure of showing Doris the setting he had arranged for the house where he would place her. Most things had been planned with her in mind. He liked to think of her slim beauty in this setting of shrubbery and flowers.

The others dawdled, exclaiming over each new thing. Finally, they were far enough back for Brent to slip through an opening in a hedge with Doris.

"Brent," she exclaimed. "It's wonderful!"

Surrounded by high shrubbery, sheltered by trees, was a tiny grassy glade with a small bright pool in which flashed tiny goldfish. "Your hide-away," he told her. On tiptoe, she held up her lips for his kiss.

The others were coming now, and the two stepped out and joined them. They moved to the very end of the garden, where a single un-draped female figure stood. She was a fountainhead, a thin stream of water emerging from her pursed lips. Forbes broke the silence.

"Very artistic, Brent," he commented. "It bears out what I've always said, that there's no suggestiveness about the undraped figure."

Brent's mind flashed back to that figure in his bedroom. From a corner of his eye, he saw Mrs. Forbes' tightly pursed lips. He had often enough heard the family opinion of artists and their fellow workers. Mrs. Forbes was a Puritan, despite her social activities.

Lunch was perfect, a midday dinner, in fact, and Mrs. Walcott's niece served it skillfully and quietly. They all enjoyed it, from Doris to her mother. The hour slipped by, and it was nearly two when Forbes glanced at his watch.

"Brent, you've led us astray. Your cook is a marvel. Now, we haven't much time. You know the women will want to look over the house a bit, then we'll have to fly."

"Right," Brent agreed. "I'll show them about; I want them to see everything."

"Even the bedrooms," Doris teased. "Mother, he was scandalized this morning when I tried to peep. Then you helped him out."

"Oh, Doris," Mrs. Forbes chided. "I know what your father's room would be like if he lived alone."

He led them to his studio, hoping that he could keep them safely busy until Forbes became impatient to start. There he showed and explained the models of estates he was landscaping, tiny things in scale. "That's the Goodwin place," he pointed to one. They gathered round with delighted exclamations as they recognized, in miniature, grounds they had seen.

"I'd like to play with it," Aunt Sue declared.

"Lovely," Mrs. Forbes agreed.

They were back in the living room when Mrs. Walcott appeared. "Mr. Caldwell, there's a man to see you."

Brent frowned. "Tell him to wait, Mrs. Walcott, I—"

"Beg pardon, sir, I did. He claims it's pretty important." From her tone, he knew something significant was meant. This would be no ordinary caller, and he excused himself. Outside the kitchen was Officer Fallon of the local police.

"Well," Brent demanded. "What's up now, Fallon."

The officer produced a notebook and thumbed it open. "Mr. Caldwell, you were in a hurry this morning. That new car of yours is pretty fast—"

Brent drew out a bill from his pocket and closed the policeman's fingers on it. "Sorry, Fallon, my fiancée and her parents were coming. I was in a real hurry. Take this donation."

Fallon grinned and put away his notebook while Brent raged inward-ly. He did not want his guests alone.

"I'll forget I saw you. But—I almost forgot. Did you see that crazy Aldice today?"

Brent knit his brows. For a moment, he did not remember. "No, Fallon, I don't believe I did."

"Well," the officer rumbled on. "This morning, he was doing some-thing suspicious like."

"Sorry, Fallon," Brent interrupted. "Some other time, tell me the sto-ry. Only if you catch Ted doing things that seem suspicious; just run him in. It'll do him good. I'll bail him out."

Fallon laughed, and Brent darted inside. He was too late; he saw that at once. The group was in the small reception hall. The door of his bedroom was open, and Doris was emerging.

Doris Forbes was modern enough. Brent knew that, but no mod-ernism would be proof against what she had seen; he knew instantly from her face. Some imp of perversity had impelled her to look in. Mrs. Forbes, only a step or so away, saw Doris' look.

"Doris," she demanded. "What's wrong?" Instead of stopping at her daughter's side, Mrs. Forbes pushed open the door and immediately came out again, closing it. Brent ran forward.

"Really," he cried, "I can explain!"

Doris's eyes flamed, but she kept her voice low, steady.

"No doubt, Brent, no doubt. But we mustn't disturb your friend. She's so peaceful in there, so cool."

Forbes looked around the group. "What's going on?" he boomed. His hand dropped on the knob, but Mrs. Forbes pushed it away.

"No, John, you'll not go in there," she said firmly.

"Why?" he demanded, and Aunt Sue nodded, craning her neck.

"Because the man to whom our daughter is engaged has a friend in there, a woman. And she has forgotten to bring her clothes. She's—she's—" Her control snapped, and she shrieked the last word, "Naked!"

"Come on, Mother; we are really disturbing the poor thing." Doris' voice was icy. "Goodbye, Brent. The lunch was lovely, and, really, you have lovely taste in views, trees, and—models!"

Brent followed them outside, the women with their heads in the air, Forbes mystified but indignant. He left the group on the walk and went for the car. Doris drew off her engagement ring and handed it to Brent.

"Here, Brent. Sell this, and buy the poor thing a nightie."

Brent turned the ring over and over in his palm, stunned. Someone was crossing the lawn in the rear, but he scarcely recognized him other than to see that he entered at the kitchen door. Forbes had brought the car around when Ted Aldice appeared on the porch, carrying something wrapped in a sheet over his shoulder.

"Brent," he announced as he came down the steps. "I had to borrow a sheet. That fool Fallon nearly arrested me this morning, so I had to park Milly in your bedroom."

He stopped, sensing the tenseness of the group. They stared. To Brent, Doris, and Mrs. Forbes, the thing over his shoulder was obviously the figure that had slumbered on the bed.

Ted bowed. "Brent should present me, ladies. I am Ted Aldice, sculptor. I make life-sized mannikins for dress designers and the like. This is Milly." He jostled his burden, partially displacing the sheet. "She's my best job. I was taking her down to a fellow to have him box her up, and I ran across Fallon. He complimented me by thinking I was carrying a lady in the altogether—" Aldice grinned into their shocked faces.

"Well, I ran into Brent's place, parked her on his bed, and just now came back for her. Officer Fallon can't see beauty in the undraped, you know, at least not when he thinks anybody is looking." He winked. "I'll have to run now; much obliged, Brent, for looking after Milly."

Leaving them staring behind him, with the figure bobbing grotesquely over his shoulder, he hurried away down the street.

BLOOD IS THICKER

THERE HAD been no firing for the past half hour, and it had become very still on the top of the bluff. An occasional puff of warm breeze whispered briefly in the thin needles of the jackpines and rustled the leaves of the bushes.

The three men lay in a rough triangle. To see each other, it would be necessary to stand, and the skirmish line down below had demonstrated that standing was risky business. Red lay to the extreme left. By his side was a scattering of short blunt cartridge cases. His automatic lay before him. He seemed half asleep. Butch was on the right, the vicious muzzle of the "Tommy" gun thrust through a clump of laurels. His heavy face was expressionless, but his small bright eyes held the watchfulness of an alarmed snake.

The third man lay where he could look down on the wreck of their car. From time to time, he moved enough to draw up his ankle and touch it with his fingertips. It was swollen now so badly that opening his shoe gave him no relief. His thin face was white, drawn.

Below, in the flat fields and brushland, the skirmish line of police and deputies could be seen. Men moved from it to the long lines of cars parked beside the concrete highway. One of the jack pines shivered suddenly; something droned away, bark fell, then the crack of the rifle came to the three.

The third man began to crawl to the left, moving slowly and with a care for his ankle. Red looked up with a scowl.

"What's up, Clem?"

The third man shook his head. "Nothing, but we're in a hot spot, Red."

The leader eased himself on his side. "You tellin' me? Anyway, you ditched us."

Clem was still a moment, then said, "The wheel just snapped out of my hands. You drive and know how it is with a car. Me, I was the one who got hurt."

Red snorted. "Seems to me, Clem, you've lost your nerve. We stick up this rich bank, the guy in it gets strong, and Butch drills him. You look sick, but we're all set, the dough and all. You're the driver; you lived in these parts once. Then you ditch us five miles out. Now, look at the army down there."

Clem nodded. When he spoke again, his voice was flat, colorless. "Red, there used to be an old guy live back of this bluff by the river. He had a boat when I was a kid. I was thinking-"

Red twisted around in excitement. "You was thinkin'. You cut it out and scram down there. We could get over the river; there's timber—"

Clem shook his head. "Red, this leg's killing me; I—"

"Oh, alright, punk. I'll go. You hold the fort with Butch. Them guys down there get hot; put it to 'em. Try to get a bull."

Red moved away rapidly on all fours. The ghost of a smile flitted across Clem's thin lips. It might work. From below, a rifle cracked, and men moved about. A minute dragged by, then Clem crawled again.

Butch's scowl was savage. Clem had ditched them, spoiled the plan. After the scowl, he looked back over his gun.

"Butch, Red's got the dough, ain't he?"

The gunman moved a little. "Yeah, what of it?"

"Well," Clem's voice quavered a little as though he was afraid. He laid a thin hand on the big man's arm. "Butch, Red slipped away, back over the bluff. I was afraid he was letting us hold the bag. Mebbe he wasn't, but—"

Butch studied a moment. Ideas came slowly to him, but now his face was murderous; his teeth showed, and blood suffused his face. He caught Clem's arm and gripped it until the smaller man writhed.

"You saw me settle that bank guy, didn't you?"

Clem nodded and nursed his ankle again.

"Well, I'll go down to Red. He and the Tommy gun can argue a little."

He moved away rapidly. Clem lay looking through the bushes until all sound stopped. He saw a spur heavily covered with brush swung away from the bluff and dropped to the fields. He closed his eyes wearily.

"Wade," he whispered softly. "You was the youngest. How was I to know you was in that bank? Wade—I'm settlin' for you—"

Back of him, in the direction of the river, came the sound of a pistol shot, then a single burst of machine gun fire. Once more, the pistol spoke decisively.

Something was moving on the little spur, closer and closer. Clem opened his eyes and looked, then he took the clip from his automatic and jacked the shell from the barrel. The movement was closer now. He saw the rifle barrel before the man.

"Wade," he breathed softly. "You was the youngest," then he rose to his knees and threw up the pistol. The flat crack of the rifle split the universe. Clem dropped to a crumpled heap.

Twenty minutes later, the hilltop was full of men in police uniform and others with deputy shields. A big man moved among them confidently.

A policeman came up and saluted. "Both dead, sheriff, down over the bluff. That makes the three."

The sheriff nodded, moved over to Clem's body, and kneeled beside it. Slowly he turned it over, then he started.

"God," he said in surprise. "God."

The other officers surrounded him and looked down at his shocked face. "Men, you know the cashier's name was Wade Benton?"

They nodded without understanding. The sheriff went on. "I been in office here more'n twenty years, know the folks. All the Benton boys, but one, was good men. Wade was the youngest. The oldest, though, was bad. Left these parts years back."

Still, they did not understand. He stood up slowly. His voice had become toneless with implications, flat.

"I know this man. He was Clem Benton."

REYNARD OF THE RIDGES

FROM MY PERCH at the top of the cherry tree, I had heard the dogs, of course, but I had paid little attention. Finally, I realized they were coming out of the fringe of the woods into the weed-grown field, and they were growling almost as loudly as they barked. I parted the branches and saw them almost at once.

Neither dog was much larger than a good-sized fox terrier; in fact, the tan dog was largely terrier, while the white one owned a distant ancestor that was probably a beagle. The two animals traveled together, and in the woods, the white dog was as useful as a Royal Coachman fly. You could see where the chase was going by him.

Both dogs were backing up and extremely worried, telling the whole world their state of mind by their outrageous clamor. Coming slowly toward them was the reason, a big gray fox!

If ever a beast of the field tried its level best to preserve an ingratiating manner, it was this animal. I had often heard that a fox would play with a little dog but had discounted the stories. Now I was seeing the thing.

The fox moved forward mincingly as though doing the preliminary steps of some dance movement. His red tongue lolled out; I am satisfied he was trying earnestly to smile. In the best fox circles, that expression would have been worth a good portion of stolen chicken.

The dogs retreated grimly a rod or so into the field. The white one was directly in front of the fox. Presently the tan tried to flank the too-friendly stranger, but the fox wheeled to face him, tongue still lolling. It was a case of: "There, there, you can't escape my smile."

From my high perch, I watched, so fascinated I nearly spilled the cherries I had picked. I wanted to see what would happen when the dog and fox touched their noses. The trio rounded a stump and came into a clearer space. A two-yard radius would have taken in the three. It was then I remembered my duty to the chickens. This fox moved on familiar ground. I tried to be careful sliding down that tree. The dogs clamored when I touched the ground and ran for the house and a gun. But when I emerged with the weapon, they came up the lot. The fox had departed with that swift, silent manner of which he is a past master.

Since the fox was gone, I had to charge the thing to education. Once again, Mr. Fox had lived up to tradition. Of all animals, he is the most satisfying this way, even to nursery rhymes. He is slick, fast, clever, and unbelievably sly.

Conceding these qualities to the gentleman of the glorious brush and the slim muzzle, whether he be red or gray, there is one point where he fails as the wiseacre of the woods. Why does he insist on crossing like a deer? For foxes use well-known regular crossings when going from one side of a ridge to another, and particularly, crossing roads.

I have had the occasion to follow a mountain road during the winter many times. At one place, a low bluff shoulders the highway toward a ravine; at another, the road winds around a point of rocks. After the snow, when the foxes are moving, one always finds well-tramped trails there. Of course, there are scattered tracks along the road. Hard pressed by hounds, he will still cross at these places, and hunters get him there.

But he who would hunt the fox of our hills as it is done in my section with dog and gun must agree to several things. He must shoot quickly and straight, and he must know the crossings. I remember one gray fellow who tried us on both these points.

The dogs, one of them the tan which had resented the too-friendly advances made under my observations, and another, Mike the terrier, had started the fox somewhere in the thickets down by the creek. The third dog, a big lumbering hound, was baying, and Mike sang his savage yapping song. The dogs were doing well, but we made the mistake of being together.

It's music to hear dogs after a fox. There is an abandon to their barking; even a cur howls as though he is at least first cousin to the best Kentucky hound ever whelped. They came closer. We advised the man carrying a rifle to get up on a stump. He had boasted of his skill with a rifle and of the foxes he had shot.

Presently the fox was in sight, a gliding gray shape along the bank. Without the snow, we would not have seen him. Mr. Rifleman on the stump prepared to do his stuff. I don't know the yardage, and neither did the rifleman, but as his first shot whipped out on the frosty air, the fox accelerated in that deceptive slouching way he has. Our expert had missed it, and he was angry. His second shot produced the same result, a fine noise but no fox, and I am certain his third shot missed by a full six feet. The fox disappeared; the dogs came into sight.

The man with the rifle stepped down from the stump and grinned sheepishly. I ran forward with my shotgun for the place where I should have been stationed, and the fox timed his arrival to mine. Believe me, his braking system is excellent. He stopped in a yard, doubled his direction right back upon itself, and left. My snapshot clipped a sapling just four feet by measure above the snow. The safety margin of the fox was at least three feet four inches, even if he was a reasonably tall animal.

Half an hour and a good mile away, "the real woodsman of the trio, the owner of Mike, shot the fox" on a logging road. I had a real twinge of conscience. It seemed to me that the fox had been in sufficient jeopardy before.

Watching one of these fox crossings isn't the sinecure it seems. A man must keep his eye on the ball every second. I watched the point of rocks one afternoon. We had a good hound, one of those organ-voiced fellows that will stick until the fox is either dead or run to earth.

The dog was coming. I held my gun ready, for the fox must come that way. Minutes passed; the dog came nearer, nearer, then, to my discomfiture, appeared and poked his nose in a hole in the rocks. There was blood there and tracks. The fox had reached his burrow directly under my eyes. I had a hard time explaining to the others how I failed to see the game.

How he survives is a mystery to me, for he has few friends. There is a price on his head, and all hunters itch to see him across their sights. But, if you doubt his presence, try to raise chickens in our hills and leave them unprotected even in the daytime. Or listen on a frosty night to his sharp derisive, jeering "Yap, Yap." One's eyes stray to the rifle in the corner and come away. He is hard enough to get in the daytime.

This fall, I drove through a fourteen-mile stretch of state forest late at night. Halfway through, I saw something move on the edge of the path of my lights. A quick swerve—there was a gray fox. He crossed the road deliberately. That was one. In less than a mile, I shot up on a little hill and dipped down again. My lights picked out two pairs of lights. Two more gray foxes scuttled leisurely into the safety of the brush. Actually, three foxes to the mile! How many ruffed grouse and foolish hill rabbits would it take to support this trio?

The fox makes his living where apparently there is none, and he covers the ground thoroughly. He cannot afford to miss chances, or he goes hungry. That he survives is a tribute to his efficiency as a hunter. But nature caters to the efficient; an animal with the percentage of efficiency of the average man becomes just another meal. He makes a mistake only once—he gets no second chance.

I cannot help but believe the fox is increasing, particularly in our hills. Of course, I refer to the gray; the red is comparatively scarce. Trapping, even poisoning, doesn't help much. The only thing I know to reduce his numbers is to increase the value of the gray's pelt.

With the evening shadows, one of these gentlemen emerges from his burrow in the rocks and climbs to the ridge summit. There he stands with one foot raised; this foot too large for his slim shanks. His red tongue lolls out; he tests the echo with his sharp jeering bark. When I see him across the sights of my rifle, I must remember my duty to the ruffed grouse and the scrawny mountain rabbit and press the trigger. But down where I live, I have an unconfessed affection for this slim, hungry, marauding freebooter of the hills—with the fighting, challenging heart.

TONGUE TIED

DAN SELBY smoothed a rumpled bit of turf with his boot as he talked, his words coming slowly, giving the effect of a drawl. "No, Ed, I'm not on my own anymore. Sold the old ship and bought a pint-size cottage about a mile from the home field. Prue likes it a lot; I'm home practically every evening."

Ed Lamphier smiled suddenly, perhaps at the thought of Dan Selby sleeping two nights in succession in the same place. He started a sentence and then checked himself.

"Is she still . . ."

Dan noted the red coming up on his friend's face. "Never mind, Ed. I know what you were going to ask. Prue's the finest little woman in the world, but she's a mite jealous. Sort of flatters me, but that's why I gave up the junketing about with the old bus taking up passengers, hitting the fairs."

"How is this racket?" Lamphier gestured in the direction of the plane over beyond the club shrubbery. "Does it pay you, Dan?"

"It's right enough. I get a fair salary; I'm supposed to be a test pilot for the Brent Aviation Company. Fultz is the field manager. I never met the higher-ups, but if they like me as much as he does—my name'd be Dennis. He's just waiting to get the wind up on me, then goodnight. The ship over there is sort of queer; that's why I'm down here. Your club has a good landing field, all right. I didn't want to take a chance of cracking up. This is no time to jockey with a good job."

A few minutes later, Lamphier turned back to the clubhouse, and Dan moved through the shrubbery in the direction of his plane; but he had not gone a rod before a small figure darted from behind a clump of bushes. It was Dan's turn to smile, but he didn't, even though the girl was easy to look at from the crown of her trim hat to the tip of her almost tiny slipper. She looked astonishingly like a small child, dressed up, until one looked into her eyes.

"Dot," he announced slowly. "I knew that ship would get me into trouble, and here you are."

His half-whimsical smile didn't take away the real sting of his remark. The girl made a pouting mouth at him and tapped the ground with her slipper impatiently.

"For goodness' sake, Dan Selby. Are you still mad after a year and a half? I saw the papers, and you and Prue are married, all right. You know I only wanted her to be jealous, Dan. I liked Prue."

"Prue doesn't understand women—" Dan stopped clumsily, and she went on.

"Like me." She snapped the word viciously. "Anyway, Dan Selby, I didn't come down here to make Prue jealous. I'm in trouble, and I heard up at the club that you were here with a plane."

"You're usually in trouble, Dot, aren't you?"

She ignored the thrust and hurried on. "I'm married myself, to a perfectly satisfactory husband. We live on an estate, and it bores me sometimes. So, yesterday I got out my roadster—he was away—and drove down here. Well, a truck wouldn't turn out, and my machine's a total wreck. I came on here. I wasn't much worried, but just an hour or so ago, my maid called me and said a telegram had arrived, saying my husband would be home this evening. It's a matter of hours, Dan, and I've got to be home when he gets there; that's flat. I've sort of tried his patience before."

Her small features showed that she was really worried now. For once, she wasn't acting or trying to do so. Suddenly he saw by the bush a small ornate overnight case and realized what she had come to him for.

"And you want me to take you home, Dot. That's the poison."

She nodded her head vigorously. "That's it. There's a good field back of our house. We live at Chetwold, just a mile or so out of Sunbury. You can't miss it."

Dan turned from her. "I'm sorry, Dot, but this ship's a little sick. Another thing, I haven't a passenger license. Besides, I'm flying for my bread and butter. There's absolutely nothing doing."

She ran forward and caught him by his lapel as he moved toward the plane. "Dan, you old bear. I've tried to get a car, but it's too late. Besides, none of the men at the club is sober enough to drive that far and fast. Prue's jealous—well, so is my husband."

There were tears in the depths of her violet eyes. Two things in Dan's makeup were dominant. The first was that he couldn't stand feminine tears. The second was he could keep his mouth shut. He had picked up a smattering of three or four languages over there, and he could keep his mouth shut in any of them.

A club mechanic was standing by the plane. By the time they had reached it, Dan had given in. He boosted her into the second seat and tossed her his parachute. He climbed up and buckled her into it and the safety belt. Just before he gave the mechanic his signal, he glanced back and was disgusted to see she was powdering her nose. That was just like Dot when she had her way.

The motor answered the gun well enough, but once off the ground, the machine climbed unevenly, adding to Dan's concern. He was risking too much, the plane, his job, and two lives, all because this girl-woman behind him had made a fool of herself first and then him. Once before, Dot had nearly come between Prue and him; if something happened this time, there would be no explaining to his wife. If the plane crashed, Fultz would have what he was looking for, a man in Dan's place.

Finally, Dan shrugged his broad shoulders. He settled himself into the serious business of flying this plane, which had suddenly turned docile and responsive to the stick. He shoved the throttle wide open and turned her nose in the direction of the thin line of blue hills. Cotswold, he knew, was just beyond Sunbury, and something more than an hour in the air would do the trick. He fell to speculating whether some chauffeur on the estate could help him get away. Below, the panorama of hills and streams and fields drifted by.

Just north of Sunbury, the thing happened, and altitude was the only thing that saved them. A strut parted with a report like a shot. There was a rending noise of fabric parting, and the plane slipped into a spin, plunging down like a weighted leaf. From then on, Dan was too busy to note details. They crashed, all right, and ripped off part of the landing gear. They came to rest miraculously right side up, but with the nose of the plane buried in the soft ground of a field.

For perhaps a minute, Dan fought for the breath knocked out of him against the side of the cockpit. Then he clambered out and unstrapped Dot. She was breathless but entirely over her fright.

"How perfectly thrilling," she cried then her face grew long. "Just think—a crash, and I daren't tell a soul. Isn't it awful?"

Dan fought back the things that he wanted to say. This spoiled little thing had no thought for anything but herself. A thrill, that was all it meant to her. His predicament meant absolutely nothing. He left her powdering her nose and walked to the side of the field and the concrete road. A decrepit car drew up and stopped.

"Trouble, buddy?"

The young man's face was none too clean. It bore smudges of oil, but they did not begin to hide the engaging grin.

Dan grinned back. "All cracked up. Say, will that thing carry a passenger?"

"Sure thing, Mr. Airman. She's a good buggy."

Dan turned and beckoned to Dot, who had clambered out. When she joined them, Dan boosted her over the fence.

"Take this lady to Cotswold. She'll pay you well."

Dot tried to argue, and Dan was almost sharp. "You've time enough. Hurry!"

The mechanic's car started away smoothly enough in a cloud of smoke, and Dan breathed a sigh of relief. That was one less trouble, anyway. His duty now was to notify the home field by telegraph. Fultz would know at once he was away, out of bounds. He returned to the plane and started to inspect it.

Half an hour or more passed. He was too busy sizing up the motor to note that a car had stopped, and he did not see the two men until they were by the side of the plane.

"Brent Aviation Company," The man was reading the inscription in a high-pitched, singularly irritating voice. Dan looked him over, a man of his own height but thin, with a peering-looking face. He had a notebook in his hand. The other man kept back of him, a burly, surly-looking individual. The man with the notebook tendered a card when Dan looked up.

"I'm Brown of *The Item*," he explained. "A farmer telephoned us there was a crash, and we hurried out. What's your name?"

Dan ignored the request in his irritation, and the pair moved around the plane, taking their time, and approached Dan again.

"Name, please."

This time Dan gave it, and the reporter wrote busily for a moment. "Now," he said brusquely. "Where's the lady, was she hurt?"

Dan looked at him, surprised. "I'm alone," he said gruffly.

The reporter held up a small vanity case. "Aviators are getting lady-like all right. Need a bit of touching up after a crash, likely."

He studied the small box Dan recognized as the one Dot had used in her irritating fashion. "Initials don't jibe. You gave me your name as Daniel Selby; these initials are D.F. Maybe that was your maiden name."

"Now see here," Dan gritted. "That's about enough. I crashed because a strut busted or something. I'm alone. Keep your dirty tongue straight."

The reporter paid no attention for a moment but wrote on his pad. Then he read aloud. "'Crash Ends Aerial Joy Ride. Aviator Refuses to Talk. Female Companion Escapes.' Nice headlines—no, don't start rough stuff. This man likes them rough and tough."

Dan had lunged forward, but the other man who had been directly back of Brown stepped in.

"You'd better talk, young fellow. I know your superintendent, Fultz. This story will look fine in the city papers. I'll see they get it."

Dan had stepped back to the plane. In a moment, his head and arm came out of the cockpit, and he held part of a baseball bat. The two men turned and ran, beating Dan to the fence, and their car, by scant yards. Dan was left to curse his folly in not speaking out, frankly.

He had been foolish enough to take up a passenger; it had been almost as bad to get in wrong with this newspaperman, but the cumulation of irritation had been too much for him. He walked around the damaged machine several times. Things were bad enough there; the job business was settled. There remained the biggest worry, Prue. Ever since her serious illness a year before, she had been unreasonably jealous. Even before, it had been bad enough. Now this story would bring things to a real head, and Dan loved her.

There was plenty of time to think things over. Telegraph orders from the flying field told him to remain with the plane until a truck could reach him, and it was more than forty-eight hours before Dan reported to Fultz at the flying field. One of the mechanics gave him the wink outside.

"The old man's got the wind up on you, Selby. Handle him easy."

Fultz reached for a newspaper when Dan entered and tossed it across to the flier. Brown of *The Item* had kept his word, and it was a complete job. No insinuation had been omitted, and the headlines were as Brown had sketched them on the field. Dan read in silence. Fultz scowled.

"Who was the woman?" he demanded savagely.

Dan's only answer was a slow, exasperating smile. Fultz's face became almost apoplectic. "Now, my fine bird, you cracked up a plane, joy riding—no license at that. You're fired."

Dan turned slowly, but Fultz was not done. "You, a married man, cracking a fifteen-thousand-dollar plane . . ."

Ordinarily, Dan Selby seemed to move slowly, but now he was over the superintendent in a flash, his big hands open, itching.

"Not another word, you clipped crow, or I'll change your map all around. Just shut up—tight."

Fultz permitted his erstwhile subordinate to leave without further word.

It did not take long to run down to the little cottage he and Prue had selected with such care and furnished so lovingly, but there was no one there. Inside he found she had carried the thing through in the best melodramatic way. The paper with the item about the crash was ringed with a pencil mark. Her note was short: "Of course, I've gone home to Mother."

In the following weeks, Dan learned the far-reaching effect of his crash. He went, after the first two or three days, to a half-dozen places to apply for work, but he met the same refusal everywhere.

"Sorry, our planes are expensive, Mr. Selby. We can't take chances."

There were times when the whole story trembled on Dan's lips, but he held it back. Several times fellow airmen questioned him, but he always made the same reply: "Sorry, I've nothing to say about that yarn."

He had been paid shortly before the unfortunate trip and had left most of his money with Prue. He was glad after two weeks to get work as a mechanic in a garage. There, grimy and oily, Rob Davis found him with the news. Davis and Dan had been friends since A. E. F. days.

"Been hunting you for days, Dan. Fargus wants to see you in his office tomorrow at ten. It's important."

"Fargus," Dan wiped his hands on his overalls. "Never heard of him. What's his line?"

Davis grinned. "He'll be good for what ails you, old top. Don't miss him, and be on time."

Dan was punctual. The office was on the tenth floor, and outside the number, there was no lettering to indicate what the concern was. Several people were waiting, but at the stroke of ten, a business-like girl came out from an inner room and made her announcement.

"Mr. Fargus had an appointment with Mr. Selby. Is he here?"

He followed her trim back through another waiting room and was ushered into a huge room furnished sumptuously, where a man with huge shoulders and iron-gray hair worked at a broad desk. He rose and extended his hand.

"Glad to see you, Selby. My name's Fargus."

Dan liked him instantly; he was as tall as he, a great bulk of a man with tiny wrinkles about his eyes and a mobile mouth over a square chin. He took the chair to which Fargus had gestured. The big man got to the point at once.

"Mr. Selby, I own the Brent Aviation Company, of which you were lately an employee. I'm letting Fultz out there, go, for a number of reasons. There's no blood in the man. I've looked you up, war service and all. You're a good man, Selby, and a real flier. Two weeks ago, though, you cracked one of our planes outside Sunbury. There was a news story that there was a woman with you."

He stopped and looked at his former employee for a long time before he went on more slowly.

"I'm prepared to offer you Fultz's place as superintendent of the flying field."

Dan half rose, his pleasure shining in his eyes, but Fargus waved him back to his seat.

"On one condition. We know this much, that you were giving a service to a woman who was involved in an escapade of which her husband disapproved; that your wife left you in consequence; that you were discharged. So far, you have not told anyone the name of the lady. Fultz's job is yours—just as soon as you give me the woman's name."

Silence dropped like a garment into the office. The outside noises seemed not a part of this place. At last, Dan rose wearily, faced the big man back of the desk as though he wanted to say something, then he moved toward the door.

Fargus leaped up and moved around the desk. "Just a minute. I want to tell you a little story. Sit down."

Dan eyed him suspiciously but finally took a chair. "All right, but hurry. I ought to be at work."

"Several years ago, I left the lumber business out on the coast and came here, buying this company. I met a girl and married her rather suddenly. Maybe, she fell for my money."

He laughed shortly and glanced at a door as though he feared an interruption.

"Of course, she was so much younger that she liked things I didn't. I was willing for her to have a good time, in reason, but I got a little jealous. I ordered her about. I tell you, this jealousy business is fierce; it hurts both ways. I tried to keep her name out of the papers after her escapades, but it was a hard job. Some reporter was always snooping around. Now I feel the woman you helped was someone rather like my wife, young, headstrong. I want to know who she is so I can go to her husband and tell him not to be foolish, that things are all right. Now, the name of the woman, please."

Both men were standing at the same time. Dan's scowl met a quizzical smile. He spoke slowly.

"You and your fairy stories can go to—"

Fargus' long arm shot out; his hand grasped the flier's shoulder and spun him half about.

"Good boy," he shouted. "I need you. Report to the field in the morning. Your pay started a week ago. Selby, don't be so damn mad. The woman you were protecting is my wife!"

Dan stared, in something like sheer dismay, as to what to do. Fargus pressed a button. A side door opened, and into the office came two women. The first was Dot, in all her glory.

"Sorry! Dan, old thing, for the jam I got you in. But I did my best." She stepped aside, and the next instant, the other woman, Prue, was folded close in Dan's hungry arms.

"I'm so sorry, Dan," she sobbed on his shoulder. "I'll never be foolish again. Mr. Fargus hunted me up, and I'm so proud of the way you stood up under it all."

Fargus broke in after a minute. "My car's waiting, people. We're running out to my place to celebrate, out where you were taking Dot. Now don't forget one thing, Selby. Here in the presence of my wife, I'm saying it. She thinks I did all this for sentiment, but the fact is we're developing a new plane. I needed a man who could be tongue-tied, sometimes, even under the gaff, and I've found him."

He grinned happily. "Selby, I'm proud of you. Old man, I'd have squealed long before."

BOGUS

FOR THE LAST quarter of an hour, Loring had given over all pretense at reading and sat, leaning forward a bit, intently watching the dog. This was the third night the animal had been uneasy. Now it sat before him, staring into the darkness of the tiny kitchen, its upstanding ears pricked forward. To Loring, the thing was beginning to take on an eerie quality. Somewhere outside beyond the zone of his own hearing but still within the compass of the canine ear, something was moving about.

Minutes slipped by. Once, the dog growled softly deep down in its throat; a moment later, it rose to its feet, moved slowly across the living room of the cottage, and stood poised for a moment like a pointer. Only a moment, then it whimpered and retreated as it had done on the other nights, under the couch.

In spite of himself, Loring felt the hair on the back of his neck stir a little; then, suddenly, the telephone shrilled sharply across the silence.

All of a minute passed before Loring managed to pull himself together. Thoroughly ashamed of himself, he took down the receiver. It was a woman's voice.

"Yes," he answered the inquiry. "This is Loring, Cade Loring."

Broken, excited sentences reached him over the wire. Unconsciously he echoed them.

"Lock my doors—danger—keep inside!"

Just that, and the wire strummed in his ears. He jiggled the hook rapidly, and finally, the sleepy operator answered with an irritating, "Number, please."

No, the operator did not know who had called. She was sure, however, that it was no one from the hotel, probably from one of the other cottages. Loring hung up the receiver, exasperated.

The dog remained in his place of retreat. He studied the animal for a moment. He had bought him in a pet store before coming up here; an unusually large fox terrier. Beyond the animal's name, Rex, he knew little of the dog.

He moved over to the table littered with magazines. Near his pipe lay a snapshot photograph of a smiling girl. He picked it up and stared at the face for a moment. Could the voice have been hers? Suddenly it occurred to him that she might be in danger; there was always something queer about these Russians. He snatched up his hat, his pipe, and a slim walking stick and went out.

Even in his excitement, he paused a moment on his little porch. Bathed in pale moonlight, the scene before him was beautiful. The long, dark, pine-clad slope dipped slowly down to the distant lake, shining in silver patches under the moon. Here and there was the spark of light in a cottage. Far over by the lake, the hotel's lights blazed.

Ten minutes of walking along a narrow road brought him in sight of the cottage where the girl lived. Loring had started with the full intention of going to the cottage. True, he had never been there; for some reason, she had never invited him. Now, outside, his fears had passed; it seemed ridiculous here, so near the big hotel, with cottages almost everywhere.

The windows of the small rambling building were blank. He remembered now that it was after twelve. The telephone call was some hoax. He turned and walked slowly back in the direction of his own cottage. He was almost there when he passed what had once been a small field that ran up across the hill. Loring stopped short and stared.

Sharply silhouetted against the moon-flood beyond, a man had passed the open space and with him, tugging at some sort of leash, was an animal that did not move like any dog Loring had ever seen.

Several times during the rest of the night, Loring found himself awake, each time listening intently, but he heard nothing he could definitely identify except the tiny gossipy noises that moved among pine trees.

The morning came in with a riot of gorgeous sunshine that streamed in through Loring's windows. He lay there in his bed luxuriously. The thought came to him that his vacation ended the next day. He had enjoyed his stay in the mountains immensely this year. The last week or so had been particularly pleasant; something about this girl, Sonia, was tremendously alluring.

Staring out at the sunshine, he allowed to pass in review his meetings with her. First, he had surprised her sketching just back of his cabin, and she had been so prettily alarmed to think she had trespassed. Later, the walk to show her a view. Again, she had sketched back of his cabin; that was only two or three days ago. He had invited her into his cabin to see some prints he had brought with him. He smiled when he remembered one incident. On one of their walks together, he had removed his light coat. Stopping to rest, he had thrown the garment down carelessly, and a packet of bills had fallen from the inner pocket. How her eyes had widened as he stuffed it back carelessly, explaining that to a banker, money is merely a commodity.

"I am supposed to be an expert on currency," he had explained. "Those bills were sent to me to examine the engraving."

She had listened so carefully and made a little face as he put the money away.

Rex was himself this morning and accompanied his master on his walk over to the hotel for breakfast. Loring talked with several people at the hotel but did not see Sonia. Sometimes she came over with the big, bearded man whom he presumed to be her father. Loring had seen them quite frequently at dinner. They did not mix with the people there. He remembered that he did not know the girl's last name—neither had she shown any desire to tell him about the man with whom she lived in the cottage.

Just a little before noon, Loring was loafing on his back porch, staring off at the mountains. Suddenly Rex barked sharply. It was Sonia, and she was hurrying, almost running.

Loring leaped up and went forward to meet her. "Sonia, good morning, but what's your hurry?"

She did not smile in answer. Instead, she looked nervously over her shoulder. "Oh, my friend, I have hurried. Take me inside at once, I—"

He led her into the cottage. She flung herself on the couch. It was quite evident that she was breathless, that she had been running. The dark hair that framed the oval of her face was a bit disarranged; her bosom heaved. Loring stared at her, at a loss what to do, then she began to speak rapidly, almost incoherently.

"It is Alex," she panted, "and I am afraid."

Loring leaned forward. "Sonia, did you telephone me last night?"

She nodded. "He, Alex, was out last night. I was afraid he would come here."

"You see," she hurried on after a pause. "He has been spying on us. He knows that I have been here, in your house."

She beat her breast dramatically. "He—he suspects everything, and he is Russian. He does not understand that in this country, men and women can be just—just friends. You know he is an animal trainer. The day after I was here—in the house—he took the car and drove away. When he came back, he had with him a leopard. The beast is up there—he prowls with it at night. In the daytime, I can hear it walking up and down, up and down. I cannot stand it any longer. I must go away—now, this very day."

She sprang up from the couch and crossed to Loring, her dark eyes swimming with tears. "You—will help me, my good friend. There is no one else."

Impulsively Loring placed his hands on her heaving shoulders; she nestled close like a frightened bird. He began to stroke her hair.

"He keeps me without money. I could take the car, but—"

Loring cleared his throat. "But, Sonia, I have only a little money here; I—"

She looked up at him suddenly, a look of pain in the deep wells of her eyes. "Why," she almost whispered. "Only the other day, you had a package of bills—oh so big. I thought money meant nothing to you."

Her slender shoulders were heaving again. "You don't understand, Sonia. That money was sent to me by the bank for which I work. If I gave you that money, I should be a thief. It was sent to me to examine. Do you wish me to steal?"

Suddenly another thing occurred to him, the natural thing, but he had been so disturbed by her trepidation he had not thought to ask.

"Listen, Sonia. You called this man Alex; who is he? I thought he was your father?"

She drew away from him and stared up into his face. "Don't you know," she said wonderingly. "Alex is my husband."

A queer sense of sickness mounted in Loring. Alex, her husband, this huge hairy Russian. So that was why the man was so infuriated. Almost, he wanted to shake her for her foolishness.

Slowly she turned toward the door. "But I go. It does not matter that he kills me. A little money—and you will not give it to me. You do not value my life, and I thought you cared—a little."

Nearly all of his adult life, Loring had worked in banks. Now he studied the girl, something cold inside him. "Then you would have me be a thief—take this money that belongs to the bank."

With the quickness characteristic of her, she was at his side again, her hand on his shoulder. "No, it is not that I want you to be a thief—but since I know you, life is sweeter. I shall take the money to get away; I shall write you where I am. You will come to me, and you will forget the money."

She was smiling audaciously through her tears. Loring crossed to a bookcase. When he returned, he was holding a packet of bills banded around with paper in the fashion of banks. On the paper was printed FOUR THOUSAND DOLLARS. Her fingers closed on the packet, which she thrust into the bosom of her dress.

Suddenly her arms were about him. Her lips were like a flame against his. "You are not sorry," she breathed. "You are saving Sonia for yourself. You try to act cold, but Sonia will thaw the ice."

She was gone the next moment. Loring stood there in the middle of the floor. Perfume lingered in the room. He felt old, tired, futile. After a few minutes, he went out and returned a half hour later, breathing rapidly as though he had been running.

During the remainder of the day, Loring was amazingly busy. First, after lunch, he conferred with the hotel manager during the greater part of an hour. Then the manager called a certain quiet, unobtrusive individual who sat by, occasionally prompting, while Loring talked over the long-distance telephone. That done, he returned to his cottage.

Loring was one of the rare men who traveled with a great deal of luggage. It took him all afternoon to assemble his things and pack them carefully in his trunks. Whatever he possessed of household gods, he carried with him. The last thing he stowed away went with his more personal belongings into a pigskin bag. It was a rather large leather case. He opened it and glanced inside with satisfaction; in it were several powerful lenses or reading glasses, several pairs of delicate dividers, and a micrometer.

A little after dark, Loring retraced the steps he had taken the night before, but this time there was a light in the cottage occupied by the Russians. He approached with deliberate steps, and his rap was greeted with a gruff command to enter.

The man Loring knew as Alex had risen from his seat back of a table as his visitor came in. In the rather faint light, he was a huge, almost terrifying, figure with his thick beard and heavy torso.

"Ah," he boomed. "It is Mr. Loring that honors me," his teeth showed white in his beard as he gestured in the direction of another chair and sank back into his own.

"You have the advantage, Mr.—"

"Georgevitch," the man replied quickly. "That is not exactly my name, but it is the best Americanized form of it I can supply."

Loring cleared his throat. The big man's eyes never left his.

"Thank you, Mr. Georgevitch. I am leaving tomorrow morning, which compelled me to force myself upon you this evening. The truth is, I half anticipated a call from you this evening. I called to ask you for a packet of banknotes. The packet contains some four thousand dollars, and it belongs to the bank by which I am employed."

The Russian threw back his huge head and laughed until the room seemed to echo. Back in another room, something stirred. Loring distinctly heard that. Then, as suddenly as he had laughed, the big man leaned forward over the table.

"You are right, Mr. Loring, quite right. I was going to call this evening. There is a little matter between us that requires discussion and—perhaps a little adjustment. My wife left me this morning, and I have much reason to believe it was because of you, my dear Mr. Loring."

Again, the teeth showed through the beard. The man's eyes widened slowly until they seemed like deep wells. Loring watched them a moment, then he nodded.

"You neglect the matter of the money, Mr. Georgevitch, and it is most important to me. Let me explain. I am employed by a bank, a rather large institution. It is my business, as a sort of money expert, to be familiar with the money of the world and to advise my institution. While I am on my vacations, considerable sums are sent to me. It's irregular, but I have been with the bank a long time, and I am trusted."

Georgevitch nodded. "I understand. You also seem to be an expert with women. Now a woman is not so much; but I dislike any interference with things that are mine."

His voice had become silky. Loring was reminded of a big cat purring and switching her tail. There was something almost hypnotic about this giant.

"At first, Mr. Loring, I was almost primitive. I thought of coming to your place and doing things to you with my hands. You are a small man, and I assure you, my hands are quite capable."

He waved them suddenly before his face. Loring noted the hairy wrists, the little tufts of hair that grew down almost to the knuckles. His voice was equally quiet now.

"Mr. Georgevitch, it is true that I enjoyed the society of your wife. However, you know there was nothing improper in our relations. I am not a seducer; the fact is I met her accidentally, and our relations were those of friendship until this morning."

"Ah, yes."

The big man's words were like a sigh. Almost it seemed the table had come closer to the visitor.

"This morning, your wife told me she was married, that you were insanely jealous, that she must go away. She asked me for funds and persuaded me, on impulse, to give her a packet of bills that were not mine. It is for them I have come to you."

Again, the man laughed, and the stir in the other room answered him, but Loring went on.

"I suspected something when your wife came to me this morning. When she left, I followed quickly. I saw her flourish the packet of money to you in your garage and saw you kiss her as she left. It was a most amiable leave-taking. Mr. Georgevitch—you will note that I continue to use the name you gave me—you probably know what is meant by the old "badger game." Your most estimable wife also took the key to my apartment in the city. You would have paid me two calls; one here, to threaten me, then you would have followed me to the city. Your wife would have been ensconced in my apartments in a most compromising way. You would have asked me to pay handsomely. You see, I have been busy with friends and the telephone. You are, of course, no more Russian than I am. You have been a cat man with a circus which explains your ability to handle your "kitty" stirring in the next room. Now, please," Loring rose, "the money."

Georgevitch rose. Loring's hand slipped from his pocket, holding something blue and heavy. "I realize, my big friend, that I was only an incident. You had planned for bigger game, but I seemed so credulous to the woman whom I shall continue to call your good wife that you couldn't resist taking me in. You failed to realize that bank men are suspicious. She will be asked to come to the police station by those who will meet her on her coming to my apartment. "Now, hand over that money."

"You fool, you poor little fool." The man's voice had lost all its suavity. "What do you take me for? You stole the bank's money. You'll keep mighty quiet. No doubt those bills are numbered and registered—"

Loring nodded. "Every one of them."

"By this time, Sonia has changed all of them. She'd move quick. You're still holding the bag, Loring." He stepped back suddenly, and Loring whipped up the automatic.

"Stand still. I am counted a pretty good shot. Besides, we don't want you to call your kitty out here. I mean the leopard you have in the back room that you have been prowling about with at night."

Georgevitch swore savagely. "You little shrimp. You're running a bluff. Kiss your money goodbye. Besides, I'll get you right before you leave this resort—"

This time Loring smiled. "No, Georgevitch, no. I failed to tell you that my friends are outside. I just wanted to know where my money really was. I believe you that your good wife has it. I was afraid we might have trouble finding it. Your reference to the plan to have Sonia get the money changed in a bank helped a lot. The warning has gone out, and she'll be arrested on the spot. The police want you both, you know. Keep your hands on the table, big boy. My friends will come in as I leave. Be very, very still."

Loring backed slowly to the door and opened it with a hand thrust back of him to admit a uniformed policeman. He lowered his weapon as the officer pushed forward. Loring smiled into the face of the furious man.

"I must tell you something more, Georgevitch. Your interesting wife caught me rather unprepared. I had to give her what money I had. You will remember that I am supposed to be a sort of expert. Well, unfortunately for you and the charming Sonia, the money I gave her was—counterfeit."

GAUNTLET

FOR THE LAST half hour, Brent had been fighting his way down through the brush. From the ridge top, he had seen the buildings in the clearing. Dog tired, he was plunging forward with his head down. He did not see the man or the menacing rifle until he was less than ten feet away.

The roar of his motor still deafened the airman's ears. He did not hear the gruff command to halt but stepped forward with a smile.

"Sure glad to see somebody," he began with a smile. "I—"

Only an instinctive quickness saved Brent, for the man had whipped up the rifle and fired at the airman's second step. Next instant Brent dived forward with a tackling spring that swept the man off his feet and hurled the rifle a dozen feet away. The mountaineer fought like an animal, better down than standing up toe-to-toe. Back and forth over the brush and leaves, the two rolled. Brent was trying to swing his fists; the other was scratching and clawing, trying for a throat hold on his adversary.

Rolling against the trunk of a small tree broke their grip. Both sprang up. Brent's face was stinging from scratches; his temper was boiling at the murderous unprovoked attack. The other man moved forward slowly, cautiously. Brent rushed, his fists swinging savagely. The mountaineer staggered under a blow, Brent's toe caught in a root, and the two came down with a thump. The airman felt a tugging thumb on his cheek. His wrench-and-roll brought the other on top, clawing away like a wild cat. Fair play was out this time. Brent took no chances; he twisted, brought his knees up and released them like a powerful spring full into the pit of the mountaineer's stomach, hurling him back and down in a tumbled heap where he lay still. Brent was almost spent; he came up slowly, his eyes on the silent heap in the heavy dusk. The next instant, the entire universe crashed down on his head, and he dropped forward into a well of blackness.

Minutes, that seemed hours, later he opened his eyes and stared around him, then he raised himself slightly on one elbow. He was in a lamplit room, on the floor. About him on chairs and benches were a half dozen men. Even his first glance told him these men were not mountaineers, except for one who looked battered and sick, evidently the man who had fired on him. They were a hard-bitten crew. Brent twisted round; near his head sat a big man with a square, cruel face and a leering, brutal mouth.

"Who—hit—me?"

As his brain cleared, sheer cold rage mounted in Brent. He had come down for help, and they tried to kill him. He moved his body slowly at first, then gained his feet in a rush.

"Listen!" he snapped. "Which one of you dirty cowards hit me?"

He saw one man look in the direction of the big fellow. "High, tell him."

The big man addressed as High shoved back his chair. Standing, he made a mock bow. "Yes, dearie, I'll tell you. I did it with a persuader."

Despite his lack of bulk, Brent's body was made of steel springs. He was tired, but he forgot the ache of muscles at the leering face. His swing was too quick for the big man to avoid; it crashed home, full on the open mouth. The fellow had not been set for the blow. He went backward over the chair and struck the floor like a dropped sack.

For an instant, the room was perfectly quiet. High tried to scramble up, then the pack closed in savagely, battering, tearing, pinioning his arms, tripping him. In the end, Brent was down. Someone brought a rope. They tied him until the cord cut into his muscles.

The big man's face was livid with fury. He came up to the chair where they had dropped Brent, his hands working. First, with one hand, then the other, he slapped the airman's cheeks and spat full into his face. Brent strained his bonds.

"You big hog, better kill me, or I'll break your neck!" he gritted at his tormentor.

"We'll kill you all right, Mister. No damned spy can come in on one of my rackets and get away with it. Not in High Kelly's deals."

He drew Brent up. "Now, tell me what you came for. Who sent you?"

Brent twisted to face the others. "My plane cracked up this afternoon, back a dozen miles or so in the hills. I was walking out for help. Listen, you fellows, untie me. Give me a break."

Kelly was forcing him toward the table where the kerosene lamp stood. Brent's hands were tied back of him. Kelly turned him. Brent could feel the heat of the lamp on his hands.

"I'll fry it out of you," Kelly snarled.

Over on the far side of the room sat a man, smaller than the others, with a thin, hard face. Brent saw him move slightly; a vicious-looking revolver gleamed in his hand.

"Cut it, High; no burning goes."

Kelly released his victim and whirled around. "Put up that rod, Whitey! I'm running this show." His teeth showed in an evil snarl.

The small man rose and came forward slowly. "You listen, High. I'm in on this deal, and I'll go through, but no burning; none of this third-degree stuff goes."

The others were moving uneasily. Kelly took a step in the direction of the little man, whose pistol, held low, did not waver. "I'll break your damn—"

The little man grinned. "No, you won't, High. You make another pass, and I'll blow you so full of holes, the wind'll whistle through your guts."

The pistol muzzle jerked slightly. Kelly winced and stepped back. He turned to some of the others. "You guys put this bird down cellar where he'll keep. Ankers," he gestured in the direction of the mountaineer, "you see he don't get away. Drill him if he does."

The cellar was pitch dark, but the man who took him down cut the rope off his hands and feet and left him a small piece of candle. Then, he piled some sacks on a long box. This fellow had red hair. He leaned close to Brent just before he left.

"Don't rile High anymore, buddy. He's poison when he's mad!"

Brent tried to grin in answer, but it did not go over well. His body ached too much, yet when he stretched himself on the sacks, he could not keep awake. He tried to speculate into what sort of den he had blundered. Drowsily, he noted the sound of footsteps above, then he slept the deep, dreamless sleep of exhaustion.

He woke to find some light coming in at low windows, set where the sills of the building rested on the walls. A little later, the fellow called Whitey brought him some breakfast. Brent ate hungrily. The little man would not talk; he was surly, uncommunicative, and left the prisoner inside of ten minutes.

Alone, after he had finished eating everything brought to him, Brent reconnoitered through the boards that partially closed the two little windows. Outside one was a close-growing bush of some sort; he could see nothing beyond it, but from the other, he could look out in the direction of the weather-beaten barn. Four cars were parked there, not the sort one would expect to find here in the heart of the hills. They were heavy fast-looking machines, all of them. Out around the corner of the house, he could see a ribbon of dusty, rutted road.

He returned to his bunk to think the thing through. Overhead was the sound of tramping about. There seemed many men, perhaps a dozen in all. After a little, they all clumped outside.

From the window, Brent saw them approach the cars; he counted nine, among them Kelly. Over by one machine, one of them bent over the hood, raised it, and peered at the engine. Kelly approached him and talked a moment, gesturing over his shoulder at the house with his thumb. There was something vaguely familiar about this man's back. He tried but could not get a glimpse of the man's face.

Twenty minutes slipped by, then there was a fumbling about the cellar trap door. It raised, letting in a rectangle of light, and a man came down. Brent stared at him; his eyes were better suited to the semi-gloom, then suddenly, he cried out.

"Dan, Dan McLeod, what are *you* doing here?"

Brent thought he could see the tall man's freckled face suffuse with color as he strode forward. "Brent," he grunted. "My old captain, by all that's holy."

For a long minute, they pumped each other's hands. Dan had been his mechanic overseas for nearly all of an eventful year. Brent told his story briefly and to the point. Dan seated himself on a box and listened without interruption, but Brent saw his big hands clench when he told of the fight in the room above.

"Knew he was some sort of swine," Dan commented, "but I was after the easy money, a hundred a day he's been paying me." As briefly as his former superior, Dan explained he had been up against it almost and thought he'd have to sell his car when High Kelly had hired him to run booze. He'd made two trips, then was told to report here.

"There's something fishy, Cap." Brent smiled at the nickname. Dan had called him that; he'd always had a fine disregard for rank or suitable titles. But, he could make an engine sing and was a good man to have at your back.

"Kelly told me to come down here and pump you. Course, he didn't spill who you was. Said he thought you was some kind of a spy, a revenue officer. Listen, Cap. They've got a bunch of fast cars, and there ain't any booze in sight. Kelly says I'm to drive them to Lock Haven tonight; stay in the car and be ready for a fast getaway." He saw I was doubtful and I'm being watched. Bootlegging is bad enough, but I'm no crook! What shall I do?"

He rose and came over to Brent's bunk and sat down. Brent studied a while before he spoke. "Well, Dan, I don't know what to do. All I wanted a while ago was to get loose and get somebody to help me with the ship. It's back in the hills, maybe a dozen miles. I footed it in here, and first, one guy shoots, then I go through the mill. Now I'd sure like to spoil Kelly's game somehow. You get a chance to pry them boards loose at that window, so I can get out when I want to. Pretend to fall in with what they want, and when you're on, tell me. I'll try to figure then."

Dan left. Brent had forgotten to ask how far it was, but he knew the town of Lock Haven. He must be in the forest reserve to the north and west of the town. The miles of brushland he had seen since he left his machine would indicate that. He went back to his window. Out by the barn, there were ten men now. Dan was with them, and Kelly was talking earnestly.

The day dragged on. Dan had not loosened the boards. Lunch was brought in by the red-headed man who had first brought him down;

then, things lagged again. Brent's watch had run down and stopped. It was three o'clock, or nearly that when there was a fumbling at the boards of the window with the bush. Then the aperture was cleared, and Dan's freckled face appeared.

"Listen, Cap. I've got it now." Dan swung himself into the cellar. He was excited, mad.

"This is the lay of it. It's Saturday night. They open all the banks in Lock Haven on Saturday nights, so the farmers can come in. Also, the town's lights come in from Graden Dam, up here in the hills. This Kelly's got a man posted along the line, and he'll cut the wires somehow, going to use some kind of explosive. When nine o'clock comes, this bird back in the hills'll do his stuff. Town lights blink out. In the confusion, they'll clean all three banks and get away. We park just across the bridge and wait for the mob. Cap, I'm going to beat it to town and warn the police! Come on, most of the bunch is asleep."

Brent shook his head. "No, Dan, that won't do. I want to get Kelly. If you run for it, they'll all beat it clear. We must trap them. How far is it to Lock Haven?"

"Twenty miles," Dan answered. "But that's by the road. There's old trails right back of us that'll take you there in about twelve miles or so. Why?"

Brent leaned forward and whispered excitedly. "I can do it," he finished. "I'll have to stay in here until supper time, so they won't have time to suspect anything or find me gone. Your job'll be to come on just as they wanted. I'll get there or know why not!"

Dan crawled out the window. Before he left, he stuck in his freckled hand and gripped Brent's. "Listen, Cap. If you don't show up down there at the bridge, I'll shoot it out with them. I want to even up with Kelly for what he did to you, Cap."

Before Dan slipped away, Brent set his watch. He got somewhat vague directions regarding where the old road ran, back of them. Dan thought it ran along the ridge. Alone, Brent gave himself over to various misgivings. First, he had to get out in time to cover twelve miles or more on foot. That would take nearly four hours. Second, finding that road would be something of a task. And, finally, he knew that what Dan had said was true. Failing to find Brent at the bridge meant a one-sided fight for his old friend.

The place was pretty quiet; perhaps now was the time to try for the break. It was nearly four o'clock. Brent took one look out the window where the cars were. Ankers, the mountaineer, sat there, his rifle beside him. Dan was out there, too, tinkering with his car. There were four men in sight, one of them Kelly. Brent decided; and crossed to the other window.

The bush was part of a mass of lilacs that had gone wild, covering half of the shabby little house. Brent edged along to the corner. Kelly was not in sight, but some men were coming out of the barn. He lay there a full ten minutes studying the lay of the ground. Back of the barn, the fields, overgrown with weeds and brush, sloped upward toward the ridge top. Midway, they also sloped toward a deep, tree-lined gully leading to the ridge. He wanted particularly to know the whereabouts of Kelly. Suddenly Dan turned and faced the house. Brent knew his friend saw him, and one of his hands moved in a slight gesture. Now the airman looked up the gully. There was Kelly! He was following a path that led up to the woods and was a scant dozen yards from the brush.

Dan McLeod was something of a strategist. He noisily opened the hood of his car, looked under, then slammed it down again. "Come here, you fellows!" he called. "I want to show you this car's pickup."

The men sauntered forward lazily. Dan directed them to pace off a distance. He had started the motor. Three of them piled in with him; others began to pace the distance. All the while, Dan was loud in his claims for the machine. As he stepped into his car, his hand twitched in a short wave. Brent interpreted it to mean "Go."

He was around the barn in a flash, running low and trying to keep to the shelter of the bushes, but he had not realized how open this hillside was. His last glance back showed him the men about Dan's car. He doubled down into the gully, suddenly obsessed with another idea. Kelly had gone that way.

Halfway up, though, something happened back at the buildings. A chorus of yells came, then a revolver cracked spitefully, to be followed immediately with a fusillade. Brent kept on going. A dust spot kicked up near his feet, then another, but shooting with a revolver would be chancy at this distance. Suddenly a rifle cracked. Brent had no difficulty noting the different sound—like an angry bee buzzing into the brush. For once, he was lucky; almost immediately, he stumbled just as the rifle cracked again. This would be Ankers. Brent crawled on all fours into the shelter of the trees.

Brent had taken the gully for two reasons: it offered a little more cover, and Kelly had gone this way. Brent had hoped to catch the man away from his gang when things would be more even with him. His blood boiled at the memory of the slaps and the way the gangster had spat in his face. Now, with the whole gang down there streaming after him, there would be little time to settle with the leader.

Not ten feet back along the path, Kelly was coming. He had heard the shooting, and he was hurrying. Brent swerved into the brush. Kelly's face was livid when he recognized his former captive, and the big man took after him, yelling savage threats.

Brent ran easily, thinking rapidly. He felt certain of his ability to beat Kelly, but it would take time, which would eat up his lead over his other pursuers. Kelly panted after him. It was evident at once that he did not have a weapon, or he would have fired. Brent led him easily down the side of the ridge, across the hollow and up the next. A glance back showed him the first pursuers coming over the other ridge. He had about a quarter of an hour's head start. He rounded a clump of brush and stopped. A moment later, Kelly rounded the same clump and, staring ahead, missed his quarry. Brent was so close to him he could have touched him; he saw how Kelly's chest was heaving.

A moment later, Kelly turned, spat out a curse and leaped. It was the same old story, rushing tactics against the cutting skill of a boxer. Brent let Kelly swing; his face was cut repeatedly, letting those tremendous swings do the work. Kelly was breathing like a spent horse; his mouth stood open, and blood trickled over his face from cuts.

"Fight, you skunk," Brent snarled. "Get your dirty paws up and fight! I'm going to knock you out in a minute. When you come to and want more, come on over to my ship. I'll be waiting for you."

Kelly bored in as Brent taunted him. Half-blinded, he surged with all his weight forward into a savage uppercut. His eyes widened in a look of agony. He sank to the ground and lay still. It had been a reckless thing to do, Brent reflected, rubbing his bruised knuckles, yet every nerve of him thrilled. He had beaten this brute down, marked him, at least.

In another half-hour, he knew he had distanced the pursuit. He heard the men gather around Kelly. From then on, he put distance between himself and them. The only problem was that he was forced to take a long detour to the north. His time was getting short.

Before long, the going became abominable. He swung on a long arc south but could not cut the line of the trails Dan had said ran to the city. He dared not go further, for he knew that the road the robbers would take made an arc; his route must cut that if he expected to cover a dozen miles in the few hours remaining. He was crossing ridge after ridge, all of them laced with underbrush, where they were not mere ledges of rocks. At every ridge top, he slowed up to look about. Once, he thought he saw the smoke of a town, but it was almost due east, too far north for Lock Haven. In the end, he traveled toward it.

The tangled nature of the country cut his travel speed. He was already beginning to tire. The rough handling of the night before and his strenuous combat with Kelly had not helped him. He came to a stream, stumbled, and barked one knee on a sharp rock. The pain sickened him, but he pressed forward, fearful lest it stiffen. Nightfall came on him as he passed through a ravine where the timber was a bit bigger. Plunging forward through a tangle of cat briars, his feet struck a solid roadbed which he followed with relief.

Down the defile along a brawling stream, the road led him for a mile, then came out on another road. Directly before him was a house with a faint light upstairs. Lying about were piles of what he took to be railroad ties, and his heart leaped to see the unmistakable shape of a car under a rough shed roof.

He pounded on the door for a long minute before anyone answered, then a window went up. "Is this the way to Lock Haven?" he called.

He was answered in some foreign tongue he could not distinguish.

"Take me to Lock Haven," he called. "I'll pay you well."

Again, the gibberish. He tried French and German, the extent of his linguistic ability, to no avail. Angry and impatient, he ran to the car and leaped in. To his surprise, it started! At the thrust of his foot, it woke to shuddering life. After a moment to turn on the lights, he rocked away to a chorus of frantic yells. Then a shotgun boomed twice, and little lead pellets rattled on the top of the car.

The machine demanded all his attention. Its one good quality was that it was quick to start. It took all the muscle he had to steer the thing; it evidently suffered from a bent axle. He was not destined to go far, however. On a long twisting grade, it spluttered and died. Nor would it start again. The gas was all out.

Leaving the car, Brent hurried up the hill, then his heart sank. Below him and to the south, what seemed miles away, were the lights of a town. He dared not look at his watch. There was Lock Haven, and he knew he could not make it, but he plunged into the brush again. He fought through a hollow and saw another group of lights on a large building.

He had no clear recollection of what followed. It was down one hill, up another, all through the underbrush that caught at his limbs, whipped at his face, and stung him to frenzy. His breath came in gasps; he was weaving on his feet when he emerged from the woods into a broad field. He saw a building blazing with lights, which he first took for a hangar.

Five minutes later, he was inside, collapsing into a chair. A man in the uniform of a captain of the National Guard was bending over him with a drink. Men in uniform clustered around. "Where am I?"

"Armory of Troop K," the officer answered. "This is drill night."

Brent sat up, refreshed by the drink. "Tell me, what time is it?"

The officer glanced at his wristwatch. "8:40. What's up?"

Brent told his story as quickly as he could. His heart leaped as the captain made a decision.

"Lieutenants Hafer and Cross. Get three cars; take six men apiece. Lively."

In a matter of minutes, they were outside in cars. Headlights boring through the night, they shot away like great eager animals. "Don't worry," the captain assured him. "We'll make it."

They shot round the corner of the hill, now in plain sight of the city's lights. Suddenly, when the spider outline of the bridge was in sight, the lights winked out as if a giant hand had thrown a switch. The captain as suddenly switched off the lights of his machine. Brent glanced back; the other cars were dark, too. Just a minute more, and their machine swerved to the side of the road. In the shadow by the bridgehead, dark bulks of cars were moving.

Brakes screeched behind them, and troopers piled out in the road with a rattle of accouterment and began running in the direction of the slow-moving machines.

There wasn't much fight about it. The robbers were too surprised and the soldiers too quick. There were not a half-dozen shots. When the lights were turned on, nine men were lined up, guarded by soldiers. Over near the side of the road were two limp figures.

"They ran for it," the captain explained to Brent.

In the light of the officer's flashlight, Brent looked down at the still figures. They were Whitey, and High Kelly.

They walked back to the prisoners. Brent pointed out Dan and explained briefly. Dan stepped out, saluted the captain smartly, and turned to Brent.

"Thought it was up to me, Cap. I was getting out my gun when the soldiers jumped us."

Twenty minutes later, they were in the City Hall. The prisoners' hearing had been before the mayor. When they had filed out to cells, His Honor turned and complimented the troop's captain. "The citizens of our town will appreciate your public service this evening. I'll see that they know."

He turned next to Brent. "Now, Captain Brent. This has been a wonderful service. I am at a loss for how to reward you. Suggest anything I can do for you."

Brent smiled. "Here's the man who did the most." He indicated Dan, whose freckled face turned brick red. His Honor laughed.

"Tell me the whole thing," he directed.

Brent sketched the thing rapidly, stressing the part Dan had played. The mayor studied Brent's scratched face, his torn garments, then he leaned forward, smiling.

"Mr. Dan McLeod. It's the sentence of this court that you be paroled, with your car, in the hands of Captain Brent." There was a sly twinkle in his eye.

"I believe you need looking after. Captain Brent, I shall see what a mere civilian can do about getting you a citation for public service. We've a congressman about here who needs a little work."

Early the next morning, with the tonneau piled with tools and materials, Captain Brent and Dan McLeod rolled north. Brent was sleepy and dozed in the seat, but Dan sat erect like a soldier and drove with infinite care. Every once in a while, his lips puckered in a soundless whistling, a paean of joy.

CHICKEN/ COME HOME

T WAS A church wedding. Cledice Waring had insisted on that, and it was going off splendidly. She thrilled with pride in it, as she stood there beside her husband-to-be, demurely facing the altar. The whole business was abundantly satisfying; the rehearsal had paid off, she reflected, for there had not been the slightest hitch, and in a matter of moments it would be over. She stole a covert glance at the man by her side, to whom she was now more than half married. Back in the church she knew the women would be saying how distinguished he looked with the touch of grey at his temples and his square, erect shoulders.

She faced the minister again. Elliott did look a little fussed. His fingers seemed to be fumbling. Her heart checked a bit—suppose he dropped the ring! For herself, Cledice was not in the least nervous but then, this was not her first venture. In a minute or so, her second marriage would be accomplished. Then, there had been that other episode—"I pronounce you man and wife."

Even Cledice had a faint flutter in the region of her heart when she heard Doctor Bowman's deep voice intone the words. It was all true and settled. She was now Mrs. Elliott Warren before all the world, and she had something of the thrill of the runner who has just broken the tape. Now her husband was turning toward her, bending over her with a smile. Demurely she held up her flushed face to meet his kiss. Cledice's greatest assets were her wonderful complexion and that ability to show the surprised innocence of a child, just when she wished. She was likely to possess both for a long time.

The rest of the day was delightfully breathtaking: passing back through the aisle full of crowding friends, the shower of rice, and the quick trip to her home for a change of costume. Then, she was back in a car with her new husband, and they were slipping away, out of town.

For two weeks they had drifted through the country southward, out of the chill of the northern autumn into sunny southern countryside, on to the blue water of the Gulf. There, a day or so, and then a leisurely rolling north again. Elliott could spare less than three weeks for the honeymoon.

It was chilly in Virginia again, and Elliott bought her a fur coat in Washington. She already had one at home, but he insisted, and she wore it as they drove up the Cumberland Valley. Cledice knew that this time her choice had been wise—very wise indeed. Colonel Waring had been an old man when she married him, and a most considerate husband, but he lacked certain things that Elliott Warren had. To begin, the colonel's legal practice had been ample to allow them to live well, but this sort of living had only stimulated Cledice's desire to live better. As Mrs. Elliott Warren, she would not need to count the cost—ever—and he was generous. She had noted that carefully in their brief courtship.

She had intended to be a good wife to the colonel, and she had apparently succeeded to his satisfaction, but there had been little thrill in the business. On the other hand, she was genuinely fond of Elliott; as nearly in love with him as she would ever be again with any man.

Then, in Harrisburg, they went to the theater. Elliott made a distinguished figure in his dress clothes. She liked the way he tied his tie, the careless air of ease about him and his quick, instinctive courtesy. The curtain went down on the last act. Elliott lifted her wrap over her smooth bare shoulders in a way that made the action a caress. She took his arm and moved very close to him as they went down the aisle and into the foyer. They had been purposely a bit slow in going to allow the crowd to precede them and when they stepped out to the pavement, the throng had thinned. Elliott was lighting a cigarette when Cledice saw the man.

For a moment, the thing shocked her into a frank, frozen stare that Elliott would have noticed if he had not been occupied. It was Tom Brandes—there was no mistaking the tall figure, the sun-tanned, aquiline features. And he recognized her, too, though it was the first time they had crossed paths in ten years.

Tom had stopped, faced her. For a paralyzed moment, she was sure he was coming up to them and she pulled Elliott's coat sleeve.

"There's a taxi, dear."

He followed her obediently into the cab, the door slammed, and they shot away from the curb, leaving the tall figure standing there in the bright lights with a puzzled look on his face.

Back in their hotel rooms later, Elliott turned to her.

"Why were you in such a hurry when we left the theater, Cledice? You know, you almost jumped into that cab."

She crossed over to him, slipped a smooth bare arm about his neck and kissed him. "I just wanted to be alone with you, Elliott, I guess."

His arms went around her yielding figure, swept her off her feet, and for a moment he held her so.

"You know," she breathed. "I want to go home, Elliott, so we can settle down together."

"I, too," he told her. "But we'll have to be here in Harrisburg, over tomorrow. Then, we'll be on our way."

She could not argue the point. After all, the city was fairly large, the meeting with Tom was a mere accident. Nevertheless, that night she sank into a troubled sleep from which she woke in the small hours of the morning. The room was still but for Elliott's quiet breathing. The light from the hallway entered through a transom. She sat up, arms about her drawn-up knees, and so remained for a long time.

Tom Brandes—how well she knew him. It would be like him to get his little revenge now; to tell. He had gone away, been gone so long. She had married Colonel Waring, lived in a different town where no word of the ugly story had ever followed her, and she had been lulled into a false sense of security.

She looked at the dim figure of her husband lying so near to her, and shivered a little. He would never understand, nor forgive. And this was her chance—she had been young then. Tom had swept her off her feet.

Elliott singing in the bathroom awakened her in the morning. He was one of the few men she ever knew who was entirely happy in the morning. She thought of that and smiled. He entered the bedroom almost at once, fully dressed.

"I'll have your breakfast sent up, Cledice. I've an appointment at nine, and I can't wait. Sure that'll be all right?"

He looked at her a bit anxiously, and she smiled back at him and stretched her rounded body luxuriantly.

"You'll spoil me, Elliott," she told him, "but hurry back to me."

Propped up with pillows, she surveyed the tray brought to her, and her eyes sparkled. She had a good appetite, and she liked this luxury of breakfast in bed. Her hand was half raised to her lips with a piece of toast when the telephone by her side shrilled. She picked up the instrument, thinking Elliott had called; then the color left her face as she heard.

It was not Elliott—it was Tom Brandes; and he had not waited for her to reply. His voice came, impatient, over the wire.

"Is this Cledice Warren, Mrs. Warren?"

Cledice clutched the mouthpiece of the instrument to her breast in a sudden panic. He knew her name; what should she do? After a moment, her wits came back to her. Luckily, she had not answered, and she hung up the receiver with a bang. The thing was silent only for a little, then its bell shrilled. She waited, then took down the receiver and rejoiced to hear the operator speak.

"Sorry, Mrs. Warren doesn't answer."

Again, Cledice forced herself to wait, then she called the operator and gave instructions. "This is Mrs. Warren in Suite B. I do not wish to be disturbed by the telephone. Take no calls for me, please."

So far, she could guard against embarrassment, in case Tom telephoned while her husband was in.

Cledice was glad Elliott did not return until nearly noon. That would shorten their stay in the city for her; at least shorten the time she must risk appearing in public. She put on the fur coat and accompanied her husband to a restaurant for their lunch. There, she was glad to note, he had chosen a table more or less out of sight to the person who happened in casually.

Later, they toured the stores. Elliott had learned how much she liked to walk in and out of these places, examining things, and he wanted her to enjoy herself; but the amusement palled on her because every time she lifted her eyes, she was afraid of encountering the questioning grey eyes of Tom Brandes.

At the hotel, she found they had just missed Tom. Had they arrived a few minutes earlier, they would have encountered him. A discreet clerk leaned over the desk when Elliott had crossed the lobby.

"Mrs. Warren, there was a man here just now inquiring for you. He was a bit out of sorts when I told him you were out." He smiled. "Any instructions in case he calls again?"

Cledice leaned forward toward him, her small chin set, her blue eyes darkened. "Tell him I am out—always."

That night, she pleaded her first headache as a reason for not going to the theater with Elliott; he seemed well enough to spend the evening in their rooms at the hotel. They left early. As their car rolled out on the main highway north, she saw, in a gas station talking to one of the attendants, the man she dreaded. It was Tom all right, there was no mistaking the way he stood. She heaved a sigh of relief as they left the city and there seemed no car following them.

She liked Williamsport from the first. The town was large enough for her amusements and shopping and small enough to know people; and being Mrs. Elliott Warren meant something in his hometown. She found she had stepped into the sort of thing of which she had dreamed so long. Elliott's business took him out of town quite often. She even liked that; there was a delightful thrill in the uncertainty of his returns that gave zest to them.

A month slipped by; Elliott was away. There was an upstairs room she frequented a lot because it permitted her a view through bay windows up and down the street. Today she was lolling there when she saw a huge coupe swerve from the center of the street and roll up in front of the house. Cledice got up promptly, as she knew it was the maid's afternoon off and the cook would not answer the bell. She glanced out the window again. A tall figure had stepped from the machine—it was Tom Brandes!

Tom scanned the number on the house for a moment then came up the steps with his springy stride. The doorbell clamored with his long push on the button.

For a long five minutes, she stood at the head of the stairway. What if the cook came to answer the bell? What could she do?

But Mary Sonnberg stuck to her kitchen, as she declared she always did. The bell shrilled again; then there was a step on the porch. Tom reappeared, going down the steps. He crossed to his car, jumped in; and, in a moment, the machine shot out on the street and away.

Thereafter, Cledice knew little of complete peace. When Elliott came home he inquired if she was ill, and she denied that, but it was hard fighting down this dread that was with her all the time. She knew Elliott, with his social position, would never stand for the story Tom could tell if he chose; and she was forced to think he had some sinister purpose in pursuing her.

Then a letter came. Elliott found it in the hallway and tossed it to her with several others. Under his eyes she tore it open and read the brief line or two.

"Dear Cledice: I must see you, have a talk with you. I'm up against it. Please make an appointment with me."

She managed to put the thing down carelessly, pick up another letter, and talk casually with her husband; but her head was ringing with the thing. So he meant blackmail, he was "up against it." Just one approach on Tom's part and things would be all over, her peace of mind, the luxury of her present life, Elliott, and all. And Tom would have proof—those damaging letters. That would be the way he would force her to help; could use them. Only three; but they would be damning, and he had sworn he would use them some day.

There was another letter the next day, and another two days later. They were all insistent. Elliott had left for a ten days' trip, and Cledice found no zest in bridge; she mooned at the country club, and the theater was no distraction.

By her second day alone, she capitulated. She would see Tom, try to beg off. At first, she thought of telephoning, but someone might overhear on the house line. She wrote a note but tore that up. Tom would have more written evidence if she did that. She solved her quandary finally by driving out to a rather questionable roadhouse where she would not be recognized, and there put in a long-distance telephone call to the address Tom had given in his several letters. His impatient voice answered with startling suddenness.

"Thought you'd come to your senses," he declared almost truculently. "It'll be good for us to get together. Shall I run up to your home?"

"Oh, no, no!" She exclaimed, and he laughed.

"That's right, Cledice. Keep up the front always—all the time. Then, meet me in Scranton tomorrow evening. Get a room at the hotel." He gave her a name and address. Scranton was far enough away, she thought. No one could know her there.

Cledice assented and heard him hang up. It was as though he had ordered her, and now that the showdown was coming, she felt something like relief. It would be something to know just what he wanted, then she might be able to get him to be merciful.

The hotel was not the sort she liked. It was on a side street, quiet and a little dingy. The clerk smirked when she told him she wanted a room for the night, and that there would be a caller. She was angry, the blood rushed to her face, but she said nothing.

Alone, she studied herself. Years before she had been able to wind Tom around her finger when she chose. She looked at her image in the mirror, a calculating smile curving the corners of her lips. The traveling clock she had set there said it was seven-thirty. Suddenly she became full of energy. She flung off her clothing, turned on the taps in the tub. In the bath, she hummed a little.

About twenty minutes later, there was a rap on the door. Swinging a negligee about her, she came into the main part of the room.

"Who's there," she called.

"Tom Brandes. I came up alone."

Cledice studied a moment. "Tom, you're early, I was dressing just now."

"Hurry it up. You know I can't loiter here in the hall." She could hear his low chuckle. "It doesn't matter to me, if you're dressed."

Suddenly, she was ashamed. Elliott's face appeared in her mind. Even if he never knew, she would know. She pulled on her clothes. She couldn't be vulnerable in front of Tom. She must be strong, calculating. Feminine wiles might have helped her, but they also gave him the upper hand. She must find a way. She drew a deep breath and opened the door.

"About time!" he snapped and pushed roughly past her. She shut the door and turned to face him.

"Now, look, Tom, you simply must stop this pestering of me!" She could hear a small quaver in her voice and prayed he didn't notice.

He whirled on her, grabbing her shoulders. "You don't get it, do you, Cledice?" He shook her a little. "I'm up against it, I tell you, I—"

At that moment there was a harsh knocking on the door. Cledice had not locked it, and as they turned to look, it swung open, and admitted Elliott Warren, followed by two police officers.

Elliott rushed to Cledice, who tottered, feeling faint. "Are you all right, did he hurt you?" He wrapped his big arm about her and kept her upright. She couldn't look at him.

The policemen had subdued Tom, with very little effort. He stood, feet apart and head hanging as if resigned. Suddenly he stiffened, and his head came up with a wild, defiant gleam.

"You'll get me out of this, Warren. You'll do it to protect your precious reputation, your little wifey that you're so proud of," he snarled. "The things I could tell you, will tell anyone—"

His voice was stopped by the force of Elliott's blow. Tom's head snapped back, and the policemen caught him and dumped him into a chair. He sat woozily, a trickle of blood sliding down his chin.

Elliott's voice was scornful. "No one will believe the word of a criminal. And where you're going, Brandes, no one will care."

The policemen lifted Tom Brandes to his feet. "Thank you, Mr. Warren. We'll be in touch." One on each side, they half-dragged the man out the door.

As the sound of their steps faded, Elliott turned back to Cledice, sitting on the side of the bed, her head in her hands. "He didn't hurt you?" he asked her in a solicitous tone. She shook her head, unable to speak as the tears dripped from her chin. She couldn't look at him.

"Cledice, why didn't you tell me? It took a while for me to figure out what was going on. Not until Sergeant Tompkins contacted me that Brandes had been driving by and hanging around our house, did I realize why you had become so skittish." He sat down on the bed beside her.

"I couldn't tell you," she sobbed. "I knew you'd never stand for it, for me!"

He took her chin in one big hand, turning her face to his. "Cledice, I know all about it. Did you think I wouldn't look into you when I started thinking of marriage? You never brought it up, so I didn't mention it. I thought it's all in the past, and it would have been, except that Brandes turned up like a bad penny." He took her hand in his. "You can't be blamed for things that happened when you were a child. You moved on, grew up, and changed. You became the woman I love. I will stand by you in the face of anything."

His eyes searched hers, and a tiny flare of hope grew in her heart, along with a love she hadn't realized was there. A deeper, mature love of a woman for a man, not a foolish girl for a charmer who turned her head. She knew then that she could love Elliott Warren with all she was for all her days.

WHIJPER VALLEY

DAN BECKWITH'S fingers fumbled for his watch and remembered it had stopped in the crash. He pushed the smooth metal case back into his pocket and stared ahead, weariness pushing his shoulders forward. His flying suit was in tatters and hung sack-like about him, and his 'chute was still in place, for he had not thought to remove it.

Twenty-four hours since the crash, he figured, but nothing was very clear to him. Early evening the day before, he had lifted his plane through the light fog at the airport. Now, a day with no hint of the sun gave way to a crowding night.

Dead leaves, stirred by a hint of a breeze, rustled near him; and his tired muscles twitched as he listened. It had been like this through the long hours he had fought the brush since bewildered, half stunned; he had staggered away from the wreck of the ship. Always there was a stirring in the leaves. When he had tried to sleep, it had been that way, and he found it better to drive his weary muscles than to lie and listen to these ever-closer stirrings nearer when he lay still.

The fog at the airport had thickened when he climbed for the ridges; then, the mountain's grim black mass had leaped up like a great dark beast. He had cut the switch with wheels skimming the red brush and tried to relax his body, then the crash and momentary unconsciousness.

He knew, now, he should have remained by the plane. The flashlight had died in the first mile, and he had no idea of his location or how far he had come in the dragging hours. He moved forward again, his tired feet moving downward, following the ghost of a path. Then he found himself in pines. The fluttering of the oak leaves gave place to the soothing whisper of pine needles, and he drew a deep breath of relief. The path entered an old logging road. After a little, there was a tiny stream across it, and Dan drank deeply of icy water.

Rising, refreshed, he saw something else on a stone—a tin lunch box. Ravenously hungry, he opened it with trembling fingers and devoured to the last crumb, the scraps of a lunch. Having eaten, he drank again and rose stronger, some of his weariness falling away. There must be men close, and that meant help.

Dusk was thickening rapidly here in the pines, and a hundred yards or so farther on, the road turned left. Beyond the turn was the loom of a small cabin set on a slope. The roof sagged, but yellow light gleamed through a window frame guiltless of a sash. He hurried.

Dan's footfalls made little noise on the pine needles. Some vague impulse of caution stopped him near the window. The light was from a lantern set on a packing box by which two men stood. One had bristles of a stubby red beard all over his face and, with huge hands, was making three tiny piles of something bright on the box. The other, dark, squat, powerful, watched. Both men were grimed with mud and incredibly dirty. The piles finished, the red-bearded man looked at his companion, a mocking light in his eyes.

"Cal," he called. "Come in and see the split."

Too late, Dan turned, but the world exploded in a shower of sparks.

There were ropes on his arms and legs when he came to consciousness, and a thin line of yellow light glared into his aching eyes. His head throbbed, and he was glad to lie still, but after a little, he did try to rise and came up sharply against boards. He lay back and fumbled with his bonds.

This was different, though, than the rustling in the brush. Contact with men, even though enemies, was better than the vague things that had torn at his nerves. These men knew little of ropes, anyway; for in a matter of minutes, his arms were free, then his legs.

It was the same room he found, into which he had looked before, and there was a third man, tall and skinny, like the others mud-stained. This would be Cal. The man with the red beard was announcing a decision.

"No, boys, we're in bad enough now. We'll leave this bird tied up. We'll be done in a day. Anytime he makes trouble, you boys can swing a pick on him."

The squat man growled. "There'll be folks in here hunting that flier, Ben; best use the pick now."

Dan moved back from the crack and explored with his fingers. He was shut in a small lean-to, half-filled with firewood. There was a board that seemed loose. He was careful lest the sound of a nail would warn his jailers. The first board was clear. He tried the next, then he stopped, the hair rising on the nape of his neck; for a hand had closed about his wrist.

A long moment, then a sibilant "Shh!" Dan made no reply. A whisper came through the opening he had made. "You Beckwith?"

This time he answered, and the whisper came again. "Hurry with the board; no time to fool."

Another minute, and he was free. A hand was on his wrist again, and he was being led away rapidly into the dense blackness of the pines. Ten minutes later, the hand released him.

"Now you follow close," the voice directed. "Things'll pop here, any minute. Me and you'll have to be pretty far off when they do."

Dan followed as best he could. The pace was fast, and his breath came in wheezes before his rescuer paused. Carefully, the man lighted a match and held it cupped in his palms. Dan caught a glimpse of drooping sandy mustaches, eyes gleaming, and heavy wrinkles at their corners. A little man dressed in worn corduroy. Even in the brief glimpse, there was something vibrantly alive about the man.

"You're Beckwith, alright. I was kinda doubtful. Look pretty used up. I was a little late, saw that bird land on you with a club. I'm Rand, county detective."

Dan knew that name; he had once heard it mentioned in the airport. This was the fellow that took the Humphreys. He extended his hand and found it gripped in iron fingers.

"Grateful you came at all."

Rand caught his arm and pointed. Way back, where the cabin must be, was a yellow light; but there was something else. Dozens of pinpoints of light were flickering to the right and left of the greater light. Dan turned.

"What's going on?"

Rand chuckled, but there was no mirth in the sound.

"Everything, for your playmates back there. That cabin stands at the mouth of a ravine; those little lights are torches setting a fire. This'll be a sort of deer drive. Everything'll be driven up this ravine."

"And we're in it," Dan interjected.

"Right. I found your plane and tried to locate you. Figured I could get you out of this three-ringed circus."

"But, Rand, what's the use of running away? Let's go back; I have to report—"

Back at the cabin, a rifle cracked, followed by a long scream of agony.

"Listen," Rand's voice was cold, hard. "There's maybe forty men back there and on the ridges. Nothing is going to be left alive here tonight to talk. Those fellows can shoot. Maybe you've been in tight spots, but this is the tightest for you that'll ever come. Maybe there's somebody ahead, too. Come on."

Dan stopped arguing. He needed his breath to follow. They were taking a long diagonal toward the nearest ridge. The belt of pines thinned out; it was open and rocky here. Then, suddenly, a flashlight gleamed for a moment. Rand went into action like lightning. His fist crashed home on the holder. The flash dropped to the rocks and went out. A revolver spat sound and yellow flame. Rand snatched at his arm, and they sped back down the hill.

Their attackers did not pursue. "Looks bad," Rand jerked. "They figure no one can get over the ridges; they're watching them."

"We'll go on up the ravine," Dan panted in answer, and Rand chuckled.

"Can't; there's a sort of jumping off place, three hundred feet down. Even in daylight, we could hardly get down."

Dan was stubborn. "Then, let's wait for daylight."

Rand stopped. "Young fellow, you don't get things. You figure that's a mob back there, with some good people in it. But they don't want any witnesses. There won't be any daylight for us. Listen."

From down where the cabin was burning came two rifle shots, deliberately spaced, then again the scream of a man hard hit. The long line of torches was moving slowly toward the fugitives. On the hilltops, more torches gleamed. This time they sped to the left-hand ridge. Once again, they narrowly escaped a group of men. This time rifles cracked.

The torches were coming faster. This time men were after them in the dark. Rand urged Dan on, doubling back like rabbits. The detective seemed made of steel springs. The aviator was ready to collapse. Finally, Rand stopped. Dan flung himself prone.

"Well, I guess the jig is up." Down the ravine, the torches were making a great Y and drawing closer. "They're closing in," Rand went on.

Dan staggered up and dislodged a stone with his feet. He heard it bound downward, down, down, but he could not hear it strike bottom.

"Mr. Flyer, if we had your plane, maybe we'd have a chance. This is the jumping-off place. Those fellows back there know they've got us caught."

Closer, the torches were closer. Again, rifle fire, three shots this time, no scream.

"That's all three," Dan muttered. "Is this cliff straight down?"

"No," Rand answered, "some places, it's straight. Me, I've no head for height. Maybe a man could get down in the daytime."

A queer, low, strong, muttering like a growl came from behind the torches. Dan set his jaw.

"Give me your belt, Rand." Working rapidly, he fastened the detective to him with the belt. "Come on, Rand, let's go over."

He could feel the detective stiffen, then they went over, sliding down a steep slope a dozen feet or so, coming to a stop with a jerk. Again they slid over, their fingernails breaking as they clutched at the bare rock. They stopped again with a jolt.

This time, Dan felt Rand fumbling at the leather belt. "Me," he muttered. "I'm sick, guess I'll stay here."

Dan did not give him time to finish but slid off. The officer grunted and slid forward. They were shooting down sickeningly, clutching at bushes that gave way, and bumping into rocks. This time, they crashed into a tree in a bone-jarring bump.

It was a full minute before they could move. Rand said nothing, but Dan could feel him shivering.

"Hurt, Rand?"

"No, just kinda sick."

"Ready?"

Rand retched, then his voice came back. "Yes."

Dan tapped him on the shoulder. "You're game, all right." Far above them, pinpoints of light lined the cliff edge. A light breeze swept up from below. Dan could hear the sound of a stream that seemed miles away, straight down.

Once, a boulder tore loose beneath their scrambling, bounding twice, then fell far below with a muffled crash. Down, down, clinging to brush, clutching at rocks. Nails broken, faces raked with whipping branches, feet searching desperately for purchase against the sickening sliding, they went on.

Another ledge stopped them. "Rocks at the bottom," Rand panted.

Dan fumbled at his 'chute. Not drop enough for it to open, but—he tore at the wrapping, shook the thing clear. It might catch on to something and help them a little.

Over a big rock, against a ledge that crumbled, then down, this time with a sickening rush. Brush thrashed them savagely with blind blows; then the chute caught with a wrench that nearly tore Dan in two.

They had struck in a pine top. The chute tore loose; they fell again, landed with a thump and stopped. After a long moment, Rand spoke. "You all right?" Dan grunted in assent, and the detective went on. "Well, I felt around; seems level."

Despite his aching body, Dan had to grin at the relief in Rand's voice. They staggered to their feet and cut away the chute ropes. Far above them, the cliff edge showed against the sky. No torch showed way up there. At their feet, a brook babbled.

Presently there was a woods road. "Know where we are now," Rand said. "My car's up here a piece. I walked into Whisper Valley." They found the machine and made some repairs with salve and torn garments. There was a thermos of coffee.

Later, they drove up to a farmhouse, and Dan was able to report. It was difficult to escape the farmer's hospitality. They offered no explanation except that the plane had crashed and that Rand had come in and rescued him. Neither said anything of the cliff.

Outside, Rand fumbled with the switch of the car. "Beckwith, I was listening. You didn't say much about what happened, about the mob and the men. You figure you owe me anything?"

Dan laughed. "Only my life, that's all."

"Well," Rand went on. "I was wondering if you could maybe forget about the whole business; just say you crashed, and I found you."

Dan looked at the weathered face sharply etched by the dash light. He extended his hand, and the detective grasped it.

"Guess I'd better tell the story. That place back there is called Whisper Valley. One time it was farmed, there's lots of little farms back there, deserted now. All the houses are gone now; nothing left but the old cemetery. Folks moved out to better land. Descendants of those folks live all around."

Rand paused. "Last summer, they put a state road through near here, and a lot of hard guys came in for the work. Some of them picked up a story about the old people that lived up in Whisper Valley. It was that whenever they buried a member of the family, they put money in the coffin. It would be silver or gold money. It was something like how we send flowers nowadays. The old folks didn't mean anything; only it was their way. These state road toughs picked up the story."

Suddenly, Dan understood. "Those men were robbing those graves?"

Rand nodded. "And word got out about it. I expected trouble. Relations of those old folks went in there to settle those men. They were good folks but didn't want to get the law to help. I went in and found your plane. You and me got out in time. Those farmers wouldn't want any witnesses."

Dan shivered and remembered the narrow valley, the whispering trees, the shots, the screams.

"I got friends in this section and figured them grave robbers likely got what was coming to them without costing the county a cent. That's why I figured you and me'd just keep quiet."

Again, Dan thrust out his hand. In twenty minutes, they were at the airport. Rand's car swung in and stopped near the office. Doors opened. Men were coming out, shouting Dan's name. Rand stopped and leaned close.

"Beckwith, there was one more reason I didn't give you. The fellows that tipped me off something'd happen up there in the valley figured I ought to know."

He paused. Men were all about the car now, shouting.

"You see," he whispered. "My old granddad's buried up there."

Then Dan's fellow fliers and the ground men were pulling him from the car, carrying him on their shoulders and thumping the rescuer on the back as they went into the lobby.

THE WITHDRAWN HAND

ROSS KLEBER waved a huge hand awkwardly to the driver of the battered car now rolling down the lane and turned toward the house. He liked Luke Daniels despite the stories about him. But then, he was Hilda's brother.

Her low call brought him to the bedroom. There, his wife, Hilda, lay, propped up by pillows. His hands were deft as he smoothed these a little. She settled back where she could look out of the window.

"You waved to Luke," she said with a smile.

Ross grinned. "Luke's like a kid, always waving, grinning. I just answered him. Didn't want to hurt his feelings."

Her face was thin from her illness, but her eyes were alight and so blue they seemed to cast a shadow on her thin cheeks. Now her voice was thoughtful, touched with regret.

"You like Luke, Ross?"

He nodded. "Always did, from the times we were kids and him, older. Guess I looked up to him. He was always doing what we thought couldn't be done. Anyway, he's your older brother."

She nodded with another smile for his loyalty. "Yes, and he's on my mind. You know he's no good. Now he's been gone five years—maybe he's been in prison. I'm so worried he'll drag himself down and his friends and relations with him. Ross," her eyes became wide, startled. He kneeled by the bed, took her frail hands in his.

"What's wrong, Hilda?"

"He's been in prison, twice. Once, he shot a man. It scares me so. Almost I wish he was dead. He comes here and visits, laughs, talks."

Ross patted her thin shoulders. "Hush, Doctor Holt says you mustn't be excited."

"But" she hurried on, "I'm so afraid he'll kill somebody else. Why did he come back? Do you think he's planning something?"

He shook his head. "No, he wouldn't do that. He just wanted to see us."

Now she leaned forward. "He's my brother, and a criminal, and I believe you forgot you're the constable. What if he goes out, does something?"

Ross whistled softly. He had forgotten. Nor had he thought of it while Luke was there. What she said was true, but—

Her voice was insistent, almost shrill. "If anything happens to him, Ross, it might be a good thing. Only not by your hands—I couldn't have that come between us, to lie by your side and know. Promise—"

"Hilda, you're just being foolish. Luke's gone; he just visited us. There won't be trouble." He laughed. "I've got to arrest some apple borers, not my wife's brother. You get these ideas out of your head."

Out in the orchard, working down the long rows, he thought of what Hilda had said. Luke did have a bad record, and he, Ross, was constable. But Luke had never done anything criminal around here.

Three days passed. Hilda was better, more cheerful. Doctor Holt said that was her trouble; once things were quiet, she'd regain her strength. Perhaps in another month, she might walk out. But—nothing must disturb her. Too much shock might easily be fatal. She must be guarded.

He was in the back field with Paul Breon. Paul, with his witless face, could work for Kleber, who had taught him to hunt apple borers as a sort of game. That, the boy could do, and shoot a rifle like a veteran marksman. Paul was proud of both accomplishments. Now he stood and stared vacantly while the messenger told the news.

The bank down in Mooresburg had been robbed. Norris, the cashier, was dead; shot through the brain. Kleber was to come; he was the constable.

Something unsettling stirred in the orchard man as he hurried down the lane. Hilda must not get this story. He'd just slip away and send word that he had to get some machinery repairs. He scarcely noticed that Paul followed.

The little town was seething when he arrived and pushed through on his way into the bank. Norris's body had been taken away, but there was still a pool of blood on the floor. Norris was a hard man; but he had been shot down like a dog, and he was an old man.

The safe door was open; papers were scattered about. Ross Kleber was thorough. He asked questions. The robber had entered just as the bank had opened for the day. One man had been seen to leave. He drove a battered-looking car. Methodically, the constable stepped about. Over by the vault door, in a pile of papers, color caught his eye. He bent, and picked up the object, a handkerchief.

"Mr. Kleber, that's yours—"

Paul was by his elbow, smiling, pointing. Ross felt again that awful sickness. No doubt about it, Hilda had made the handkerchiefs out of some soft red stuff. Luke had taken one away with him, and dropped it here.

There were powder burns on it. Likely it had been used to mask the revolver. Now, Ross remembered how Luke had hated Norris because of a beating the older man had given the boy years ago. Likely this morning, that old hate had cropped up. Norris had reached for the pistol under the counter, and Luke had fired—just once.

There were many things to do. He sent a messenger back to make an excuse to Hilda; then he called the sheriff.

"Get some men, try to follow," the sheriff told him. He was given Norris's car. Two or three men stepped forward, and volunteered. Now before him was Paul again. Somehow, he had his rifle. Likely he had darted home while Ross was busy.

"I'll go, Mr. Kleber. I can shoot."

Ross was going to refuse. Then Springer, one of the volunteers, said, "Better take him, Ross. He can shoot. You taught him. Next to you, he's the best shot in these parts."

"All right." Five minutes and the car darted away in the direction the robber had taken, but they hadn't gone a quarter of a mile when a police car approached them, its siren going. The car swung across the road, and a man in the uniform of a state policeman jumped out.

Ross stepped out. The officer spoke rapidly. "Car's wrecked down here about three miles. We came up, and the fellow opened fire with a rifle, and took to the woods. I want some men to round him up." He looked at the revolver in Ross' belt, the shotguns, and rifles.

Springer told what had happened. The officer whistled. "So that's it. I thought it was fishy. Quick—you, Mr. Kleber, Springer. Say, can that boy shoot?"

He looked at Paul and the fine rifle he carried. Paul's face was alight; all the vacancy was gone. "You just ask Mr. Kleber; he taught me."

A moment and they were tearing away in the police car. The other was turned back for the sheriff's use when he should come.

The car had not made the elbow turn and had crashed into a concrete culvert post. It was demolished. The driver's license was tucked into the dash pocket. Springer nodded as he saw the name. "We figured it was Luke Daniels, Ross. Did you?"

Kleber nodded. Springer went on. "He always hated Norris. I haven't seen him for years. When did you last hear from him, Ross?"

Kleber was saved a reply by the call of the policeman. There was no dodging; it would have to come out that Luke had visited at the Kleber home. He and Hilda would be dragged into a trial. Her brother on trial for murder and robbery!

The officer was beckoning. He joined him, and moved across the field to where the other officer was waiting.

"Fellow has a rifle and can use it. He cut bark not two inches over my head. Don't get too close; that bird's just plain murder."

Ross turned to Springer. "You wait for the sheriff; tell him where we went. You ready?"

The policeman nodded. "I'm Sergeant Craig of the police; this is Private Robbins. I'll take charge if you don't mind."

Ross was glad for the man's officiousness. In the next hour, they sighted the fugitive just once. He was limping, carrying a rifle. By noon they had crossed two ridges, and it was plain that Luke was following the old buffalo path. That Ross could understand, but Luke must be hurt, or he would have won clear long before this.

Through Kleber's brain was a tiny line of something like fire. "Not by you," Hilda had said. Almost it would seem she had looked ahead and seen this situation coming. Just a few months ago, he had taken office, held up his hand, and sworn to do his duty. He was proud then, determined. Now he was following his wife's brother through the brush, hunting him down against her pleading. And he liked Luke, liked his winning smile, his way of doing things. He did not believe the man had come there to plan a robbery. It had been a thing of the moment. Just so Norris had found his death. Luke would have beaten him to the draw.

When the buffalo path reaches Shriner Mountain, it goes up on a sort of switchback winding through the rocks that are here piled up in masses; there spread out like rough paving. Thickets are scarce on the north side. On the top, the land spreads away nearly level and is covered with a tangle of red brush.

Ross knew that once in this brush, it would take an army to rout their quarry out. And he wasn't sure he cared if Luke did reach the crest. Arrested, Luke's presence in his house must come out. The trial would be slow death to Hilda.

But two-thirds of the way up the mountain, they brought Luke to bay. They saw him moving slowly up the slope, and the policemen had elevated their revolvers and made the slope unsafe to cross. Now their quarry was behind a rock pile.

Ross listened while Sergeant Craig talked. But he was thinking of Luke as a boy, thinking of him just lately, how he smiled at Hilda, how he waved his hand in parting. He could remember the big boy who always did things better . . . .

"You fellows with the rifle, keep him busy. Robbins and I'll flank him, drive him out."

The officers crawled away. High above the crest against the brassy sky, a hawk wheeled, dropping from his height with a thin, reedy whistle. Heat waves shimmered on the rocks. Behind them, they could look back, down through the gap to where a stream sparkled in a small clearing.

"I'm kinda dry, Mr. Kleber."

He had almost forgotten the boy. He was rubbing the stock of his rifle, a beautiful weapon with its short heavy barrel and micrometer sights.

Paul had refinished the stock until the dark walnut was beautiful. Now he slipped back the bolt, looked at the ready cartridge, and closed it again.

"We should have brought some water, Paul. You could go back down to the stream and get a drink." Ross spoke dully, his mind churning over the problem of his brother-in-law.

"I could suck on a pebble, Mr. Kleber. That would help for a while." Paul's voice was eager to please. He liked to show off his knowledge; it gave him a sense of being like others. Often, he seemed not to be aware that his mind was childish. But he must sense it sometimes.

The boy turned away, laying his rifle aside as he searched for just the right pebble. Ross scanned the hillside, watching for movement. He hoped Luke stayed put, and didn't try again. Ross must do his duty, but the cost to Hilda! He shook his head.

He glanced back at Paul, who had picked up several small rocks and considered them, then tossed them aside. As he turned back to his watch, there was movement in the rocks! He snatched up Paul's rifle and aimed. Suddenly it was as though Hilda was whispering in his ear, and he jerked the gun up, the bullet going high, hitting the rocks above and to the left of where Luke had hidden.

He felt sick. If he shot her brother, Hilda would never forgive him. But a trial would kill her just as surely. He loved her and couldn't imagine life without her. He couldn't lose her!

He felt Paul settle back down beside him, mouth working a rock. The boy picked up the rifle and exclaimed in horror, "Oh, no, you've scratched it! You've ruined it." Tears stood in the boy's eyes, then as he looked at Ross and saw the sorrow and worry etched on his face, Paul said, "It's all right, Mr. Kleber, I can polish it out. It'll be ok. Did ya shoot him?"

"No, Paul. I missed. I guess I'm not as good a shot as you are." He smiled weakly, but Paul beamed at him.

Ross thought the officers must have nearly made it up to where Luke was hiding by now. "Watch close, Paul. They'll be reaching him soon. He'll have to make a break for it, or surrender." He hoped—he didn't know what he hoped. Any way it came out, they would lose. Luke would lose his life or his freedom. Hilda would lose her brother and probably fade away. Ross would lose Hilda; his own life would be meaningless.

A voice called out above them, hard to understand. Something about surrender. Then it all happened at once. Movement, the roar of a shotgun above, and the loud explosion of Paul's rifle nearby. A figure rose out of the rocks and fell, sprawling down the slope. It was Luke!

Ross and Paul made their slow way up the ridge to join the policemen. His ears ringing, heart pounding, Ross stood over the still form of his brother-in-law, lost in the memories of their childhood. A sound made him turn.

Paul had dropped to his knees beside the dead man. Fat tears rolled down his face. "I'm sorry, I'm sorry," he sobbed. He looked up at Ross. "He was a bad man. He shouldn't have shot Mr. Norris. He shouldn'ta made me shoot him."

The police officers moved uncomfortably, and Sergeant Craig stepped forward. "Young man, you are right. Luke Daniels was a bad man, and he had hurt more than one person in his time. You stopped him. It's nothing to be proud of, but you shouldn't be sorry, either. It was just your duty." He helped Paul to stand, and they made their way back down the mountainside. Ross handed Paul his handkerchief and took his arm.

It was nearly dark when he reached his home. He washed his hands and face in the kitchen and realized he was stalling, not wanting to give Hilda the news. Her voice, faint and quavery, drifted to him. "Ross, Ross, is it you?"

"I'm coming, Hilda," he said, dried his face, and walked to the bedroom. Her eyes, huge in her wasted face, searched him. She looked even more drawn than she had when he left, and he knew, somehow, she had figured it out. He breathed deeply and began. "Hilda, it's bad, I'm afraid. Be brave, darling." He took both her hands in his. Her eyes filled with tears, and she caught her breath but lifted her chin and met his eyes squarely. "It's Luke, dear. He held up the bank in Mooresburg, and dear—I hate to tell you—he killed Mr. Norris."

A tiny wail escaped her, and she fell against him. He held her for a moment, then she mastered herself and looked up again. "Tell me all of it, Ross."

"He's dead, Hilda." Her chin quivered, but she kept her eyes steady on his face. "He cracked up his car and ran for it." He remembered the moment he swung the rifle on Luke's form, and sickness rose in his gut. She clasped his hands hard, harder than he could have believed.

"Was it you, Ross? Was it—you?" she cried.

"No, Hilda. It wasn't me. It was Paul." He dropped his face onto her shoulder, remembering the boy's tears. She held him and stroked his hair.

"That poor boy." He didn't know whether she meant Paul—or Luke. "It had to be done. All we can do now is go forward." Her thin chest heaved, and he held her close. "I'm so glad it wasn't you."

CAUTION: SOFT SHOULDERS

THE ENGINE roared powerfully, the sound preceding the car, as Scott stood along the road. He stepped out from beside the road sign that read CAUTION: SOFT SHOULDERS. The engine slowed and as the big coupe neared, he could see a woman driving alone. He cursed his luck, she probably wouldn't want to stop here, risk sinking her car. Perhaps she could pull off up ahead. As she came alongside, he could see her tip-tilted nose, a wave of hair under her hat. Suddenly, she sped up and was gone.

Later, he heard the familiar roar and turned, hoping. It was the same car, and the driver slowed and stopped by him. The girl craned her slender neck toward him, her eyes laughing as she said, "Hey, aren't you the fellow who I passed up, back near Bellefonte? I hope I didn't get you mad then! Hop in and I'll take you a ways."

Scott eased his lean length in beside her. "You did get me, when you passed me up," he explained. "But I made good time, came the back way. I've had a good half-hour's sleep."

She eased the big car into motion skillfully. "I don't often pick up people," she explained "but I don't exactly fancy going through these mountains ahead alone."

To the east, the line of wooded mountains was faintly blue, and the road stretched toward them, a lazy gray ribbon strung over the rolling hills. Scott glanced at his watch.

"Five o'clock," he told the girl. "You can be through before dark, you've two hours or so."

She nodded, but the car kept showing a scant thirty on the speedometer. If she was in a hurry or anxious, she certainly was not trying to hasten the experience. It took them most of an hour to reach the small village of Woodward a mile or so from the first of the mountains; and here she turned in the drive of a country hotel.

"I'm hungry," she told Scott. "Will you have dinner or supper or whatever they have with me?"

The food was first-rate, but it had been a long time coming. Scott found the girl excellent company. Together they laughed, chatted, and did full justice to what was set before them. Finally, the woman who served them set their dessert before them, and left the dining room. Almost suddenly, the girl thrust aside her plate. Her face was tense.

"Listen," she said, her voice taut. "Haven't I seen you somewhere before?"

Scott met her gray eyes fairly. "No," he said slowly. "don't think you have. At least, I've never seen you."

"Are you some kind of officer?" she demanded.

This time he laughed banteringly. "I'm a hitchhiker, my dear young lady, my name's Scott Milroy. By the way, what's yours?"

"Doris, just call me Doris," she answered. "But I set out to do something, and—I'm sort of afraid. I thought you might help."

He sat silent for a moment, the lamplight on his lean bronzed face. His brown hand lay on the cloth, turning a spoon over and over. "Yes," he answered without emotion. "I'll help, can you tell me just how?"

Her brows drew down a little. He was almost sure he had offended her and sat forward a little. He liked the level look in her eyes, liked the way her hair waved where it showed under her hat.

"Well," she began doubtfully. "Down in these mountains is an old farmhouse off the main road. I must go there and ask one question. I thought it'd be easy but—"

"You want company," Scott said with a smile. "I know something of these hills. It would be just as well you had someone along."

She drew a long breath, then smiled and drew her dessert toward her. "I feel better, Scott," she pronounced the name doubtfully. "Now, I'm in a hurry."

Outside it was dark with the first heavy dusk of the evening. The mountains loomed ahead, a dense dark mass. Doris, as she called herself, drove rapidly and Scott finished his cigarette. When he tossed the butt aside she drew to the side of the road.

"Now, it will look better if I seem to come alone. Will you get down in the rumble, and keep your head down?"

He stepped out obediently, clambered into the rumble seat, and found room for himself on the floor. "Now," he called, "straight ahead a mile and a half, then turn left on a dirt road over the hill—"

"What?" she demanded, surprise in her voice. For a moment she seemed to study with her slim fingers on the gear shift then the car moved ahead.

In the dark of the rumble, Scott wondered. She seemed all right with those gray eyes. Yet—he eased down the robe he had found so he would not bump against the side. He'd see the thing through.

Ten minutes later, the big car swung left and began to bump along a dirt road. The thing was crooked, the machine swerved and rocked, tossed Scott back and forth. The girl was going pretty fast for this kind of going.

A mile or two, now the car was climbing, and the grade was hard. The road was angling up the side of a ridge. She slipped into second and the powerful motor's beat echoed back at them. Scott straightened up. Far to the west through the hills he caught a glimpse of the twinkling lights of Woodward. Some more turns and they were up, gears purred, and they were again in high.

Scott had been up here before. He was practically certain where the girl was going. Her speed, he felt, was reckless on these turns. There had been rain the day before. If she slid into the ditch, she'd stick.

Suddenly, the girl slammed on the brakes, the car slued drunkenly, slid into the ditch, crawled out again, and came to a stop. Somewhere out front a man was swearing. Then the arc of a flashlight swept across the car, came to a stop on the girl.

"You," a man's voice demanded. "What d'ye want up here?"

Scott crouched down. He'd play the role the girl had assigned him.

"Looking for the old Dale place." The girl's voice was steady. She had nerve, Scott granted from his huddle. The man with the light approached the machine.

"What?" he demanded.

"Looking for the old Dale place. Want to see a man they call Patch."

"The hell you do," the man grunted. "Sister, this is a private road. Sure you don't just want to turn round and go back?"

Suddenly Doris laughed, and the man unlatched the car door.

"All right, sister, it's your show—but move over, I'll do the driving. Ed, you stay here."

The man's bulk settled into Doris' seat, and the car moved forward slowly, kept going for what seemed like ten minutes.

"This is the Dale place," the driver grunted. "Get out."

Scott raised himself cautiously. The pair was moving across what had been a wide lawn broken with clumps of shrubbery and trees, in the direction of a shadowy house that showed two yellow squares of lamp light. Cautiously, he clambered out of the rumble and stood sheltered by the car.

When the couple ahead had about reached the door, he followed cautiously, keeping to the dense shadows of trees and shrubs. The house door opened for a moment showing a streak of light, then closed. Now Scott saw something else. An old barn bulked to the rear of the house and here a half dozen men were working by lantern light, loading two trucks. For the moment, his attention was divided. Should he watch these trucks, or try to see where the girl and her escort had gone. He moved toward the house.

The windows were low down. Near one a huge fragrant lilac offered concealment. He looked in the window. Doris was there, standing straight in the middle of the floor. A man was entering, a huge figure with a queerly twisted mouth and a heavy brutal face. He scowled when he saw the girl.

"What d'ye want?" he growled. "Mat says you wanted to see me."

Scott thrilled to see her little chin go up. He could just catch the throaty tones of her voice. "If you're Patch Tibbens, yes. I came to ask you where—"

Patch Tibbens scowled, cursed savagely, then turned on the big man who had brought her in. "Mat, what'd you bring this damn skirt in here for. We're loading and I can't have any sniveling spies about. Take her upstairs, lock her up till morning."

Doris stepped forward. "Please," she begged. "I'm not a spy. I came to see you about—"

Patch gestured with his thumb. "Take her upstairs!"

Mat stepped forward, laid a hand on the girl's arm. They disappeared through a side door. Scott clenched his fists sharply. He'd give a great deal to crash a fist home into that brutal twisted face.

Two more men entered the room. Patch swung on them. "Listen, you guys. There's a skirt here asking questions, let's hurry with the trucks. There may be some dicks following her."

Scott edged away from the window. On his side of the house a door opened, and the three men came out. Without warning one of them switched on a flashlight, swept it along the house. For one second it flared on Scott's face blinding him. There was a savage yell, then Patch's deep voice boomed.

"Get him, boys!"

A pistol flared. Scott dodged round the lilac bush, darted away in the shadow. Desperately he rounded the house. A second shot, a third. Here it was thick with high growing weeds and brush. Another huge shrub grew close to the house. He dodged behind it, crouched down close to the wall. The chase streamed by into the brush. Patch was yelling, the men from the barn came running, swinging lanterns. Someone turned on the truck lights. For just a moment, he crouched there. Doris upstairs would have heard the shots, he could get away but—

Cautiously he edged back. A big tree of some sort grew near the front door; likely, too, this door was not locked. A minute later he was on the narrow porch, the knob turned under his hand. Slowly the panels swung back. He was in a hallway and a handsbreadth of lamplight showed from the room where Doris had spoken to Patch.

Keeping on his toes, he climbed the dark stairway. Mat would be up here somewhere, and Doris. This was a hallway, and he could see three doorways, one door stood ajar and from it shone yellow lamplight. A heavy step, then Mat's voice.

"Got to lock you in, sister. Guess Patch was right. You was spying."

Scott edged back against the wall. Mat's huge bulk came out backward. The man switched on a flashlight, drew the door shut, turned a key. Then, just as he turned to come along the hallway and even, Scott struck, putting everything he had behind the blow. Mat dropped with a thump of relaxed muscles.

The key was in the doorway. Next instant, Scott was in the room. Doris' eyes were wide with fright.

"Come on," he ordered. "We'll have to be quick."

His heart sank as footsteps drummed on the porch. Men were coming in. He caught the girl's hand, drew her out to the hallway, around a corner and into another room. Hastily he reconnoitered from the window.

"Clear here," he whispered. "I'll drop you from the window. You race for the car. I'll be right after you. Got your keys?"

He saw her nod in the faint light and thrust up the window cautiously. Her hand was on his shoulder. "Oh," she breathed. "I got you into this."

Scott chuckled softly. "Don't worry about me. Get to the car, start it."

He lifted her through the window, let her down. Her arms slipped through his strong fingers. She was a scant five feet from the ground when he had to let her go, but she struck running in the direction of the machine. Scott waited until he could not see her, then leaped back into the hallway and yelled.

There was an instant of silence, then oaths. Men streamed into the hallway, started up the stairway. Near Scott was some sort of small table. He hurled it down at them, leaped back into the empty room, and dropped out through the window.

Just as his feet struck in a clump of weeds, he heard a motor wake to life. But Doris would have to turn the car! Pandemonium rocked the old house. Once again Scott yelled, and the men piled out on the lawn. This time he circled the place. Shots crashed; the beams of flashlights searched the lawn.

Five minutes later, the friendly lilac bush helped Scott the second time. He edged along the building again, came out front. Suddenly, a figure loomed before him. He heard Patch growl a curse, saw his hand come up.

Scott leaped forward with a savage diving tackle. The raised pistol cracked, but the big leader was swept off his feet, and his head crashed against the tree as he fell. Scott sped across the lawn like a rabbit, reached the road. Then he swore. As he ran, a small figure was running toward him.

He caught her hand and swept her round. "Foolish," he snapped. "Why didn't you stay in the car?"

The motor was running, and the machine was turned. Thankfully he picked her up and dropped her in the seat, then sprang in and slipped into gear. Behind them, pistols cracked, and frantic yelling sounded over the roar of the engine. The big car leaped ahead along the sandy road. Scott set his jaw and drove for it.

They passed the place where the lookouts had stopped them. The man left had just time to leap out of the fan of the lights as the big car hurtled past. Scott laughed; excitement half intoxicated him. Patch Tibbens and his crew licked without a gun.

In a few minutes, he slowed for the steep road down the ridge. Doris caught his arm. "Faster," she begged. "They'll be after us."

"Not they," Scott assured her. "That crowd won't come outside." The lights picked out the place where they had turned from the highway. "Which way?" he asked.

The car coasted to a stop. He turned and looked at Doris for a moment. She was frowning, then she looked up, met his look.

"How did you know where I was going?" Scott fidgeted with the gear shift. "Did you hear what I asked Patch?" There was strain in her voice. He shook his head, remembered that she could scarcely see him. "No, I didn't hear it all, and I'm afraid I can't tell you how I knew where you were going."

He gestured. "Back to Woodward, or east?"

"East," she almost snapped and obediently he turned the machine, let it shoot ahead over the smooth concrete.

Neither spoke for several miles, then Scott turned a little. Doris sat huddled against the door. She seemed very far away on the wide seat. He repressed an impulse to draw her closer, she looked so small and lonely.

"No," he said slowly. "I couldn't know what your errand was. You see, I only know your name, that is, your first name."

She didn't reply. He drove another mile. They were coming out of the hills now into a farming country. Almost suddenly, she spoke.

"You know, I'd feel better if I drove."

Scott stopped the car so suddenly that it skidded a little.

"Fine, I just forgot."

He opened the door, and stepped out. She slipped into her place behind the wheel. "Go round back," she directed in a voice almost a whisper.

The starting car left him so suddenly he almost fell into the road. Scott stood with his mouth open in sheer chagrinned surprise until the taillight was a mere pin prick of red down the straight road.

About midnight, a very hot, still pretty angry Scott Milroy entered an office in Milltown. One man was sound asleep in a chair; another was yawning over a newspaper.

"Well, well," the man with the paper announced. "Here's our playmate. Come to life, Dan, here's Milroy."

Scott scowled. "Come alive, you guys. We can have Patch Tibbens with the goods in two hours. Rout out the others."

Dan went to the telephone. Mills, the man with the paper, stared at Scott. "One week more to serve and you've the luck to get him. How about this girl you were to watch?"

"She's nothing in it," Scott announced. "I was to watch for a girl in a big brown coupe. Don't believe there's such a dame. Step on it, Mills, I want to help in this pinch before I go back to the bank."

Twenty minutes later, a big touring car loaded with men slipped out of town, bound west.

* * *

Every window of the Lock Haven Country Club showed lights. Out on the broad porch that overlooked the moving water of the broad creek, an orchestra played softly. Scott Milroy parked his car and listened for a minute or two. He liked the music, liked the silver paths of light on the water. But he was late.

Mildred Davis was near the door when he entered. "Why, Scott," she cried. "I am glad you could come."

A half dozen people crowded round laughing, shaking his hand.

"How goes the bank stuff, Scott?" Fred Melton asked. "You've had two weeks of it. Are you a partner yet?"

Scott laughed. "Well, Dad's happy anyway, he always hated the service."

"But you got the Tibbens crowd," Mildred Davis interjected. "You see, I know a lot that's going on."

He nodded. "But let's let the bank and the service stuff rest. I want to dance. Who's new tonight?"

Mildred looked through the wide living room to the porch. "All the old crowd, Scott. Oh yes, Doris Wheaton from Williamsport is here. Don't believe you've met her."

Then suddenly a girl was coming in the door. Her head was turned toward her escort. She laughed, and Scott started. Then she turned, and he saw her face. There was the little tip turn of her nose, the laughing eyes. Scott remembered the receding taillight.

Wheaton, Wheaton. He remembered the name with a start.

"Doris," Mildred was calling. "Come here; we have our lion cornered. We'll present you to him. Mr. Scott Milroy, late foe of John Barleycorn, now a rising young banker at his father's urgent bidding. Miss Doris Wheaton, Mr. Scott Milroy. Now, Scott, tell her long stories of your adventures."

Her hand was in his, and it was absurdly small, but Scott felt trembly as though he held something dynamic. "I believe—"

Doris' wide grey eyes were on his, almost as though they asked a favor. "I believe I saw Miss Wheaton's back once—but—she was going away."

It was an hour until he could get her away from the others, and then he led her down a path along the creek to an old stile.

She sat down. "Well," she began. "I suppose I must ask you to forgive me."

He shook his head. "I know, now, what you wanted of Patch Tibbens. You wanted to ask about your brother."

She nodded gravely. "Yes, you see, there's just Fred and I. When he didn't come home for a week, I was desperate. He told me how you and some of the men got him away and put him in a hospital for a week."

Her hand fell on his sleeve. "And I believe he's going straight now. And I'm so grateful. That night I thought—well I thought you were mixed up in it someway."

"So, you ditched me!" He threw back his head and laughed.

"Listen, Doris. Do you know the first thing I noticed after you drove off?"

She shook her head.

"It was one of these highway signs. It said: CAUTION SOFT SHOULDERS."

For the second time that evening, her laughter rang out, silver like the moonlight on the broad dark creek water.

"Doris, I have a sort of confession to make, too. I was on duty that day. Our office had word that a girl in a big car had been looking for Patch Tibbens. That was why I was so peeved when you passed me up the first time near Bellefonte. We got Tibbens that night with his whole outfit, trucks, booze, money, and all. But I wonder—"

"What?" she asked when he did not go on.

"Whether I captured the girl."

She seemed to sway toward him. His arms caught her close, held her.

"Scott, Scott," she whispered. "I've been so miserable since I knew what you've done for me, but I was too proud—"

He stopped her with a kiss. "I love you, Doris. I have ever since you stopped that second time."

He caught her shoulders in both hands, and held her away. "Soft shoulders," he laughed exultingly.

"Caution," she countered softly.

He drew her close again. Below them the water rippled softly, the muted music of the orchestra reached them, thin strings of melody.

"Oh, my dear, my dear." he breathed.

9798888190906